The HE grenade blew the door off its hinges

As the triad overlord sprawled across a sofa, bleeding from a gash below his hairline, he fumbled in vain for the semiauto pistols he'd dropped when he was taken down. He stared up into Mack Bolan's eyes.

"Who are you?"

"I'm your judgment," Bolan replied, dropping the grenade launcher and whipping out his pistol, drilling the man with a 9 mm Parabellum round between his arched eyebrows. The overlord sagged and slid off the couch, leaving his final thoughts spread over the upholstery.

"Back out the way we came," Bolan advised Bizhani, brushing past him on the short run toward the service stairs. He now had the Steyr AUG in hand, prepared to greet gunners waiting on the flights below.

Job done, and all that remained now was for the Executioner to get out of here. Alive.

Don Pendleton's Mack
Bolan®

China White

A GOLD EAGLE BOOK FROM
WORLDWIDE®

TORONTO • NEW YORK • LONDON
AMSTERDAM • PARIS • SYDNEY • HAMBURG
STOCKHOLM • ATHENS • TOKYO • MILAN
MADRID • WARSAW • BUDAPEST • AUCKLAND

Recycling programs
for this product may
not exist in your area.

First edition July 2014

ISBN-13: 978-0-373-61570-4

Special thanks and acknowledgment to
Mike Newton for his contribution to this work.

CHINA WHITE

Printed in U.S.A.

Justice should remove the bandage from her eyes long enough to distinguish between the vicious and the unfortunate.

—Robert Ingersoll,
1833–1899

My eyes are clear. I recognize the guilty. They have judged themselves.

—Mack Bolan

For Staff Sergeant Clinton Romesha, U.S. Army

PROLOGUE

Confucius Plaza, New York City

Tommy Mu was starting to get nervous. He was due on Mott Street, at the Lucky Dragon, in ten minutes, and he wasn't sure that he could make it. Being late was bad, particularly with the product he was carrying. It could mean punishment.

But getting killed along the way was worse.

He had been followed from the pickup, though he hadn't seen the stalkers on his tail until his taxi had crossed Henry Street and rolled into Chinatown. He had begun to let his guard down, relaxing as he made it back to his home turf, and then he'd spotted it: a jet-black SUV he'd glimpsed before, while he was getting in the cab, and hadn't thought to watch for on the ride downtown.

Stupid.

He should have paid closer attention, should have known there might be watchers, what with all the other crazy shit that had been going on the past few weeks. The SUV's windshield was tinted just enough that Mu couldn't make out *who* was trailing him, but he felt safe in ruling out the DEA. If they'd been on his case, they would have swooped in at the pickup, grabbing him with the product, his supplier with the cash he'd handed over. Get the whole damn ball of wax.

No. This was someone else.

Which only made it worse.

If he'd been busted, Mu could have called his lawyer, posted bail and started thinking about where to run and hide in lieu of facing trial. But these weren't cops. And that meant, if they took him in, the odds of him coming back were nil. He might wind up in the East River, or he might just disappear.

Whatever. Dead was dead, and Mu wasn't ready for it.

So he'd told the cabbie that he'd changed his mind about going to Mott Street. He had the hack stop at Confucius Square, where there were people all around, making a snatch more hazardous.

Back in the old days, Mu understood, New Yorkers might have stood and watched him be slaughtered on the street without lifting a hand or bothering to call for help. These days, post–9/11, things were different. Someone would definitely call the cops, and likely film the snatch squad on his or her cell phone at the same time. Now that he was back in Chinatown, someone might even recognize him and call Jimmy Wen.

Not that his boys could reach the scene in time.

The good news: Mu had his equalizer with him, just as always. He preferred the SIG SAUER Mosquito, light and fast, packing ten .22-caliber Long Rifle rounds, its muzzle threaded for attaching a suppressor if he had a special job to do. It wouldn't knock a man down from a block away, but it would kill him, hell yeah, if you hit him in the right spots, and it didn't have the shocking recoil of a larger caliber.

The question: would he have a chance to use it if the stalkers moved on him?

The plan: cross Bowery westbound and walk against Bayard Street's one-way traffic, so the hunters couldn't follow him. Make them drop down to Pell and try to keep up with him, wondering the whole time if they'd come this far to lose him altogether.

Psy-war, man, he thought. Just hope it works.

If not…

He made the move; dodged into traffic, barely checking left or right, and made it to the other side intact.

So far, so good.

"YOU'RE LOSING HIM," Ahmad Taraki growled.

"What can I do?" Babur Kazimi asked him from the driver's seat. "You see the one-way sign."

"Turn that way!" Taraki shouted, then cursed with feeling.

He pointed south, toward Pell Street, one-way westbound. They could track their pigeon that way, farther into Chinatown, and pick him up on Mott Street when he tried to cross.

"You sure?" Daoud Rashad asked from the backseat. "He could go some other way or—"

Furious and nearly shouting now, Taraki told his driver, "Do as you are told!"

Kazimi made the turn, horns blaring at them, and Taraki gave them all the finger. He wished he could have sprayed them with the AK-105 he was carrying and shut them up forever. That would be a satisfying moment, but he couldn't spare the time, much less risk drawing in police before his job was done.

Pell Street was half the length of Bayard and deadended into Mott. Taraki had a fair idea of where his boy was going, and their task would be to cut him off before he got there, thus avoiding any payback from his homeboys. It was meant to be a simple job, decisive, not a running firefight through the streets.

"Hurry!" he snapped at Kazimi. "If you let him get away, it's your ass."

"Two more minutes," the driver answered. "But I can't stop him from going someplace else."

"Then pray he doesn't, for your own sake," Taraki said.

As if God gave a damn whether they caught the man or not.

But Wasef Kamran cared. And if Taraki failed him, there would certainly be hell to pay.

TOMMY MU FELT BETTER; thought he might have made it after all. Some of the people he passed on Bayard Street were likely wondering why he'd been running past them, jostling a couple here and there, but no one challenged him. They knew better, could recognize him by his hair-cut, clothes and haste as someone dangerous. They'd be thinking he wasn't a person to mess with, and their in-stincts were correct.

Approaching Mott Street, he slowed to a walking pace, figuring the SUV could still be fighting traffic down on Pell. And if it wasn't…well, he didn't want to blunder into anything. The package underneath his arm was worth more than his life to Paul Mei-Lun.

Something to bear in mind.

Mu was cautious as he cleared the last few yards, keep-ing his right hand underneath his jacket, near the Stinger, ready for a quick draw if he needed it. It would be better for him if he ditched the hunters, rather than start a shoot-ing match on his home turf, but he would do whatever was required to make it back alive.

Mott Street was his salvation, one-way traffic running north to south, so even if the SUV caught up with him, its driver couldn't turn against the flow and follow him to the Lucky Dragon. He'd be safe then, with his brothers all around him, making the delivery. If he was not on time, at least he would be close and no one would have taken the package away from him.

Arriving at the corner, Mu felt sweet relief—until he saw the SUV parked at the corner to his left, downrange. He was about to flip them off, laugh in their faces, until he focused on the black car's open windows and the weapons angling toward him from inside. Mu wasn't sure if he should run or pull the Stinger, and before he had a chance to make his mind up it was already too late.

The bullets hit him like a pelting hailstorm, ripping through his stylish jacket, through his flesh, lifting him off his feet. The package underneath his arm burst open, powder rising in a cloud around him as he fell, no longer snow-white as it had been when he'd taken delivery. It was all red and clotted now, with Mu's blood. Beyond him, farther down the street, the slugs struck others, killing, wounding.

Mu was dead before he hit the sidewalk.

The SUV turned south and vanished into traffic as the first screams rose in Chinatown. Sirens would take a little longer, and they'd be too late.

The war had already begun.

CHAPTER ONE

Manhattan Cruise Terminal

Waiting was the hard part, if you weren't accustomed to it. Early on, Mack Bolan, aka the Executioner, had acquired the gift of patience, something schooled into him by his military training and experience in war zones where a hasty move meant losing everything. It came as second nature to him now, a part of life and every mission that he undertook. He couldn't always be proactive. Sometimes it came down to sit, and watch, and wait.

Like now.

The ferry from New Jersey was on time, no problem there, and he'd picked out the guys who had been sent to meet it. The two young males were Asian, Chinese American presumably, although they could be FOB for all he knew. Fresh off the boat that was, in common slang, although their journey from Hong Kong, Macau or points west on the Chinese mainland would have brought them to New York by air, or maybe overland from Canada.

No matter.

They were here to do a job, the same as he was. Not the *same* job, but the three of them were waiting for the same boat and the same guy, carrying a suitcase full of misery.

Bolan wasn't concerned right now with how the heroin had reached the States from Southeast Asia. He would find that out in time, by one means or another, and pursue the powder trail. This day, right here and now, his job was to follow this shipment to its destination somewhere in the heart of Chinatown and to make sure it went no further.

Ten keys, maybe twelve, as pure as any lab could make it. Ready to be stepped on and distributed to addicts citywide at a tremendous profit for the men in charge. At last report, a kilo went for sixty thousand dollars, wholesale. Cut to 50 percent purity with powdered vitamin B or some other nontoxic substance, it doubled in volume and was then packaged into thirty thousand single-dose glassine envelopes for sale to street dealers at five bucks apiece. That was ninety thousand dollars profit to the cutters, while the dealers turned around and sold each dose for ten to fifteen bucks, somewhere between three hundred thousand and four hundred fifty thousand on the street.

Simple arithmetic. Ten kilos would be worth three million, minimum, in street sales; maybe four point five, with any luck. Who could resist a deal like that?

There would be risks, of course. City and state police, the DEA and FBI, all would be hungry for a major bust to raise their profiles, justify their budgets and convince a weary public that the war on drugs was still worth fighting in these days when the United States jailed more people than any other nation on the planet, at a cost some said was hurting the already-bruised economy.

And then there were the hijackers. Why spend six hundred thousand dollars on a suitcase full of smack if you could rip it off for nothing? Make a score like that, you clipped the rightful owner for the wholesale cost and cleared a cool three million, minus whatever it cost to cut the product. All you had to risk was life and limb.

The pickup team would be well armed, and so was Bolan. On the shotgun seat beside him in his gray Toyota Camry, a Heckler & Koch MP5K submachine gun with a 100-round Beta C-Mag drum lay hidden in a canvas tote bag. Beneath his left arm hung his backup piece: a Glock 22 chambered in .40 caliber, with fifteen rounds in the magazine and one in the chamber. In a crunch, Bolan could empty both guns in something like ten seconds, leaving devastation in his wake.

And he had something else the two young Wah Ching Triad soldiers couldn't match: experience. He had been fighting for his life before the pair of them was out of grade school. He'd sent hundreds of mafiosi to their graves during his one-man war against the Cosa Nostra, by the FBI's best estimate, and no one had been keeping score since he had pioneered the war on terrorism, operating on behalf of Uncle Sam.

All that since he had "died"—on paper, anyway— roughly a half mile from the spot where he was parked right now, in Central Park. Broad daylight, he'd been shot to hell, incinerated in front of a flock of witnesses.

Or so the story went.

And maybe it was true what people said. You couldn't keep a good man down.

He saw the ferry coming now, making its slow and steady way across the broad East River. In the old days, Dutch Schultz and his ilk had dropped their adversaries into that gray water, their feet set in concrete. How many skeletons were down there, even now, their eyeless sockets gazing upward at the ferry as it passed?

Good riddance, Bolan thought. There'd always be a new crop lining up to fill the slots dead mobsters left behind.

As the ferry docked, he raised a pair of compact field

glasses and focused on the gangway, waiting for his target to appear.

"WE SHOULD'VE SENT somebody with him," John Lin said, watching the ferry as it nosed into the pier.

Smoking a cigarette beside him, Louis Chao said, "He was covered in New Jersey, all the way to boarding."

"Still, after that shit with Tommy—"

"Nobody's about to jump him on the ferry," Chao said, interrupting him. "They can't get off the boat until it docks, and there'd be cops all over, waiting for them."

"Right. Sounds good, unless you're dealing with a bunch of lunatics."

"Hey, *we're* the lunatics, remember?" Chao was smiling at him through a haze of smoke. "And payback's gonna be a stone-cold bitch."

"I don't like all these cars around here," Lin complained.

"We're in a parking lot, for Christ's sake. What did you expect?"

"I mean, they could be anywhere, you know? Just waiting."

"Then you'd better keep your eyes peeled, Johnny Boy. Be ready for them."

Lin was ready, even looking forward to it, with his Uzi cocked and locked, ready to rip if anyone looked sideways at the courier they'd come to meet. He was another Wah Ching brother, Martin Tang, who'd carried cash across the river bright and early, met his escorts on the Jersey side, and called home when the deal was done. Now he was on his way back with the skag, and it was Lin's job to deliver both—the man and what he carried—to their boss in Chinatown.

So Lin was strapped, backing the Uzi with a sleek

Beretta Px4 tucked underneath his belt, around in back, and for insurance, in an ankle holster, a little Colt Mustang .380. If none of that worked, he had a Balisong knife with a seven-inch blade in his pocket, sharp enough to shave with or to cut off some miserable lowlife's head.

All that and Chao still had him outgunned. He'd brought a Bushmaster Adaptive Combat Rifle, made by Remington, and wore a double shoulder holster bearing a matched pair of Glock 33s, chambered for .357 SIG rounds. That still was not enough for his partner, though. He also carried a 4-shot COP .357 Magnum derringer, and just for luck, had put two M-67 fragmentation grenades in the glove compartment of their black Ford Focus.

They were ready for war, and as much as John Lin ached for payback, he hoped they could make it back to the Lucky Dragon without killing anyone along the way. Or getting killed themselves.

"I see him," Chao said. "He's just starting down the ramp."

Tang was younger than Lin by six months or so, but had proved himself in action for the Wah Ching Triad. Nothing super-hideous, a little cutting and a drive-by, but he'd passed the test and this was graduation day. He might be nervous, but it wasn't showing as he ambled down the ferry's boarding ramp, keeping it casual among the tourists and commuters, careful not to jostle anybody with his suitcase full of powdered treasure.

It had come a long way from the Golden Triangle, halfway around the planet, to wind up in New York City, where it would keep several thousand junkies flying high and looking forward to their next fix, and the next one after that. Between times, they could rob their neighbors, prostitute themselves, do whatever it took to raise the cash for one more in an endless series of departures from reality. Lin knew the drill and didn't care what kind of suffering the product ultimately caused, as long as he was paid his share to make it happen.

He was all about free enterprise.

Lin thought of Tommy Mu again and scanned the parking lot with restless eyes. He had a fair idea of who had taken Mu down, and no one he had spotted so far looked the part. They might have hired white boys to do the dirty work, of course, but as Lin understood it, Afghans weren't averse to bloody hands.

It was something they had in common with the Wah Ching brotherhood.

Tang had disembarked, had seen their car and was moving toward it at a normal walking pace. The trick was not to stand out in a crowd, whether you had a package to deliver or were closing on a hit in broad daylight. Look normal, even boring. Fly under the radar.

"Hey, man, how'd it go?" Chao asked as the courier put his bag in the backseat and slid in next to it.

"No sweat," Tang replied. "This end?"

"We're cool," Chao said.

Lin thought things were okay so far, but kept it to himself.

Two minutes later they were rolling south along 12th Avenue, which would become the Lincoln Highway once they crossed West 42nd Street. From there it was a straight run to the juncture where Canal Street paralleled the Holland Tunnel, and a left turn through Lower Manhattan on their way to Chinatown.

An easy trip, unless you were at war and being hunted.

Lin drove well, obeying all the laws, watching the traffic up ahead and flicking frequent glances at his rearview mirror, watching for a tail.

Eternal vigilance was the price of running an illegal business in New York.

BOLAN TRAILED THE Ford south at a cautious distance. Taking out the couriers was not part of his plan. He wanted them to lead him home, show him the drop and let him scout the neighborhood for angles of attack.

It wouldn't be the simplest job he'd ever done. White faces were anomalies in Chinatown. Locals could spot the tourists, often coming by the Gray Line busload, trooping in and out of cheesy shops to drop their money. But a round-eye snooping on his own meant *cop* or worse, and he'd get nothing in the way of information from the members of that closed community. Start poking into corners on his own, and he could meet resistance well beyond a simple wall of silence.

Picking up the Jersey shipment was a coup of sorts. He'd had to squeeze a dealer for the intel, then make sure his source was in no shape to rat him out to the higher-ups. Call that the first kill on his latest visit to New York, but not the last. Before they found the dealer's body, Bolan reckoned he'd be finished in Manhattan, likely on his way to some more distant battleground.

But he was taking care of first things first.

There was a war brewing in New York City, ready to explode between the Wah Ching Triad and a gang of interlopers from Afghanistan. Two syndicates financed primarily by the sale of heroin produced in their respective bailiwicks had come to blows, and the prognosis was for worse to come. In other circumstances Bolan would have been content to stand aside and let them kill each other, but the action had already claimed civilian lives and that was where he drew the line.

Police were on it, sure, along with Feds from several agencies. For all he knew, the Afghan angle might be setting off alarms at Homeland Security back in D.C. That made it doubly dicey, jumping into the middle of a war *and* dodging cops of all persuasions in the process. It was nothing that he hadn't done before, but still a challenge.

One more chance to do or die.

The Ford was making good time, rolling south with Lincoln Highway turning into West Street once they got past Barrow. Bolan knew they'd likely take Canal Street, veering off southeastward from the river on its way to Chinatown, just south of Little Italy. He'd spent his share of time in *that* vicinity, as well, when he was hunting killers of a different complexion, but the local Mafia—whatever might be left of it—was safe from him today.

Next week…who knew?

Part of the deal this day was to watch out for other tails. A shipment on the road, ten keys at least, made an inviting target for the other side. The last thing Bolan wanted was to get caught in a cross fire or, worse yet, to see the delivery go up in smoke before he marked its final destination. Later, sure, he'd torch the smack himself, and everyone associated with it.

So he was watching when the midsize SUV with three male passengers became a fixture in his rearview. Bolan made it as a Chevy Trailblazer, as black as the Ford that he was following, hanging behind him in no rush to pass. It could be coincidence, since Bolan hadn't seen the vehicle at the ferry terminal, but he already had that itchy feeling he'd learned to trust in situations where his life was riding on the line.

A tail, maybe. He bumped it up to *definitely* when the

shotgun rider shifted in his seat and let the muzzle of a weapon rise above the dash for just an instant. It was there and gone but Bolan caught it, and he didn't think it was a pogo stick, a fishing pole or the antenna on a satellite phone. Those were hunters in the SUV. The only question now: were they on Bolan's tail or following the heroin?

He got his answer as they closed in on Canal Street where it split, divided by Canal Park's wedge of greenery between the west- and eastbound lanes. The Chevy made its move then, swinging out to pass Bolan's Toyota, speeding up to overtake the Ford. Some kind of hit was going down in front of him, and Bolan had to make a split-second decision.

Should he intervene or wait to see how good the Wah Ching gunners were at self-defense? How many innocent civilians on their way home from a job or shopping errand would be placed in danger if he sat it out—or if he jumped into the middle of the game?

Scowling, he pulled his MP5K from its canvas tote and stepped on the Camry's accelerator, playing catch-up on a one-way ride to Hell.

"You want to take them here?" Babur Kazimi asked.

"Not yet," Ahmad Taraki answered. "Wait until we're past the park and all the little kiddies, eh?"

"Closer to Chinatown," Kazimi told him in a cautionary tone.

"Not that far," Taraki replied. "Just be ready when I tell you."

Turning to Daoud Rashad in the backseat, he said, "And you, too."

"I was ready when we started," Rashad answered.

Taraki had taken some heat on the last hit about the civilians who'd been in his way when they'd taken down the target, but that was a risk of street fighting. The goal had been achieved regardless, and a message had been sent. The Wah Ching Triad was on notice that their days of peddling heroin outside Chinatown were coming to an end. There was a new force to be reckoned with, and the gang would have to step aside or face extinction.

Taking down this shipment from New Jersey, after it had traveled halfway around the world from somewhere in the Golden Triangle of Southeast Asia, would drive home the lesson while putting a cool three million dollars, give or take, into the coffers of Taraki's crime Family. If he went back without the drugs, there would be no forgiveness from Wasef Kamran. In fact, it would be better if he did not return at all.

Kazimi made the left-hand turn onto Canal Street, rolling past the park. Taraki saw the children playing there, some adults walking dogs, oblivious to what was happening around them. They existed in a world as different and distant from his own as life on Jupiter, believing that their trivial concerns were all that mattered. Braces on the kiddies' teeth, a raise at work, a plastic bag for dog crap in a purse or pocket when they took a stroll. The daily grind for wage slaves in the city.

But somewhere within the next half dozen blocks, before the Wah Ching couriers had crossed the borderline of Chinatown, Taraki meant to give the drones around him a surprise. A little glimpse of life in *his* world, where the struggle for survival meant exactly that. If someone got between Taraki and his target...well, they'd simply have to die.

Stopping the Ford was no great problem. Shoot the driver, shoot the engine, shoot the tires. The operative word was *shoot*. But at the same time, even knowing that the Ford was bound to crash, its occupants riddled with bullets, getting to the heroin remained Taraki's top priority. He couldn't let it burn, and he would get no thanks if he returned the suitcase shot to hell, blood soaking through the plastic bags inside it. He'd been ordered to deliver, and the shipment had to be intact.

Case closed.

"Remember what I told you," he advised Rashad, half turning in his seat.

"Head shots. No problem."

Rashad could shoot, no problem there. Back home he'd been a member of the Afghan National Army Commando Brigade, created by the U.S. and its Coalition allies to hunt members of the Taliban. Taraki didn't know how many men Rashad had killed before the brass cashiered him, citing his excessive zeal in clearing rural villages, but no one ever questioned his ability or willingness to pull a trigger. Stopping him once he got started was another matter, thus the warning in advance to keep it clean and not indulge in sloppy overkill.

"No damage to the suitcase," Taraki said, driving home his point.

"I know the difference between a suitcase and a man," Rashad gruffly replied.

Taraki let it go. Making his backseat shooter angry, seconds prior to firing on the enemy, would be a foolish move.

Instead he turned back to Kazimi. "No collision with their car, remember," he commanded.

"Paint chips. FBI lab. Yodel-yodel."

Meaning *yada-yada,* Taraki thought, but correcting the driver was a waste of time and energy. He'd never come to grips with English slang, habitually garbling what he learned from television.

They were approaching Hudson Street and its intersection with Canal. A block beyond it lay another park, this one located on Taraki's right. The neighborhood was called Tribeca—meaning, as Taraki understood it, "Triangle Below Canal Street"—sprawling out immediately west of Chinatown.

This was their last chance for a hit outside Wah Ching Triad turf.

Taraki cocked his AKS-74U carbine, the shortest and lightest Kalashnikov made. It measured nineteen inches with its skeletal stock folded to the left side, and weighed six pounds without its magazine containing thirty 5.45 mm rounds. Its automatic rate of fire was 700 rounds per minute, but he'd set the fire selector switch for semiauto, playing safe. A clean shot through the head was better than a spray of fire to shred the driver's body while the Ford went racing like a rocket sled across the park.

But could he pull it off?

Taraki hit the button for his window, instantly rewarded with a rush of warm air in his face, and twisted in his seat, tracking the driver with the V-notch of his weapon's open sights.

As soon as Bolan saw the rifles jutting from the Chevy's windows, he immediately had a choice to make. He could hang back and let it happen, let the trackers and his targets fight it out, then maybe waste the winners, or he could attempt to intervene.

For what?

No matter how it played, once shooting started, the Wah Ching gunners would not be leading him to their HQ in Chinatown. That move was foiled the second that the third car joined their little caravan and made its move to strike. Beyond that plan, he didn't care if the young gangsters lived or died—would probably have wound up killing them himself, in time—but he *did* care about the innocents going about their business, motoring along Canal Street as it turned into a battle zone.

He let the Camry drift, came up behind the Trailblazer and gave its right rear bumper just the slightest nudge, then backed away. It was enough to spoil the shooters' aims, their first rounds jarred off-target, gouging shiny divots in the black Ford's roof.

The Wah Ching driver gunned it, rapidly accelerating, while his backseat passenger—the one they'd picked up at the ferry terminal—rolled down his window, ready to return fire.

Bolan rolled down his window and reached across with his left hand to lift his submachine gun, even as he checked his rearview for patrol cars. They were clear so far, but every driver and pedestrian along Canal Street likely had a cell phone and was fumbling for it now, to punch up 9-1-1 and shout some garbled message about gunfire on the road.

No time to waste, then.

Bolan swung his MP5K out the window, bracing it against his wing mirror, and fired a 3-round burst into the SUV's lift gate. The 9 mm Parabellum rounds shattered the tinted glass, one of them flying on to crack the windshield while another ripped the backseat dome light from its socket. Bolan knew the hunters had to be going crazy in there, wondering who had brought them under fire, just as the Wah Ching gunner who had brought the heroin from Jersey started popping at them with a semi-auto pistol.

Bolan swung his stuttergun around to fire a burst across the Camry's hood, stitching three holes across the Ford's C-pillar inches from the triad gunner's face and shooting arm. The young man lurched backward, out of sight, just as his wheelman tried to milk more speed out of the Ford's 2.0-liter Duratec engine. A short burst from the Chevy's shotgun rider ripped across the Ford's trunk as it fled, while Bolan saw the backseat shooter leaning well out of the SUV to bring his Camry under fire.

He swerved back to the left-hand lane, putting himself behind the Trailblazer just as his adversary loosed a burst, his bullets wasted on thin air. Bolan responded with another three rounds through the lift gate's yawning maw, putting them roughly where the SUV's tail gunner ought to be. This time the Chevy veered off to starboard, running up behind the Focus in Canal Street's right-hand lane, its left rear window gliding down to give the soldier in the rear another angle on his mark.

Bolan was faster, falling into line behind the Chevrolet and pumping three more rounds into it. When the SUV began to swerve, he guessed he might have winged the driver, but it straightened out again in seconds flat and Bolan had to duck a short burst rattling through the blank space where the lift gate used to be. Most of the bullets missed, but one punched through his windshield near the upper frame and sent his rearview mirror flying somewhere toward the seat behind him.

It became a duel then, Bolan swerving back and forth to keep the Chevy shooter guessing, ruining his aim, and all the while returning 3-round bursts that scarred the SUV's tailgate, rattling around inside the passenger compartment. In the driver's seat, wounded or not, the Chevy's driver did whatever he could think of to evade incoming rounds, while still pursuing his intended targets in the Ford.

They'd nearly cleared the park when the Trailblazer swung around as if to pass the Wah Ching vehicle, then swerved hard right to slam the Ford along its driver's side and force it off the pavement onto sloping grass. Tires churned brown tracks across the turf, lost traction, turned them into long sidewinding loops, the Chevy following the

Ford and both cars spitting gunfire. Civilians scattered, ran for cover where some scattered trees provided it, or simply hit the ground and prayed.

It was not what he'd hoped for, but the Executioner had long since mastered adaptation in adversity. Without a second thought he braced himself and swung off-road, trailing the two combatant vehicles into the wedge-shaped park between Canal Street and Sixth Avenue.

CHAPTER TWO

Two Days Earlier
Winchester Regional Airport
Frederick County, Virginia

"I could have driven down," Bolan said to Jack Grimaldi after their handshake on the tarmac.

"What, and miss the pleasure of my company?" Grimaldi replied, smiling.

"Point taken. Any idea what we're looking at?"

Grimaldi shook his head, saying, "I got a call to show up here and prep the chopper. End of story."

Sitting on the helipad in front of them, the chopper was a Fairchild Hiller FH-1100 four-seater, powered by a Rolls-Royce M-250 turboshaft engine. It was small, as helicopters went, just under twenty-eight feet long and nine feet high, with a maximum takeoff weight of 2,750 pounds. It cruised at 122 miles per hour, with a service ceiling of 14,200 feet and a range of 348 miles. It was enough to make the eighty-odd-mile trip to Stony Man Farm and back four times.

"I've done the checklist," Grimaldi said, "if you want to get on board."

Bolan secured his carry-on behind the copilot's seat, then settled in and buckled up, donning the headphones that would be required for any kind of normal conversation once Grimaldi switched on the chopper's engine. The soldier's old friend was at his side a moment later, strapped into the pilot's seat, scanning the perimeter and checking gauges, engaging the clutch switch, contacting the tower in preparation for liftoff. Once they were airborne, Bolan settled back and let himself appreciate the scenery.

Winchester was located in Virginia's Shenandoah Valley, between the Appalachian Mountains and the Blue Ridge range. They would be following the path of Skyline Drive, a 105-mile road running the length of Shenandoah National Park, until they reached Stony Man Farm and set the chopper down some ten miles north of Waynseboro.

It would be safe to land because they were expected. Uninvited drop-ins didn't happen at the Farm, the secret base of the nation's top antiterrorist squads—at least not twice for any given trespasser. Tall fences posted with specific warnings kept the normal hikers out. Those who arrived with mischief on their minds—a rare occurrence—would be taken into custody for questioning, all depending on the circumstances. Any aircraft that attempted to land on the property without advance approval would be blasted from the sky by FIM-92 Stinger missiles or shredded in flight by M134 Miniguns spewing four thousand 7.62 mm NATO rounds per minute.

It was serious business if you were on the receiving end.

Bolan normally drove to the Farm, and often spent his downtime there if he was in-country between assignments, but this time he had been mopping up a little something in St. Louis when the summons came from Hal Brognola, routing him to Winchester, where Jack Grimaldi waited with the whirlybird. Brognola would be flying down from Washington—had likely reached the Farm ahead of them, in fact—with information on a rush job he had marked for handling by the Executioner.

It could be anything, as Bolan knew from long experience. He didn't try to second-guess Brognola based on what was in the news from Asia, Africa, wherever. Crises-making headlines were normally covered by established law enforcement or intelligence agencies, while Stony Man tried to stay ahead of the curve, defusing situations that were working up to detonation or pursuing fugitives who had outwitted every other operative sent to bag them. Stony Man—and, by extension, Bolan—was the court of last resort, employed when following "The Book" had failed and nothing else would do except a hellfire visit from a fighting man who specialized in neutralizing human predators.

So it was going to be bad. He knew that going in, and focused on the woodland scenery below instead of trying to imagine just *how* bad it might turn out to be. Sufficient unto each day was the evil it contained.

Amen.

A line of white-tailed deer crossing Skyline Drive paused to glance up at the helicopter passing overhead before they bolted, seeking cover in the forest on the other side. Another half mile farther on, two motorcycles rode in tandem, northbound, trailing vapor from their tailpipes in the chilly morning air.

The flight from Winchester took forty minutes, give or take, approximately half the time it would have taken Bolan to drive down from Washington once he had cleared the capital itself. He liked the drive, relaxing in whatever vehicle he happened to be using at the moment, but if Brognola wanted Grimaldi on the new assignment that meant there would be more flying in their future, maybe international.

No problem.

He was up to date on his inoculations, kept himself informed on all the major hot spots of the world and could absorb whatever job-specific information might be necessary as he went along. Specifics varied, but his task remained essentially the same: apply force to some selected enemy or obstacle until said enemy or obstacle had been eliminated. Bolan rarely took prisoners, obeyed no rules beyond a code of conduct that was self-imposed and didn't worry about finding evidence to build a case in court.

The jobs reserved for him had gone beyond that stage of civilized behavior. Bolan's specialty was going for the jugular and hanging on until his enemies no longer had an ounce of fight or life left in them. Whether it was sniping from a mile away or fighting hand to hand, he was a master of his craft.

Thirty-seven minutes out, Grimaldi raised the Farm by radio and confirmed that they were cleared for touchdown at the heliport behind the rambling farmhouse that served as headquarters for the Stony Man teams. Once they were cleared, he veered away from Skyline Drive, flew over treetops and then swept across cultivated fields that marked the Farm itself.

It *was* a farm, in fact, producing crops in season, but the "farm hands" were selected from elite groups of the U.S. military, Special Forces, Army Rangers, Navy SEALs and the Marine Special Operations Regiment, as well as the occasional police officer or FBI agent. They worked a short rotation under oath-bound vows of secrecy, dressed in civilian garb but never without weapons close at hand. Those assigned to watch the gates were courteous but firm with wayward travelers. And if a prowler managed to intrude, well, courtesy was no longer an issue. On occasion these farm hands, also known as blacksuits, provided backup to Bolan.

The soldier saw the farmhouse now. It felt like coming home, but any sanctuary that he found at Stony Man was temporary. As Grimaldi hovered for his landing, Bolan wondered where his War Everlasting would take him next.

STEPPING FROM THE chopper in a whirl of rotor wash, Bolan saw Barbara Price, Aaron Kurtzman and Hal Brognola waiting for him on the far side of the helipad. The big Fed had begun to show his age, but kept in shape with a determined regimen he cheerfully despised. Price was drop-dead gorgeous; no change there. Kurtzman—"the Bear," to friends—was in the wheelchair where a bullet to the spine had left him when Stony Man's security was seriously breached.

They all knew Bolan too well for the standard handshake ritual, reduced in Brognola's case to a nod as Jack Grimaldi joined them after shutting down the copter. "You made good time," he observed.

"Tailwind," Grimaldi offered with a crooked smile.

"Something to eat or…?"

"We might as well get to it," Bolan said.

Brognola nodded and then led the way inside. They got a "Hey, guys!" from Akira Tokaido, the youngest member of the Farm's cybernetic team, who passed them in a hallway, doing something with a tablet.

There was room for all five of them in the spacious elevator; it was a short ride to the basement. Kurtzman led them to the War Room, his wheelchair moving silently toward a door with a keypad. He keyed in a short sequence of numbers and gained entry.

Inside, a conference table with a dozen seats stood waiting. Brognola went for the single chair at the far end, where a 152-inch flat-screen TV was mounted on the wall behind and above him. Bolan took the chair to the big Fed's left, facing Price across the table, with Grimaldi at his side.

Kurtzman rolled to the table's other end, where a keyboard controlled the room's lights and the giant TV.

"We've got a problem in New York," Brognola said by way of introduction. "There's a drug war coming, and it has already claimed three civilian lives."

Bolan decided not to ask why it was their problem instead of the DEA's or the NYPD's. Brognola liked to set the stage, and as he spoke, the giant screen behind him came alive with news footage of bodies on a sidewalk stained with blood, two uniformed policemen grappling with a Chinese man who tried to bull his way past them, tears streaming down his face.

"Mott Street," Brognola said. "Manhattan's Chinatown, two days ago. The target was a member of the Wah Ching Triad, who was carrying a key of heroin. In one shot there, you see some of it on the sidewalk."

Bolan saw it, like a sugar dusting on the sidewalk mixed with blood. A pastry recipe from Hell.

"The shooters, we believe, are from an Afghan outfit that's been growing since the DEA took down the Noorzai organization in 2008."

Bolan knew the basics on Haji Bashir Noorzai, the widely touted, widely hated Asian counterpart of Medellín's late Pablo Escobar. He'd battled Russian forces in the Reagan years and then served as mayor of Kandahar while selling weapons to the Taliban regime, then switched to aid the U.S. after 9/11, handing over tons of small arms and antiaircraft missiles to the CIA. Since then he'd made a fortune smuggling heroin, largely ignored—some said protected—by America's intelligence community. Finally convicted in 2008, he had been sentenced to life imprisonment, leaving the remnants of his empire up for grabs.

"Who's filling in for him?" Bolan asked.

"It's a whole new crew," Brognola said. "The man on

top, we understand, is one Khalil Nazari." Cue a string of mug shots, candid photos and a strip of video that showed a swarthy, mustached man emerging from a Humvee, flanked by bodyguards. "He's forty-five years old and everything a drug lord ought to be. We all know what's been going on with heroin since the invasion."

More bad news. During the Russian occupation of Afghanistan, regional warlords had financed their guerrilla war with opium, then kept it up with CIA support as they struggled to fill the power vacuum left by Soviet withdrawal in 1989. The Taliban had dabbled in drug trafficking, producing a bumper crop of 4,500 metric tons in 1999, then collaborated with the United Nations to suppress the trade, encouraged by a $43 million "eradication reward" from Washington in early 2001. Everything changed that September, and the warlords had returned with a vengeance, pushing opium and heroin production to the point that drugs accounted for 52 percent of Afghanistan's GDP and an estimated 80 percent of the world's smack supply. The Golden Crescent of Afghanistan, Iran and Pakistan had eclipsed Southeast Asia's Golden Triangle in drug exports, and Bolan knew the triads weren't exactly thrilled by that development.

In fact, it was enough to start a war.

And now, apparently, it had.

Brognola forged ahead, saying, "Nazari's front man in New York, we're pretty sure, is this guy." Cue a younger thug on-screen. "Wasef Kamran, age thirty-one. Supposedly provided information on bin Laden to the Company, but nothing that panned out."

"So they're protecting him?" Grimaldi asked.

"I didn't say that," Brognola responded, "but I couldn't rule it out, either."

"Terrific."

"On the triad side," the big Fed said, pressing ahead, "their 'dragon head' or 'mountain master,' as they like to call him, is a character called Ma Lam Chan." More video and still shots on the giant flat screen. "Home for him is Hong Kong, where it seems he's reached some kind of an accommodation with the PRC authorities."

Bolan translated in his head. The People's Republic of China had reclaimed the teeming offshore island of Hong Kong in 1997, after something like 150 years of British colonial rule. Despite Washington's fears that the Reds would wreak havoc on Hong Kong's thriving capitalist economy, little had changed overall. The worst problems suffered so far had been unexpected outbreaks of disease, each claiming several hundred lives. Meanwhile, cash registers kept ringing and the drugs kept flowing to the West.

"Chan's guy in New York—" pictures changed on the screen once more "— is Paul Mei-Lun. I'm never sure about his rank. He'd either be a 'red pole,' which is an enforcer, or a liaison officer, which they call a 'straw sandal.' Take your pick. Either way, he's in charge on our end and he's squared off against the Afghans."

"Deport him," Grimaldi suggested. "What's the problem, if you know he's dirty?"

"*That's* the problem," Brognola replied. "Somehow he came into Manhattan squeaky-clean, at least on paper. He has all the proper documents from Beijing's end, and State saw no good reason to reject his entry visa. Now he's here and all that DEA can say is that they're working on a case against him. There's nothing solid they can hang a warrant on."

"Homeland Security?" Bolan suggested. "If the Reds have bent the rules somehow to smooth his way—"

"There's still no proof of that. And while we're working on it, Chinatown's about to be ground zero in a war that's making no allowance for civilians."

"So, we'll be putting out the fire," Bolan observed.

"For starters," Brognola agreed. "Beyond that, we should think about discouraging round two, three, four, whatever. Make them gun-shy, somehow. As for details…"

Bolan nodded, thinking that was where he came in.

THE SOLDIER'S "HOME" at Stony Man was modest; nothing but a bedroom with a private bath. There were a few books on a solitary shelf, mostly suggested reading from Kurtzman, a small TV with DVD player and a laptop with a DSL connection. When his downtime found him there, it was enough.

The only ghosts in residence were those that traveled with him—inescapable.

Bolan was working on the laptop now, absorbing details on his adversaries that had been archived for future reference. He started with the Wah Ching Triad, which had surfaced in the 1970s after a rift developed in its parent syndicate, the Sun Yee On. Ironically, that translated to New Righteousness and Peace Commercial and Industrial Guild, a mouthful of nonsense describing China's largest triad "family" with some sixty thousand members worldwide. The Wah Ching faction had spun off on its own, as criminal gangs often did, and had survived the shakedown battles to establish an empire of sorts built on gambling and loan-sharking in Hong Kong and Macau, plus exports of heroin from the Golden Triangle to Canada, the States and Western Europe. Prior to the Afghan incursion on their turf, they'd fought a bloody war with soldiers from Mexico's Juárez Cartel to keep a foothold in Texas.

In most respects, the Wah Ching was a traditional triad, with tattooed members who took the usual thirty-six vows prescribed since sometime in the eighteenth century. Their structure was familiar, from the Dragon Head down to the "Vanguard"—operations officer—and "White Paper Fan"—administrator—down to the oath-bound members known for some reason as "forty-niners," and the uninitiated prospects called "blue lanterns." Up and down the chain, each member of the crime family—an estimated six thousand in all—was pledged to sacrifice himself if need be, for the greater good.

Make that the greater evil.

Their Afghan rivals, on the other hand, had no such rigid structure or tradition spanning centuries. Theirs was a tribal sort of operation, where the man in charge had proved himself by ruthless violence, eliminating his competitors, making examples of them to the world at large. The man in charge, Khalil Nazari, rarely left Afghanistan. In fact, he rarely left his fortress compound in the desert west of Kandahar, where he lived under double guard by his own thugs and mercenaries from a private outfit also known for its extensive contracts with the CIA and the U.S. Department of Defense.

Call him untouchable...unless he could be lured out into the open somehow for an unexpected meeting with the Executioner.

It was something to think about, but in the meantime there was New York City, where Wasef Kamran ran the show for Nazari, moving in on Wah Ching territory with no apparent concern for collateral damage. If they'd just been killing one another, Bolan might have been content to let the bloodbath run its course, but that was not an option in a metro area with twenty million innocent bystanders.

The Farm's computer files contained whatever information was available on the Wah Ching Triad and the Nazari syndicate from sources including the DEA, FBI, NYPD,

Interpol, Britain's MI-5, the Royal Canadian Mounted Police and Afghanistan's State Intelligence Agency, the Khadamat-e Aetla'at-e Dawlati, or KHAD. Some of it was contradictory, and some was out of date, but the archives showed Bolan faces, some with home addresses, and gave him directions to known or suspected syndicate properties. There would be no shortage of targets, and the soldier guessed he would find others as he went along, by one means or another.

The key was focus, and accepting tough realities. He'd never stop the trafficking in drugs from Southeast Asia or the Golden Crescent, obviously. Wiping out the Wah Ching's membership was clearly an impossibility, and taking down Nazari at his Afghan stronghold posed a list of difficulties that included forcing Bolan to contend with U.S. troops. When those ideas were taken off the table, what remained?

His brand of blitzkrieg, for a start, refined in battles with the Mafia, with criminal cartels and terrorists around the world. The opposition would be tough, determined, and they'd pull out all the stops to keep from losing any ground, but neither side had any practical experience with the phenomenon Hal Brognola once labeled the "Bolan Effect." Long before some White House ghostwriter dreamed up the buzz words "shock and awe," the Executioner had honed those methods to a razor's edge and taught his enemies to spend their final hours in fear.

Unfortunately, humans being what they were, that was a lesson that required unending repetition. Each new wave of predators seemed to believe they were immune to repercussions for their actions. There were always new ones to replace the fallen, endlessly recycling common themes of plunder, savagery and exploitation. They were doomed by ignorance and arrogance to replicate the errors of their predecessors, until someone knocked them down with force sufficient enough to ensure they would never rise again.

Someone like Bolan, who would do the job because he could.

BOLAN WAS STRIPPING for a shower when a rapping on his door stopped him. Shirtless and half expecting Price, he moved to let her in and was surprised to find Grimaldi standing there.

"Bad time?" the pilot asked.

"Just washing up," Bolan replied. "It can wait." He stood aside for his friend, then shut the door and slipped his shirt back on, leaving it loose, unbuttoned.

"I was thinking we should talk about tomorrow," Grimaldi said. "New York, that is."

"Okay."

"I'm thinking we can fly directly there," Grimaldi said, "unless you need to stop somewhere beforehand."

"That'll work," Bolan agreed. "I'll borrow what I need out of the armory."

"Newark's the closest airport, if you want to call about a ride."

"Will do. You want a car?"

Grimaldi thought about it, then shook his head. "I'll stick to wings for now. If we need a second vehicle for anything, I'll pick one up along the way."

"I expect New York won't be the end of it," Bolan warned.

"That's the feeling I get, too. While you're redecorating Chinatown, I'll make arrangement for a bird with greater range. The Feds have got some business jets they've confiscated. I can probably get one of them on loan."

"Flying in style."

"The only way to go. Depending on our final destination, there's a chance I can finesse some kind of gunship."

"We can wait and see on that. It might be overkill."

"Just food for thought. I'd rather have some rockets and a twenty-millimeter I don't need than wish I had 'em when they're nowhere to be found."

"You've got a point," Bolan agreed.

"So, any thoughts on where to start?"

"Find an informant if I can, first thing," Bolan replied. "If one side or the other has a shipment due, I'll try to take it down and go from there. Play one against the other if it feels right. Rattle cages. Blow their houses down."

"Same old, same old."

"Hey, if it works—"

"Don't fix it," Grimaldi said, finishing the thought for Bolan. "Right. I hear you. Want to get a beer or three?"

"I thought I'd catch up on my sleep."

"Okay. I might try that myself," Grimaldi said. "A little change of pace. What time tomorrow?"

"Six?"

"I'm there."

Alone once more, Bolan shrugged off his shirt and had one leg out of his jeans before the knocking was repeated. Opening the door again, he felt his frown turn upside-down.

"All clear?" Price asked.

"Good timing."

"Not so good," she said, brushing past Bolan. "Jack was waiting for the elevator. I almost ordered him to wipe the smirk off his face."

"I'm sure he didn't mean—"

She cut him off, saying, "You didn't have to dress all fancy for me."

Bolan glanced down at his blue jeans. "These old things? Just something I threw on."

"You want to take them off?"

"I thought you'd never ask."

"But listen, if Jack—"

"Let's just pretend Jack wasn't here."

Their intimate relationship was not a secret, in the strictest sense. They didn't advertise it; tried to be discreet within the limits posed by their surroundings and the strict security imposed at Stony Man. The rooms weren't monitored, but there were CCTV cameras in the corridors, as well as on the grounds outside. No one would question what went on between Bolan and Price, or try to second-guess them. They were warriors seeking solace, and if something more should come of it…

But nothing would.

Their lives were fixed in place, at least as far as Bolan was concerned. While Price might feel she'd had enough of Stony Man one day, might pull the pin and look for something else to do in government or in the private sector, Bolan could not walk away into a new career where everything was rosy and the storm clouds never gathered overhead.

That life was lost to him, a distant, faded memory. His father's faulty choices had evoked disaster and determined Bolan's path, an irredeemable diversion from what might have been. He'd never own a house, with or without a picket fence. Would never watch a child or two grow up, go off to school, get married, settle into a career. So what? A soldier learned that it was folly missing things that were denied him, things he'd never had.

What Bolan had, instead, was Stony Man and Barbara Price. He had a small but solid group of comrades who would never let him down—unless, of course, the good of many should outweigh the needs of one. That was a risk he had accepted willingly and would abide by to the bitter end.

And in the meantime, Bolan had a chance to make a difference. He'd made a difference in countless lives, nearly too often to recall. Someday his luck would turn, and he was ready for that, too.

Like the lady said, a happy ending was a story left unfinished.

Nobody got out of life alive.

"Sorry?" Bolan was aware of Price saying something, but he'd missed it.

"I said that you look like you're a thousand miles away."

"Nope," he assured her. "I'm right here. With you."

"Prove it," she replied, pulling the zipper on her jumpsuit down around waist level.

"I aim to please," he said.

"And since you're a marksman, hit me with your best shot."

Time enough to put the war on hold for one night and remember in the morning what he would be fighting for.

"I was about to take a shower," Bolan told her.

"I could scrub your back or something."

"It's a deal."

They moved together toward the bathroom, shedding clothes and apprehensions on the way. Tomorrow was as distant as forever and would take care of itself.

CHAPTER THREE

Canal Street, Lower Manhattan

"Keep going, damn it! Don't stop here!" Louis Chao snapped.

"No choice," John Lin answered back. "We've got a flat, in case you couldn't tell."

"Drive on the rim!"

"Too late. We're bogging down."

Those words were barely out before Chao felt the sharp edge of their left front wheel plow into grass and sod. The Focus shuddered, wallowed in the trough it was digging, then stalled as Lin kept bearing down on the accelerator.

"Stop! You're flooding it!"

The engine coughed and died then, leaving Lin to pound his fist against the steering wheel, cursing in Cantonese.

"Stop it!" Chao snapped at him. "They're coming! Everybody out!"

The car would be a death trap if the Afghans caught them in it and they couldn't drive away. Chao didn't plan on being caught inside with bullets ripping through the windows and the flimsy bodywork into *his* body. He'd already cocked the Bushmaster and held it ready as he rolled out of the car, crouching behind it with his door open, where it could serve him as a partial shield from either side. It wasn't much, but better than if he was caught out in the open by his adversaries.

Martin Tang was last out of the Ford, clutching a pistol that seemed woefully inadequate under the circumstances. He was empty-handed, otherwise, and Chao snarled at him, "Get the bag!"

"But—"

"Get it! We're not leaving it behind!"

Tang did as he was told, leaning inside the Ford to grab the suitcase filled with heroin and drag it out behind him. As he did so, Chao could hear the SUV approaching, fat tires ripping furrows in the grass someone had spent a fortune tending, and the men inside it had resumed their firing at the Ford. He wondered for a fleeting instant who the *other* man had been, glimpsed briefly in a car behind the Chevy Trailblazer and firing at it, then at Chao's car. A policeman? Would he join the fight without the usual flashing lights and siren?

There was no more time to think about it then, as the Trailblazer passed their small sedan, two automatic weapons spitting deadly fire, their bullets hammering the Ford along its driver's side. Chao cursed them and returned fire with his Bushmaster, the first time he'd been able to retaliate so far. He was pleased to see his bullets stitch a line of bright holes on the chase car's left rear fender, even if they didn't reach the men inside.

Lin was out and firing with his Uzi, ripping off what seemed like half a magazine in one long burst. Chao hoped that he had spares, firing like that, but didn't take the time to chastise Lin for wasting ammunition. Time was better spent aiming his own shots more precisely, if he could, instead of yelling at his Wah Ching brothers in the middle of a firefight.

Do or die, he thought. If they went home without the heroin, no explanation he could fabricate would placate Paul Mei-Lun. Death from a bullet would be preferable to whatever Mei-Lun devised as punishment for losing merchandise worth three cool million. Bearing that in mind, Chao braced himself and tracked the Chevy as it turned, preparing for another strafing run, this time on his side of the crippled Ford.

"Watch out!" he warned the others, just in case their nerves had blinded them somehow. He saw Lin crouching with the Uzi held in front of him, while Tang was trying to crawl underneath the Focus, making little progress with its chassis low against the ground.

"Martin! Come out and fight!"

Tang obeyed, but seemed as if he were about to weep, a pitiful display that shamed him and his Wah Ching brothers. If they had not needed him just then, Chao thought he might have shot the whining little coward.

Chao dropped to one knee, shouldered the Bushmaster's stock, and hoped that the sedan's door would prevent the first few rounds from striking him. He craved a chance to kill one of his enemies, at least, before he died. Just one would be enough to prove that he had fought with courage, done his best, and he could face his triad ancestors without a trace of shame.

BOLAN COULD FEEL the Camry start to slide on the grass and turned his steering wheel into the skid, easing his foot off the gas pedal. The chase was ending, since a lucky shot had flayed one of the Ford's front tires, and plowing over soft ground had it bogging down. The Chevy SUV was slowing, too, its front-seat shooter popping off rounds toward the Focus, while his partner in the backseat tried to keep an eye on Bolan's progress.

The Executioner made it harder for him, cranking through a U-turn that maneuvered him away from the location where the Ford had stalled and left his Camry with its nose pointed uphill, back toward Canal Street. That way, if it started taking hits, the bullets ought to spend their force inside his trunk, or in the backseat, without doing any damage to the rental's engine. He'd be able to evacuate the scene, at least—if he was still alive and fit to drive.

That was by no means certain, with the automatic fire already hammering the park, no more than thirty yards from where he took the battle EVA. Pursuing the Trailblazer any further would have made the fight a demolition derby, likely leaving him afoot when the police arrived to spoil the party. And since being jailed was not on Bolan's list of things to do that afternoon, he opted for audacity to shift the odds a bit.

Audacity, and maybe just a little bit of luck.

The MP5K wasn't heavy. Truth be told, it weighed about the same as the .44 Magnum Desert Eagle autoloader Bolan often carried as a backup piece. Add roughly a half pound for the Beta C-Mag and it still came in below six pounds, lightened a fraction of an ounce with every 3-round burst unleashed. He wasn't firing at the moment, though. The soldier was covering ground instead, closing the gap between himself and six men trying hard to kill one another in the middle of the park.

The Executioner came at the Trailblazer from its blind side, more or less, half crouching as he sprinted across the sloping turf. The shooter in the backseat tried to get an angle on him, squeezing off a burst to get the range, but rushed it so that half his bullets struck the inside of the tailgate, peppering the grass while Bolan ducked and rolled aside.

He squeezed off two short bursts in answer to that fire and saw his target flinch from the incoming rounds. Wounded? It was impossible to say, but when the Afghan fired again, his rounds tore through the Chevy's roof, a reflexive act accompanied by what Bolan assumed to be a shout of profanity.

Closer. The SUV's tailgate and left rear quarter panel were his cover now. They wouldn't stop a rifle bullet, but they kept the shooters in the Trailblazer from spotting him until he showed himself—which, as he saw it, couldn't be put off for any more convenient time.

Nine blocks from the Fifth Precinct and he was running out of time.

Bolan reached up, holding his SMG one-handed, and unloaded through the Chevy's left rear tinted window, spraying the interior with Parabellum rounds and shattered glass. A cry from somewhere near at hand told him he'd scored at least one hit before the SUV lurched forward, roaring off to make another sweep around the Ford sedan.

Leaving Mack Bolan totally exposed.

"DAOUD? *DAOUD!*"

Ahmad Taraki, bleeding from his scalp where shards of glass had stung him, swiveled in his seat when Daoud Rashad refused to answer him. The reason for his silence was revealed immediately. Fresh blood spattered the backseat of the SUV; Rashad was sprawled across that seat with half his face and skull sheared off.

Taraki still had no idea who had attacked them from behind, but he could see the bastard now, as Kazimi took them on another run around the crippled triad vehicle. The stranger was a white man, not Chinese, and he had fired on both cars during the pursuit along Canal Street, which made no sense in Taraki's mind.

The answer: kill the attacker now before he harmed them further.

But the three Chinese were firing at Taraki and Kazimi was swerving enough to spoil Taraki's aim as he tried to return fire on the drive-by. His magazine ran dry after unloading half a dozen rounds, but he was satisfied to see one of the triad gunners stagger, clutching at his chest before he fell. Taraki fumbled to reload the rifle, cursing his clumsy fingers, and then his driver had them lined up to charge directly at the white man who had killed Rashad.

"Run over him!" Taraki ordered. "Smash him into pulp!"

"I'm trying!" Kazimi snapped.

Their unknown adversary stood his ground, waiting, some kind of machine pistol held steady in his hands. Taraki snarled a curse and started firing through the Chevy's windshield, scarring it with spiderwebs before a chunk of glass the size of his own head broke free and slithered off the hood, clearing his field of fire. By then his enemy was firing back, not panicked as might be expected, but squeezing off precision bursts.

Kazimi croaked out a dying gasp as he slumped back in the driver's seat, his hands sliding off the steering wheel and down into his blood-drenched lap. His foot was still on the accelerator as he slid down in the seat, the SUV still charging forward, though it had begun to drift off course. Taraki grabbed the wheel and tried to bring the vehicle back on target, toward the man he meant to kill, but when he tore his eyes away from Kazimi's corpse, his enemy had leaped aside, out of the Chevy's path.

Taraki cranked the wheel sharply, swerving to the right. He guessed it was too little and too late, but what else could he do? Firing the Bushmaster with one hand, steering with the other while a dead man held the SUV at cruising speed, he tried to salvage something out of the disaster that had overtaken him.

Too late.

Another burst of submachine gun fire blew through the

Chevy's shattered windshield, ripping through Taraki's left shoulder and arm with stunning force. He might have squealed in pain—couldn't be certain of it with the roaring in his head—then he was slumping to his right, against his door, as the Trailblazer tipped and rolled onto its side. Kazimi, never a fan of seat belts when he was alive, slithered across the console, settling with his mutilated face jammed underneath Taraki's chin.

"Get off me." Taraki's voice grated, but he had no strength left with which to shove his former driver away, much less crawl out from under him. His left arm was a useless dangling piece of meat, his right pinned underneath his own weight and the corpse's, still clutching the Bushmaster but now incapable of lifting it.

He heard footsteps approaching; knew that it could only be an enemy, but didn't know whether it was the white man who had wounded him or one of the Wah Ching gunners. Cursing and weeping in frustration, straining with whatever strength he still possessed to raise his gun, Taraki listened to the grim approach of death.

At the last moment, with an effort that exhausted him, Taraki craned his neck to peer out through the windshield, focusing on feet and legs outside. He struggled impotently to free his weapon, mouthing curses as the man dropped to one knee and peered inside the toppled SUV. It was the stranger, naturally, frowning at him as he raised his submachine gun toward Taraki's face.

Before the world went black.

A BULLET SIZZLED past Mack Bolan's ear and panged into the capsized SUV, leaving a shiny divot in the roof where paint had flaked away. He ducked and rolled, putting the blunt nose of the Trailblazer between himself and the Wah Ching thugs who'd missed a chance to take him down.

Stalemate?

He couldn't let it go at that, with precious seconds slipping through his fingers. Sirens would be coming at him any time now, closing off Bolan's escape route from the battle that he'd never meant to fight in this location, with civilians in the way. He glanced around as best he could, saw no one raising cell phones yet to record the action as it happened, but the idea added one more level of concern.

His face on YouTube? Not a great idea.

Of course, it wasn't *his* face. Not the one he had been born with, anyway. No one would look at him and think *Mack Bolan? Someone told me he was dead!* Still, going viral to the world at large would definitely cramp his style, and might require yet another session with the surgeon who had given him his battle mask.

No, thanks.

Before he made another move against the Wah Ching gangsters, Bolan pulled a roll of silky black material out of his left trouser pocket and slipped it over his head. It was a balaclava, black nylon and ultra-thin, that fit him like a second skin, with a "ninja" oval opening for eyes alone, masking the rest of Bolan's face. Now he was ready for his close-up, if it came to that, switching out the MP5K's nearly empty magazine for a fresh one, bracing for his move.

First step: to take the triad hardmen by surprise within the limits of his present circumstance. They had to have seen where he had gone to ground, so Bolan crept along behind the Trailblazer until he reached its rear end, pausing there just long enough scout the landscape cautiously and choose his angle of attack. Behind him, twenty yards or so from where he crouched, the Camry waited for him, still had access to Canal Street if he finished his business soon enough and wasn't cut off by police.

Too many ifs.

The way to do it, he decided, was a plain, straight-forward rush, with cover fire as needed on the relatively short run to his destination. *Short* was relative, of course. Ten feet could feel like miles when a person was under hostile fire. The first step could turn out to be his last. Still, Bolan had to make the effort, or his intervention in the fight had been for nothing, a colossal—maybe cata-strophic—waste of time.

The best scenario would be a short dash, unopposed, to reach the Ford and— Then what? Killing at close quarters was an ugly business, where the outcome could go either way. One slip and he was done. There'd be no do-over, no second chance to get it right. End game.

But if he got it right…

His plan had changed, against his will, when the Af-ghans stepped in and made the hunt a firefight. Now, in-stead of following the Wah Ching thugs to their leader, Bolan had another end in mind, requiring him to face them and relieve them of the cargo they'd transported from New Jersey. Ten or twelve kilos of heroin that would become his lever for upsetting Paul Mei-Lun's enclave in China-town, with any luck.

And what about Wasef Kamran?

Bolan planned to take it one step at a time. Survive this challenge, then move on.

A final peek around the Chevy's tailgate and he was just in time to see one of the Wah Ching gunners rise and fire a short burst from an automatic rifle toward the SUV's front end. Trying to pin him down so they could make a run for it, perhaps? The last thing Bolan needed now was a pursuit on foot along Canal Street, running from the park and *toward* the Fifth Precinct.

A distant siren got him up and moving toward the triad vehicle, clutching his little SMG and hoping that his time had not run out.

"WHO *IS* THAT crazy bastard?" Martin Tang asked.

"It doesn't matter who he is," Louis Chao replied. "We need to get the hell away from here before we've got pigs crawling up our asses."

"What's the plan?" John Lin demanded. "Are we just gonna walk away from here?"

"Unless you get the damn car running," Chao snarled back at him.

"He'll pick us off, first move we make," Tang said.

"You mean he'll try to," Chao replied, and rose to fire a short burst from his Bushmaster as punctuation, stitching holes across the broad hood of the Afghans' SUV. "That lets us have another chance to drop him."

Chao didn't have a clue about the round-eyed stranger's motive or identity, was grateful that he'd taken out the triad goon, but that didn't solve his problem. They were half a mile or something from the cop house, sirens in the air now, and he couldn't lose the suitcase full of heroin. Not if he wanted to survive the day.

"Get ready," he commanded. "Switch your mags out if you're running low. There's no time for it once we start to run."

"Run *where?*" Lin challenged him.

"Just run. We get a block or so away from here, split up and make it harder for whoever's following. I'll see you at the Lucky Dragon."

Neither Lin nor Tang replied to that, both staring at him as if Chao had lost his mind. Maybe he had, in fact, but he was dead certain of one thing: staying where they were right now was not an option.

"Ready?"

Tang bobbed his head while Lin glowered and muttered to himself.

Maybe the plan was freaking stupid, but it was the best Chao could devise. He had a final thought, leaning in toward Tang and snatching the heavy suitcase from him.

"I'll take this," Chao said, not giving Tang a choice.

"Suits me."

The bag would slow him a bit, no question, but he couldn't trust it to their younger Wah Ching brother with a madman breathing down their necks and cops converging on the battleground. Whatever happened to the skag, it would be Chao's neck on the chopping block with Paul Mei-Lun. He might as well die running with it, as to show up empty-handed at the Lucky Dragon, pleading ignorance of where the dope had gone.

"Okay," Chao said. "Remember now—"

He never had a chance to finish as running footsteps made him turn and then all hell broke loose. The round-eye was upon them, spraying death among them from his compact submachine gun. Chao gasped as the bullets struck him, punched him over backward, glimpsing Lin in a fighting stance, then falling through a cloud of crimson mist. Chao couldn't see what had become of Tang and didn't care.

He'd failed his brothers and the Wah Ching Family. Whatever lay in store for him, if there was anything at all beyond this life, at least he wouldn't have to answer for his last snafu to Paul Mei-Lun.

The attacker stood above him now, face covered, bending to lift the suitcase Chao had tried to rescue, all in vain. Chao tried to curse him, nearly managed it, but felt his final breath escape as a gurgling whistle from his punctured lungs before he closed his eyes.

BOLAN HEFTED THE BAG—ten kilos by the feel of it—and turned back toward his waiting rental car. He sprinted past the Ford, beyond the SUV slumped on its side, and reached the Camry as the sirens sounded louder in his ears. He opened the driver's door and pitched the suitcase right across into the footwell of the shotgun seat. Sliding in behind the wheel, the soldier dropped his MP5K on the empty seat beside him, leaving on the balaclava while he gunned the Camry's engine into growling life and powered out of there.

Careful!

He had to hurry, but could not afford undue attention as he picked an escape route. Pulling out into the two-way traffic on Canal Street, Bolan had a choice to make immediately. Turning to his right, he could proceed directly toward the Fifth Precinct, the source of the sirens closing in on him even now, then turn north on Sixth Avenue, running one-way, or keep on for another block to West Broadway, another one-way street bearing him north. Beyond that, he'd be rolling past the cops and into Chinatown, a move that he was not prepared to make just yet.

A left turn on Canal would take him back to Varick Street and one-way traffic heading south into Lower Manhattan, renamed after eight long blocks to become West Broadway. If he passed that, his next choice would be Hudson Street northbound, or on from there to Lincoln Highway where his tracking of the Wah Ching hardmen had begun. That route would take him north or south along the Hudson River, with a choice of side streets offered either way.

Bolan turned left.

He didn't make a big deal of it, didn't screech his tires with a dramatic peel-out from the scene. If someone memorized his license plate or snapped a photo of it on a cell phone, well, so be it. He would have to ditch the Camry anyhow, and soon, then find another set of wheels to keep him mobile in New York. He'd bought insurance on the rental, so the vendor wouldn't take a hit from any damage suffered in the fight, and Bolan's fingerprints had been expunged from every file that Hal Brognola could access from his office in D.C.—which meant all files, across the board. The cyber team at Stony Man had taken care of the rest.

The danger he faced now was that of being overtaken by police before Bolan could slip away and lose himself among the Big Apple's eight million people and two million automobiles. He didn't need much of a lead, maybe a mile or so, and he could likely pull it off.

Two blocks from where he'd killed six men, Bolan ditched the balaclava and turned right on Hudson Street, slowing to match the flow of traffic moving northward. The map in his head told him that Hudson would become Ninth Street when he had cleared the next two dozen blocks, past Greenwich Village, and then continue toward Times Square and the Theater District. Somewhere along that two-mile drive he'd find a place to ditch the Camry and proceed on foot until he caught a cab and went from there.

Next stop: a different auto rental agency, where he'd present a driver's license and Platinum Visa in the name of Matthew Cooper, home address a mail drop in Richmond, Virginia, that forwarded bills and whatever to Stony Man Farm. There'd be no problem picking up another ride, and he'd be on his way.

Easy.

After that, however, things would once again get complicated in a hurry.

Bolan's plan had been diverted by the battle on Canal Street, but it wasn't scuttled. In fact, he thought Plan B might serve him better than the scheme he'd started out with. Now that he'd acquired a load of smack worth some three million dollars, he could try a new game, not restricted to the Wah Ching base in Chinatown.

Divide and conquer, right. He'd played that hand before, with good results, and Bolan couldn't think of any reason why it wouldn't work this time. At least, not yet.

New wheels, then phone calls. He would reach out to the Wah Ching Triad first, since he'd relieved them of their merchandise, then he would float an offer to Wasef Kamran. Neither would ever lay hands on the suitcase full of poison, but they wouldn't know that going in.

Hope springs eternal, even among savages.

They would believe that every person drawing breath came with a price tag, ready to abandon principle if someone offered them a payday large enough to salve their qualms of conscience. Moral ambiguity was absolutely necessary for survival of a criminal cartel. It was the mobster's stock in trade. Neither would be familiar with a man like Bolan, who regarded the performance of his duty as an end unto itself.

A rude awakening was coming to his enemies, but if he played his cards right, none of them would live to profit from the lesson.

And when they were gone, the Executioner would deal with those who'd sent them to New York.

CHAPTER FOUR

Chinatown, Manhattan

Paul Mei-Lun poured himself a second glass of rice *baiju* and slugged the liquor down, waiting to feel its heat spread from his throat into his belly. He hoped that it would calm him soon and damp the waves of anger that were threatening to prompt some foolish action he would certainly regret.

Details of the attack were vague, confused, but Mei-Lun knew the basics. He had lost three men and ten kilos of heroin, while suffering another grievous insult at the hands of foul barbarians. With Tommy Mu, that made four deaths within a week, eleven kilos lost. He did not want to think about what Ma Lam Chan would say—what he might do—on learning of the latest losses.

It was Mei-Lun's job to put things right. He owed it to the Wah Ching brotherhood and to himself, since the responsibility had to ultimately fall on him. His problem now was where to start.

Of course, Wasef Kamran and his gorillas were responsible for Tommy Mu, but someone else had interceded in the second incident. Police had found the Afghans dead, along with Mei-Lun's men, and witnesses described a seventh man wearing a mask and firing at both sides in the fight. He had been seen escaping with a suitcase—Mei-Lun's suitcase—in a car already found abandoned on Manhattan's Upper West Side, close to Central Park. Mei-Lun knew the car was rented, but he had not yet obtained the name of the killer who'd hired it.

When he did...

His thoughts stopped there. The gunman clearly was a trained professional. There was no reason to suppose that he would use his real name on a rental contract or that Mei-Lun would be able to locate him once he had the alias in hand. His task was to determine why a stranger, a professional, would leap into the middle of a firefight, tackle six armed men and kill them all.

The easy answer: for the heroin. But that was *too* easy.

To pull it off, the killer had to have known about the shipment, where it would be coming from and when it would arrive. He had to have followed Mei-Lun's people from the ferry terminal. Without the Afghans intervening, Mei-Lun reckoned that the gunman would have trailed them to the Lucky Dragon where he sat right now, the empty liquor glass in front of him. But Kamran's men *had* intervened, and even when the shooting started it was not enough to put the other gunman off. He'd gone ahead to fight six men and kill them all, then make off with the heroin.

Acting on whose behalf?

Mei-Lun's thoughts turned immediately to the New York Mafia. His headquarters on Mott Street stood a short three blocks from Little Italy, where rivals spawned in Sicily despised him, seething enviously over his prosperity. There had been clashes in the past between his soldiers and the goombahs of La Cosa Nostra, but no overt violence had flared among them for a year or more. It would be out of character for them, he thought, to send a single soldier on a mission of such gravity.

But if they had...

Beside the *baiju* bottle, Mei-Lun's cell phone buzzed and vibrated. He scooped it up and read the message: Number Blocked. Frowning, Mei-Lun pressed a button to accept the call and asked, "Who's this?"

Instead of answering, a voice he didn't recognize said, "Rumor has it that you lost a piece of luggage earlier today."

The frown turned to a scowl, but Mei-Lun kept his voice in neutral. "Luggage?"

"I suppose you're more concerned about the contents than the bag," his caller said.

Cell phones were dangerous, their airborne messages fair game under the law for anyone who intercepted them. "Sorry," Mei-Lun replied. "Wrong number."

"Okay, then," Mack Bolan said. "I'll speak to Mr. Chan directly, shall I?" He rattled off the Dragon Head's unpublished number in Hong Kong without missing a beat, as if from memory.

A trick? Undoubtedly. But if the stranger knew that much and Mei-Lun brushed him off, he might indeed call Ma Lam Chan. And that could be the end of Paul Mei-Lun.

"Perhaps I was mistaken," Mei-Lun said. "If so, I would be willing to discuss it."

"Small talk doesn't interest me," the caller told him. "I've got merchandise to sell."

"I see." There'd been no mention of the heroin, nothing that would incriminate Mei-Lun so far. "What figure did you have in mind?"

"Wholesale, I understand it runs around six hundred thousand. Call it half a mil and we're in business."

Mei-Lun wished that he could reach out through the cell phone, grasp the caller's throat and strangle him, but he restrained himself, controlled his voice. "That is within the realm of possibility," he said.

"Okay. I'll call you back with details for the drop."

And he was gone.

Flushing, Queens, New York

KHODA HAFIZ, an Afghan social club and quasi-covert headquarters of Wasef Kamran's organization, stood near the corner of Franklin Avenue and Colden Street, in a neighborhood occupied mostly by South Asian immigrants. Some old-time residents called the neighborhood Little Afghanistan, while others dubbed it Little India. Kamran, these past four years, had simply called it home.

The club's name translated in English to "May God protect you," but He had not smiled on Wasef Kamran lately, and it angered the mobster.

The loss of three good men plus failure to secure the Wah Ching shipment he had sent them to collect had Kamran simmering with rage, augmented by frustration since he had no one to punish for that failure. With no outlet for his fury—and despite the strictures of his faith—Kamran had pacified himself to some extent with a small glass of homemade liquor that included alcohol, hash oil, sugar, nutmeg, a bit of cinnamon and cloves.

It had begun to work, soothing his nerves enough that Kamran thought he was prepared to face the second-worst part of his day: reporting his losses to Khalil Nazari in Kabul. He knew approximately how that call would go, and Kamran knew his only saving grace was that the conversation would occur long-distance rather than in person, where Nazari could slit his throat.

Killing the bearer of bad news was still in fashion with some Afghan warlords, a tradition hard to shake. Kamran had done the same himself, a time or two. Why fix what was not broken, after all?

He thought about another glass of liquor, then decided it would be too much. He wished to sound composed and in control, not high and babbling incoherently. If he appeared unstable, or Nazari surmised that he had lost control, his fate might well be sealed.

No further stalling, then.

Kamran picked up his encrypted sat-phone and was just about to speed-dial Kabul, when the smartphone beside his elbow chirped its ringtone, playing the first three bars of Farhad Darya's "In a Foreign Land." Kamran set down the larger instrument and checked the smartphone for a number. He found it blocked and answered anyway, against his better judgment.

"What?"

"Your people missed today," a strange voice said, raising the short hairs on his nape.

"Wrong number," Kamran snarled, and was about to cut the link when his caller said, "That's what I heard from Paul Mei-Lun."

"Oh, yes?"

"He wants to buy back the suitcase. I'm wondering if you're prepared to beat his price."

Kamran considered what he'd heard so far. Police were fond of stings in the United States, but this seemed far too subtle and innocuous. With no mention of contraband per se, he could discuss the generalities with no fear of indictment or arrest.

"What was his price?" Kamran inquired.

"Five hundred thousand."

"That's a lot of money for a suitcase."

"Or the property inside it."

He ran the calculation quickly through his mind. Buying the heroin cost more than stealing it, but even so, he had a chance to make a killing here—and not only financially. If he could meet this caller and determine if he was responsible for dropping Kamran's men...

"I can improve on that by...shall we say ten percent?"

"Fifteen sounds better," said the caller.

That was more than Kamran wished to pay, but still some twenty-five thousand less than Paul Mei-Lun would have shelled out for the merchandise. Call it $2.4 million and change in clear profit—and the drugs might cost him nothing, if the hijacker was dumb enough to bring them on his own, without backup.

"Where shall we meet, and when?" Kamran inquired.

"I'll let you know," the caller said, then broke the link.

Central Park, Manhattan

BOLAN HAD SOME time to kill while he decided on a meeting place—he was determined not to start the party until after nightfall. Seated on a stone bench within sight of where his former life had ended and the new one had begun, he ate a hero sandwich and perused a guidebook to the city that was once again his battleground, if only for a little while.

Phase one of his campaign would end this night and he'd move on, assuming he survived. He could have skipped the New York interlude, left it to normal law-enforcement agencies, but shutting down Wasef Kamran and Paul Mei-Lun was part of Bolan's larger plan. It was step one in rattling some larger cages, putting more impressive predators on the defensive, kicking off a psy-war that would keep them guessing, sweating, while he homed in on another kill.

New York was one end of a global pipeline pumping heroin into the States. On second thought, make that *two* pipelines. One reached across the Middle East, Europe and the Atlantic, from Afghanistan. The other ran across the vast Pacific, from its starting point in Southeast Asia, to deliver poison on the West Coast, and from there across the continent. The only way to cripple both, however briefly, was to play off the existing competition between drug lords, bring it to a head, and take the top men down in flames.

Manhattan was a test case; Bolan's master plan conducted on a smaller scale to see how well it played. And so far, even with the shooting match outside Chinatown, it seemed to be on track.

Next up, he needed someplace where the warring tribes could meet without endangering large numbers of civilians, someplace midway between Flushing and Chinatown, a spot with combat stretch, where he could set his trap and lie in wait for whoever showed up. Three million dollars' worth of heroin made Bolan confident that both sides would attempt to grab the prize.

The second map he studied did the trick. Roosevelt Island, two miles long and three hundred yards wide, lay in the East River between Manhattan and Queens. At various times in its 377-year history, it had supported a prison, a lunatic asylum and a smallpox hospital. The mostly unoccupied northern tip of the island boasted Lighthouse Park and the historic Blackwell Island Light. Access points included East 66th Street passing under the river from Manhattan, the Roosevelt Island Bridge serving Queens. Once on the island proper, a person could drive around or take the tram to see the sights.

Bolan would be arriving from the west, using the tunnel, after he'd made sure no one was tailing him. From there he'd take the island's West Road all the way, until it terminated, some three hundred yards from Blackwell Island Light, which put him in the kill zone. He would start at dusk and be in place before he made the calls directing Kamran and Mei-Lun to the appointed drop site, neither one expecting that the other would be there.

One question still remained in Bolan's mind: would either of the top men show in person? He believed the odds were good, particularly if he made delivery contingent on their turning up to make the payoff. Naturally, they'd come with heavy backup, hoping to eliminate the stranger who was vexing them and claim the heroin without paying a dime. Bolan was counting on both sides to try their best at cheating him. He needed soldiers on the ground to help him with the mopping up.

And if he missed Kamran, Mei-Lun or both…well, he could take a little extra time to visit them before he moved on to the second phase of his campaign. Why not?

Anything worth doing was worth doing well.

Chinatown

"Roosevelt Island?" Paul Mei-Lun pronounced the name as if it left a bad taste in his mouth. "What's on Roosevelt Island?"

"Your shipment," Bolan replied. "It waits for you till half past midnight, then goes looking for another buyer."

"That would be a big mistake."

"I'll risk it if you don't show up."

"I said I'd be there, didn't I? The park, out by the lighthouse, right?"

"That's it," the caller said. "If you decide to change your mind, the bag goes to Kamran."

"Hey, now—"

But he was talking to dead air.

Standing beside him, almost at his elbow, Kevin Lo asked, "Well? What did he say?"

"Midnight, Roosevelt Island. At the lighthouse park."

"This whole thing smells."

"You think I don't know that?"

"It has to be some kind of setup."

"Obviously. But it's not the pigs," Mei-Lun declared. "No mention of the H at all, so far. I show up and they bust me, I can always claim somebody called about my uncle's missing suitcase."

"Okay. It's the Afghans, then."

"Three of their men got wasted, right along with ours. If they already had the bag, why call me?"

That stumped Lo, but he still was not satisfied. "So what's the angle, then? This can't be straight."

"His angle doesn't matter," Mei-Lun answered. "Only ours. He wants to dance, we call the tune."

"We go in hard?"

"As hard as diamonds, brother." Mei-Lun checked his Movado Swiss Automatic SE Extreme watch and smiled. "The meet's at midnight. That gives us four hours to get there. I want a dozen of our best men here in half an hour, dressed to kill."

"No problem," Lo assured him. "You're still going with us?"

"Kevin, I wouldn't miss it for the world. Get moving now and set it up."

Lo bobbed his head and left the office, cell phone already in hand. Mei-Lun considered changing his command to make it twenty soldiers, rather than a dozen, but that felt like overcompensating. From the early eyewitness reports, one guy had done the killing on Canal Street by himself, and he would likely come alone to claim his payoff for the stolen heroin. But if he showed up with a friend or two, so what? Mei-Lun would have his soldiers waiting at the drop well in advance of midnight, primed to waste this fool on sight.

No, scratch that. They would have to chat a little with him first, to make sure that he'd brought the merchandise.

Killing the bastard without getting back the skag would be a waste of time—and it would leave Mei-Lun at risk from Ma Lam Chan when he admitted to the loss.

A sudden thought disturbed him. What if Chan already knew about the heist? He almost certainly had eyes and ears inside Mei-Lun's Manhattan cadre, someone who would tip him off to any problems Mei-Lun tried to cover up. If word had reached the Dragon Head at home, would he reach out to Paul Mei-Lun, or simply send a team of his enforcers to correct the situation, meting out the punishment Chan deemed appropriate?

Mei-Lun peered at his watch again, counting the hours since the slaughter on Canal Street, guessing how long it would take to have a team airborne from Hong Kong to the States. As he remembered it, the flight to San Francisco took approximately fifteen hours, then they'd face another seven hours in the air, if they were fortunate enough to catch a nonstop flight from Frisco to LaGuardia or JFK. If they were airborne now, Mei-Lun shouldn't expect to see them nosing around Chinatown until sometime tomorrow afternoon.

No sweat.

He'd have the problem solved by then, the merchandise in hand, and they could tell Chan that he'd taken care of business without any interference from the East. And if that didn't satisfy the Dragon Head, perhaps they ought to meet and talk about it, face-to-face.

Maybe, Mei-Lun decided, it was time for him to think about advancement in the Family.

Flushing, Queens

"THIS MAKES NO SENSE, WASEF," Ghulam Munadi said.

Wasef Kamran shrugged in response. "This man stole

heroin we planned to steal, and now he wants to sell it. What confuses you?"

"First, that he knows the number where to reach you."

"Anyone can find a number nowadays," Kamran replied. "The internet is free to all, and this man has skills."

"Too many skills," Munadi countered. "He is some kind of policeman. I'm convinced of it."

"Some kind? *What* kind? He asks for money to return an item that was stolen. There is nothing to incriminate us, eh?"

"Until we claim the bag. Then they arrest us."

"Think, Ghulam! Would the police kill six men in the public eye, then steal the drugs just to arrest us?" Kamran did not wait for his lieutenant to reply. "Of course not! If this person *is* a cop, he's more like us. Trying to save a little for retirement, eh?"

"And what if it's a trap?" Munadi asked.

"I can assure you that it is. We seem to take the bait, then close the noose around his neck. With fifteen men, what can he do?"

Munadi frowned. "I don't like going to this island."

"Tell me what you *do* like, Ghulam. It's a shorter list, I'm sure."

"What I would like is to forget this business. Since we can't do that, I'd like you to remain here under tight security until the bag has been retrieved and this is settled."

"Stay at home and miss the show this bastard has planned for me especially? I wouldn't think of it."

"You'll wear the Kevlar, though?"

"Of course. I'm not an idiot," Kamran replied.

He would be armed, as well, with his usual sidearm for a start, a Heckler & Koch P30 chambered in .40 S&W, with a 13-round magazine. To back it up, another favorite: the Spectre M4 submachine gun with its casket magazine containing fifty 9 mm Parabellum rounds, less than fourteen inches long with its metal stock folded above the receiver. With the Spectre he could lay down 800 rounds per minute, killing anyone or anything that stood between him and his goal.

Including this killer who believed that he could dupe Kamran somehow, perhaps make off with Kamran's hard-earned money, and the heroin besides.

"Good luck with that," he muttered to himself.

"What did you say?" Munadi asked.

"Nothing. Go and make sure the men are ready. We should leave soon."

"But it's only—"

"Yes, I know the time. I want to be there, waiting, when our friend arrives. Let us surprise him, eh?"

"As you wish it, Wasef."

He was looking forward to the meeting with this stranger who had robbed him—or, in truth, who'd robbed the Chinese Kamran had meant to rob. He felt a sneaking kind of admiration for such courage and audacity, but it required a harsh response to salvage Kamran's reputation as a man whose enemies enjoyed short, miserable lives.

This one, whoever he might be, would have been wiser to go hunting somewhere else, perhaps rob the Jamaicans or Dominicans, maybe the damned Armenians. He was about to learn a lesson that Afghanis had been teaching Westerners since 1839. Kamran's people could not be vanquished in their homeland—not by England, Russia or America—and now they were expanding into every corner of the planet to assert themselves and claim their proper share of wealth.

This night, Roosevelt Island. This time next year, perhaps Manhattan. And beyond that…who could say? It was a whole new world, beyond Khalil Nazari's wildest dreams from Kabul, where the old ways mired him down. Perhaps a younger, stronger man was needed to command that new domain and bend it to his will.

Job one: collect the heroin without dispensing any cash to the audacious thief. Then, having proved himself, Wasef Kamran could think about tomorrow and the great things he was going to accomplish.

All he had to do was make it through the night alive.

Roosevelt Island

BOLAN PARKED HIS latest rental car, a Honda CR-V, in the visitor's lot at Coler-Goldwater Specialty Hospital, and made his way to the roof of the X-shaped facility's northwestern wing. From there he had a view across treetops to Lighthouse Park, where his intended targets would be showing up, at least in theory, sometime in the next three hours.

Waiting was a sniper's specialty. Bolan likely could not have counted all the times he'd lain in wait for enemies in heat and cold, under a drenching rain, while insects crawled over his skin and hummed around his ears. He'd learned to lie in perfect stillness, barely breathing, while a target took its own sweet time about appearing, stepping finally into the crosshairs of his telescopic sight and dying there, struck down from half a mile or more away, with no idea how death had come so suddenly, without a hint of warning.

He was ready now, with his weapon of choice for this phase of the hunt, an M-110 Semi-Automatic Sniper System manufactured by Knight's Armament in Florida. The rifle measured 46.5 inches with its buttstock extended and a suppressor attached, tipping the scales at just over fifteen pounds with a 20-round magazine full of 7.62 mm

NATO rounds. Its AN/PVS-10 night sight would let him place accurate shots out to 875 yards, nearly nine times the range he would be firing from this night. It should be like shooting fish in a barrel.

But these fish might be shooting back.

His plan was simple: place the Afghans and Wah Ching hardmen into proximity, both looking for the same thing, then cut loose and see what happened next. A well-placed shot or two might do the trick, but if the opposition needed any more help, Bolan had a stack of extra magazines on hand and was prepared to use as many as the job required.

Scorched earth, all the way.

He didn't need to rattle either side for information, since the next stop on his tour had been determined in advance. Khalil Nazari's opium was processed into bricks of morphine near the poppy fields he cultivated in Afghanistan. Bolan knew approximately where the morphine bricks were sent for their conversion into heroin. The details he did not as yet possess would be available when he arrived on-site, secured by one means or another to complete the next link in the chain.

This night he would be shutting down the pipeline in Manhattan. Not for good; no one could claim permanent victory in any war against a human craving for release. But Bolan *could* remove the major players in this one dark corner of the world. Maybe incite some other scavengers to take each other off the board while they were grappling to fill the power vacuum that resulted.

Doing what he could with what he had.

His field of fire was open from the hospital's six-story rooftop to the Blackwell Island Light, four hundred feet northeast of where he sat cradling the rifle, waiting. Once the action started, Bolan's enemies could break in one of three directions: toward the light, away from him; to cars parked on the left or right, against the river's edge; or back toward Bolan, seeking refuge among trees that formed a kind of horseshoe shape at his end of the park. Whichever way they ran, it would be under fire from Bolan and from adversaries on the other side, who'd come expecting to go home with ten kilos of heroin.

How many would go home at all?

Bolan never indulged in overconfidence. He trained and practiced, planned and double-checked his plans, then trusted to his own experience and skill. That recipe had kept him in the game so far, but he did not deceive himself into believing that his luck would hold forever. No one had that guarantee, and least of all a fighting man who put himself in harm's way constantly.

His greatest apprehension at the moment was that Paul Mei-Lun or Wasef Kamran might decide to stay at home, let their gorillas keep the date and see what came of it. If he missed one or both of them this night, he'd have to stick around New York until the job was done, giving his adversaries at the next stop more time to prepare themselves.

For all the good that it would do them.

Even with the news of his Manhattan blitz, they wouldn't know with whom they were dealing.

They would not be prepared to meet the Executioner.

CHAPTER FIVE

Lighthouse Park, Roosevelt Island

"Remember, everyone," Paul Mei-Lun said. "No shooting till we see the bag. It's all for nothing if we go back empty-handed."

The shooters riding with him in the Hummer H2 all nodded like a bunch of bobbleheads. In Mei-Lun's hand, a walkie-talkie crackled and a voice came to him from the second vehicle, trailing behind his, with the other Wah Ching soldiers he'd selected for the showdown.

"Got it, boss."

They were armed to the teeth and stopping for no one, including police. There could be no explaining the weapons they carried, and Mei-Lun knew he was running a risk with the Hummers. CNN had told him they were ticketed by traffic cops five times as often as most other vehicles, and Mei-Lun himself had enough citations to believe it.

But anyone who tried to flag them down this night, Mei-Lun vowed, was shit out of luck.

Truth be told, he was amped for a killing. The skag heist, the loss of four men in a week... It was all bearing down on him, making him look bad, stretching his nerves like piano wire. He needed an outlet, and whether they got back the suitcase or not, someone was bound to die on the island.

Mei-Lun could personally guarantee it.

Once they'd cleared the tunnel from Manhattan—always claustrophobic for him, though he tried to hide it—they got onto Main Street near the tram station and barreled northward, past the interchange for 36th Avenue and the Roosevelt Island Bridge to Queens, rolling on until Main Street turned into East Road. A giant hospital bulked up beside them on the left, and they slowed down, continuing along the narrow road that led out toward the lighthouse on the island's northern headland.

Looking at a map before he'd left the Lucky Dragon, Mei-Lun thought that Roosevelt Island looked like a giant condom afloat in the river, right down to what Trojan ads called the "reservoir tip." He'd started laughing, and his soldiers couldn't understand it, but he hadn't bothered to explain. Better if they believed that he was laughing in the face of death than spotting crazy shapes on a road map.

Mei-Lun double-checked the QBZ-95 assault rifle he'd chosen for their little safari. It was the latest thing from China, a bullpup design chambered for the 5.8 mm DBP87 cartridge. Smuggled from his homeland in bulk, the QBZ-95 was selective-fire, feeding from a 30-round box magazine with a cyclic rate of 650 rounds per minute in full-auto mode. The 5-grain full-metal-jacket rounds traveled at 2,900 feet per second and delivered 1,477 foot-pounds of energy on impact, their streamlined shape and steel core designed for increased range and penetration.

Not that he'd be needing any kind of long-range skills this night. The meeting ground, according to his phallic map, was no more than one hundred yards across, its only cover the arc of shade trees screening the hospital's north-facing windows from the glare of the lighthouse. Their target, whoever he was, should be clearly visible and easy to kill when the time came.

As soon as he showed them the bag filled with sweet China white.

"We're almost there," his driver said, and Mei-Lun grunted in reply. He had already seen the lighthouse standing tall against the skyline, sweeping the dark water with its beam to help the barges find their way. The Hummer's headlights weren't much competition, but they showed Mei-Lun the sweep of grass where this night's action would play out.

"We're early," someone muttered from the backseat.

"As intended," Mei-Lun said.

Then he addressed his wheel man. "Stop here. Kill the lights."

A moment later they were sitting in the near dark with the Hummer's engine ticking. From the back, again, one of his soldiers said, "Nobody here."

Mei-Lun palmed the walkie-talkie, giving it to all of them at once. "Get out and take your places. Anybody fires before I give the word, he's dead."

BOLAN TRACKED THE Hummers through his AN/PVS-10 nightscope until they parked and Wah Ching soldiers started climbing out, all clutching long guns. Bolan counted off a dozen targets armed with automatic rifles, shotguns, submachine guns, picked out Paul Mei-Lun among them, then went back to watching for the other team.

The triad boss had played it smart, coming an hour early to the meet and staking out his men to cover both approaches, east and west of Lighthouse Park. It was a sound move, sensible, maybe the best that he could manage without formal military training or a sniper's long view toward the waiting game. He had the park well covered, but he obviously hadn't given any thought to checking out the nearby hospital.

Too public and too risky. Now, too late.

Before he'd come out to the island, Bolan had detoured past a vacant lot off FDR Drive, near the Queensboro Bridge, and dumped the stolen heroin, torching it with a can of lighter fluid he'd picked up in transit. The smack was up in smoke, long gone, but still working to Bolan's benefit, drawing his targets into rifle range.

And now he saw more headlights sweeping toward the park, coming along West Road. A Lincoln Town Car led the new arrivals, followed by a matched pair of Volkswagen Phaetons. They rolled past the hospital's northwestern wing, slowing as they closed in on the park and the lighthouse beyond. The Lincoln coasted to a halt beyond the tree line, and the Phaetons followed suit.

He waited, watching through the nightscope while doors opened on the luxury sedans and more men bearing weapons stepped onto the pavement, fanning out in a defensive formation. Bolan had no trouble picking out Wasef Kamran, the Lincoln's shotgun rider, carrying a Spectre M4 SMG. The men arrayed around him were all similarly armed, mostly with variations of the tried and true Kalashnikov assault rifle.

Bolan counted fifteen Afghans below him, giving them a three-man edge over the Wah Ching team. He saw lips moving, couldn't tell what they were saying, but he registered surprise on Kamran's face when Paul Mei-Lun stepped from the shadows to reveal himself.

A frozen moment passed, then Kamran shouted something to his rival, probably a question, possibly a challenge. Mei-Lun shouted something back and stood his ground, confusion written on his face and shifting into anger as he registered betrayal, trying to decide who was responsible.

Bolan focused his night sight on the soldier standing just to Wasef Kamran's right, placing his crosshairs on the hardman's dull face two hundred feet in front of him. The range was virtually point-blank for his M-110 Semi-Automatic Sniper System—easy pickings—as he sent 175 grains of sudden death hurtling downrange toward impact at 2,570 feet per second.

The target's skull exploded, its mangled contents splashing Wasef Kamran's face and thousand-dollar suit. Kamran recoiled, raising an arm too late to keep the muck out of his eyes and mouth, looking dazed as he shouted something to his other men.

It was the signal they'd been waiting for: to open fire and turn the quiet park into a little slice of hell on earth.

WASEF KAMRAN COULD NOT believe his eyes when Paul Mei-Lun stepped from the shadows, cradling some kind of spacey-looking weapon in his arms. The Afghan mobster felt his gut churn, knew damn well the stranger he'd arranged the meet with had not been Chinese—but had Mei-Lun arranged the call? It seemed impossible, since he had lost the heroin that afternoon.

"What are you doing here?" Kamran called across the dark expanse of grass.

After a split-second delay, Mei-Lun yelled back at him, "I'm here on business. Why are *you* here?"

Kamran was considering an answer when it happened. To his right, Amir Sadaty's head burst open with a sodden ripping sound, as if someone had struck a melon with an ax. Its contents flew in all directions, warm blood spraying Kamran's shoulder, face and hair. He lurched away before the man collapsed, his legs folding under him, and snapped an order at his other soldiers.

"Fire!"

Along the skirmish line, they all cut loose in unison, their muzzle-flashes lighting up the park. Kamran saw Mei-Lun go down but couldn't tell if he was hit or merely seeking cover from the storm of bullets hurtling toward him. Kamran wiped the blood out of his right eye with a sleeve, then fired a short burst of his own toward where he'd last seen Mei-Lun standing.

And, of course, the Wah Ching leader had not come alone. In answer to the fire from Kamran's men, at least a dozen guns were sniping at his party now, their slugs buzzing around him like a swarm of mosquitoes on steroids, all thirsty for blood. He saw another of his soldiers fall, clutching a hip and firing back one-handed as he dropped.

"Behind the cars!" Kamran cried out for those who weren't already ducking under cover. "Everybody! Quickly!"

Bullets struck the Lincoln Town Car and the two Volkswagens, taking out their windows, hammering their doors and fenders with the noise of a demonic hailstorm. Kamran rolled across the Lincoln's trunk and landed on his knees, cursing the pain that lanced through them from impact with the pavement.

What were the goddamned triad goons doing here? More to the point, where was his heroin?

Kamran pushed up into a crouch and waddled toward the front end of the Lincoln, where a couple of his men were trading shots with Mei-Lun's soldiers. They would have to torch the cars when they were finished here, assuming they could even drive away, and file a theft report with the police. But first, they had to finish killing off the Wah Ching gunners who had pinned them down.

And all before someone inside the hospital summoned police.

Kamran had nearly reached his soldiers when the closer

of them suddenly pitched over sideways, knocking down the soldier to his left. Kamran had seen the blood spurt from his throat, an inch or two below his right ear, nearly shearing off his head, and knew the angle was all wrong.

He pressed closer against the car, then turned back to face the hospital. The shot had come from that direction, somehow. From the trees or someplace higher up? With all the gunfire ringing in his ears, he could not single out a given shot, but it occurred to him that Mei-Lun had boxed them in to cut off their retreat.

Mei-Lun or someone else.

Once more, he heard the unknown caller's mocking voice, directing him and giving orders, setting up the meet. A man with the audacity to kill six soldiers and escape with ten kilos of heroin, perhaps? Did that explain the Wah Ching presence at their rendezvous? Were both sides simply chessmen in his deadly game?

And did it matter now?

Embarrassed, furious, Wasef Kamran focused on the only thing that mattered to him now: escaping with his life.

MACK BOLAN SHIFTED from the Afghan lines back to the Wah Ching side of the impromptu battleground, scanning for muzzle-flashes in the night. He had no trouble finding them—he picked one that suited him and framed the shooter in his sights. It was not Paul Mei-Lun, but Bolan didn't mind. It was a numbers game, shaving the odds.

The target he'd selected was a stocky guy, mid-twenties, with the standard slicked-back hair, wearing a pair of amber shooting glasses. Bolan placed his crosshairs on the left lens of those pricey shades and stroked the rifle's trigger, holding the view long enough to see half of the shooter's head detonate in a thick scarlet spray. The corpse toppled over, still firing its bullpup assault rifle, raking the heavens with hot, wasted fire.

Bolan had no idea what kind of soundproofing they had at Coler-Goldwater Hospital, whose grounds included Roosevelt Island's former lunatic asylum, but he guessed that someone had to have heard the gunfire from their own backyard by now. Some night-shift nurse or resident was bound to call for the police, and while the nearest precinct houses were both a fair distance away—one on Manhattan's East 67th Street, the other on 21st Street in Astoria, Queens—there could be a prowl car working the island as part of its beat.

One cop was manageable; maybe even two, if Bolan didn't let himself be cornered in a killing situation. He was not about to break one of the few rules that he'd self-imposed for conduct of his lonely war.

Below him, automatic fire from the opposing sides had thinned out Bolan's range of targets. Neither group was trying to break contact yet, their leaders both presumably still fixated on salvaging the load of heroin he had destroyed, the soldiers now wrapped up in fighting to survive. Rage would be part of it, and the instinctive racial animosity that Bolan had observed in insular crime syndicates around the world. Their take on brotherhood involved a mix of blood and oath-bound loyalty that superseded any bonds of conscience and, at least in theory, placed the welfare of the group above any specific individual.

Bolan supposed that he could leave now, letting the survivors kill off one another or keep their adversaries occupied until NYPD arrived in force. But that still left the possibility of one or both leaders escaping, either slipping out ahead of the police or, worse yet, through some stupid loophole in the law. As long as he was on the scene, he meant to deal with Paul Mei-Lun and Wasef Kamran on the spot.

Now all he had to do was to locate them once more, amid the bloody chaos he'd initiated.

Tracking with the AN/PVS-10 nightscope, Bolan worked his way along the ragged Wah Ching skirmish line, past bodies sprawled in awkward, lifeless poses on the grass, seeking the faces of survivors. There had been twelve triad gunners standing when the fight began, but nearly half of them were down, the others staying mobile, firing short bursts toward the enemy and then sprinting for another vantage point. Grass stains and sweat defaced their stylish outfits, but their focus wasn't fashion now. It was survival.

Paul Mei-Lun loomed in Bolan's scope, his face a snarling mask of rage and fear. The Executioner was taking up his rifle's trigger slack when someone beat him to it, hammering a bullet into Mei-Lun's shoulder, flinging him away and out of frame.

A mortal wound? He didn't wait to see, already tracking back toward the opposing force, looking to find Wasef Kamran.

YOU NEVER HEAR the shot that kills you. Paul Mei-Lun remembered hearing that somewhere but couldn't place it. Anyway, he figured it was bullshit, since he'd heard a thousand shots fired in the park this night and one of them had drilled him through the shoulder, snapped his clavicle and left his right arm dangling, useless.

Was he dying? Maybe.

He had failed biology in high school and then dropped out a short time afterward. But he remembered something about major arteries that branched off from the heart to pump blood through the lungs, others to carry circulation through the arms and hands. He couldn't name them if his life depended on it, but he knew approximately where they were—all useful knowledge for a killer—and he reckoned that he might be bleeding out.

How could he tell? He felt cold, but that might just be the wind off the East River. There was pressure on his chest, but that could be the trauma of his wound, a slug ripping through flesh and muscle. Breathing through his open mouth, he didn't choke or feel like he was drowning.

So, what now?

He obviously couldn't fight, but could he manage to escape somehow? Walking was out; he barely had the strength to crawl, if he could even manage that. But maybe he could *drive,* if he could reach one of the vehicles and drag himself behind the wheel, stay conscious long enough to clear the killing zone—or even make it off the island, if he didn't pass out first.

Get out, and then get help. He knew a doctor back in Chinatown who treated the wounds of the members of Wah Ching without reporting them to the authorities. How far away was that? Four miles or maybe five? How many blocks? How many traffic lights and cop cars would he have to pass before he reached the Lucky Dragon?

Too damned many, but he had to try.

Thinking about the heroin, knowing it was beyond his reach forever now, Mei-Lun began his slow and agonizing crawl across the turf, back toward the Hummers, desperately hoping that his driver hadn't pocketed the keys. He knew there was a spare set somewhere, but he didn't have the strength or clarity of mind to solve that mystery.

The long crawl seemed to take forever, but he made it somehow, with the sound of automatic weapons hammering away behind him, bullets rattling overhead. If any of his men had missed him, or observed him creeping toward the Hummers, they were too distracted to assist or to try to stop him. When he reached the nearest SUV, it was an ordeal just to rise and reach the door handle, fumbling one-handed while he tried to keep his balance.

Snarling through the pain, Mei-Lun remembered all the times he'd sat through movies where the hero took a bullet in the shoulder, shrugged it off and told some babe that it was just a flesh wound. Total bullshit. By the time he'd hauled himself into the driver's seat and found the key in place—a major miracle—Mei-Lun barely had strength enough to turn on the engine and bend down to release the parking brake.

Shifting the Hummer into Drive was something else entirely. That was right-arm work, but now he had to reach across the steering wheel, left-handed, grappling with the gearshift until he got it right. The trick to getting out would be a U-turn, maybe under fire, but Mei-Lun thought that he could pull it off, throwing his whole weight into it and stamping down on the accelerator, gasping from the pain and effort as the Hummer swung around.

The shot came out of nowhere, smashing through the driver's window, shattering his left hand where it gripped the steering wheel. Mei-Lun cried out and reared back in his seat, the Hummer leaping forward, off the narrow roadway, down a steep embankment toward the river. By the time he found the brake, he was already airborne, splashing into the cold dark water that enveloped him and drowned all hope of getting back to Chinatown alive.

WASEF KAMRAN LEANED into the Lincoln Town Car, cursing as the dome light blazed above him, then redoubled his profanity on finding that his driver had made off with the ignition key. Where was he now, the stupid bastard? Kamran backed out of the limo as another burst of auto-fire peppered its far side, and slammed shut the door to kill the cursed light.

All right. One of the Phaetons, then. As he was edging toward the second vehicle in line, he heard an engine revving on the far side of the park and craned his neck, glimpsing one of the Wah Ching SUVs as it began to turn then vault forward into darkness, disappearing into the East River.

Kamran nearly laughed at that, one of the enemy going for a midnight swim, but he had lost his sense of humor when the shooting started and he realized that he would never lay hands on the heroin he'd come to claim. At least he hadn't brought the money he had promised the killer, never planning to give up a penny when he could obtain the drugs by force.

A vanished hope.

He reached the nearer Phaeton, opened its driver's door and grimaced as another dome light stung his eyes, drawing attention to the vehicle. Again, the key was missing, doubtless pocketed from force of habit. As he scuttled back and slammed the door, Kamran knew he had one chance left before he was compelled to flee on foot.

He reached the second Volkswagen, opened its door and reached around the steering column, fumbling. Finally! He raised one leg to slip behind the wheel just as a bullet struck his pelvis with the impact of a hammer blow, dumping him backward to the pavement with a wail of pain. His feet thrashed aimlessly, their movement amplifying Kamran's agony until he managed to control the spastic kicking with a force of will.

He lay still for a moment, taking stock, and felt the hot blood soaking through his trousers, smelled a rank odor that told him he had soiled himself. The ultimate indignity. And now, as bullets drilled the Phaeton where he'd left the driver's door wide open, with the dome light burning, he smelled something else, as well.

Even in his extremity, he recognized the sickly reek of gasoline.

The Phaeton's gas tank had been punctured and was spewing fuel, the fumes invading Kamran's sinuses, almost anesthetizing him before he recognized his peril. If a round sparked off the pavement or the limo's undercarriage now...

Kamran rolled to his left, sobbing in pain, and then began to drag himself along the roadway, trailing blood and gasoline where it had soaked into his slacks. He heard more rounds striking the Volkswagen, prayed to a long-forgotten god that they would cause no flare-ups, then he heard the *whoosh* of fumes igniting as a rush of heat engulfed his feet, his ankles, swiftly climbing to his knees and thighs.

More pain than he imagined might be possible.

And there was barely time enough for him to scream.

THE EXPLOSION THAT consumed Wasef Kamran closed out the show, as far as Bolan was concerned. Downrange, a handful of gunmen were still trading shots in the park and he left them to it, breaking down the M-110 SASS for travel in its padded duffel bag. It was the work of seconds for a pair of practiced hands, and Bolan eased his way into the stairwell that provided access to the roof. He paused there, slipping on a white coat he'd borrowed on his first pass through, then moved ahead as though he owned the place.

In a hospital the size of Coler-Goldwater, new faces were routine as interns traded shifts or passed to new rotations, while the residents juggled vacation time and sick leave. Add the chaos of a firefight in the park, and no one paid attention to a doctor on his way out to the parking lot, lugging a bag of laundry or whatever it might be.

Priorities.

Security was on the run as Bolan left, but they were rent-a-cops, unarmed except for telescoping steel batons worn in scabbards on their duty belts. Bolan hoped they wouldn't try to mix it up with the surviving thugs outside. The orderlies and nurses the soldier passed were scurrying to check on patients in the hospital's north wings—and, he suspected, to find out if they could glimpse some of the action from the layout's upstairs windows.

Fair enough. Many people were ghoulish in their own small way. They slowed for a closer look at crack-ups on the highway, left their drinks behind to watch a fight outside a bar, or came out barefoot in pajamas when a neighbor's house was burning. It was part of human nature, exorcised for most by watching "funny" videos of painful accidents on television, but it was hard to pass up mayhem in the flesh.

Outside, the night was crisp and cool, with just a hint of gun smoke on the breeze as Bolan crossed the parking lot and stowed his duffel in the Honda's trunk, then slid behind the wheel. He'd leave the rifle and his other hardware at a drop he'd prearranged, before he met with Jack Grimaldi to prepare for round two of his latest match.

Flight time would give Bolan a chance to rest, but he knew his enemies would not be sleeping. They might know some details of his New York blitz already, and the rest would soon be reaching them by telephone, email or Skype, whatever. Those reports would rile not one but two distinct and separate hornet's nests in Kabul and Hong Kong. The loss of lives—and more importantly, of profits—would inflame both sides.

And each would likely blame the other for the bloody mess he'd left behind.

Exactly as he'd planned.

It was, he hoped, the first step toward a drug cartel apocalypse—but not an uncontrolled explosion. Bolan, in addition to his martial skills, had proved himself a skillful puppeteer in past campaigns, adept at leading adversaries to erroneous conclusions and compelling them to act on the disinformation he supplied. A nudge here and a knife thrust there, prompting one enemy to strike against another whom he already despised and feared, unconscious of the fact that both had been manipulated by the Executioner.

Bolan had used that trick to good effect against the Mafia, the Yakuza and certain terrorists. The campaign he'd embarked upon today, however, would be played out on a larger scale than any other where he'd used his talents to divide and conquer. Whether he could pull it off, much less survive it, was an open question.

Next stop: Paris. And a whole new world of hurt.

CHAPTER SIX

LaGuardia Airport, Queens, New York

"I understand they got this baby from a sheikh," Grimaldi said. "Some kind of human trafficking tycoon, the lousy scumbag. Anyway, we go in style."

Grimaldi's "baby" was a Dassault Falcon 50EX jet, sixty feet of sleek perfection with a sixty-two-foot wingspan, powered by three Garrett TFE731-3-1C turbofan engines with a cruising speed of 551 miles per hour and a bust-out speed of 568 mph. Inside, seating for six left ample legroom, with a sleeping area and lavatory at the rear.

"Air time?" Bolan asked.

"We'll be pushing seven hours, maybe save a little if we catch a tailwind," Grimaldi replied. "Then we've got the hop down to Marseille, another four hundred miles and change."

After Paris, that would be, taking the battle one step at a time.

"You're good to cover this alone?" Bolan asked, knowing that the Dassault Falcon normally employed a two-man crew.

"No sweat, amigo. That's why God made automatic pilots."

"Not to mention parachutes."

Grimaldi barked a laugh and said, "You're killin' me."

"How long till we're cleared for takeoff?"

"As soon as we get buckled up and take our place in line," Grimaldi said.

Bolan was traveling unarmed, with no way to predict whether they'd get a customs shakedown at the other end. All of their papers were in order, passports printed on official stock with all the proper stamps and signatures arranged through Stony Man. He'd left the Cooper name behind him in Manhattan, just in case somebody traced it to his rental cars, and traveled now as Michael Stack, a man of means whose interests in assorted enterprises could be verified by contacting his office in Chicago, where all calls were automatically bounced to the Farm.

All that was for Customs and Passport Control when they landed at Charles de Gaulle Airport in Paris. From there, once they'd picked up the rental cars he had on hold—one set of wheels for each of them—he would be shopping for the kind of hardware it wasn't wise to carry on a plane these days. The vendor he had dealt with on his first visit to Paris was deceased, but others had stepped in to fill the void. Like any other major city on the planet, Paris offered everything a person could desire, if there was ready cash on hand.

No problem there. The Farm's "black" budget was substantial, and the Executioner maintained his own war chest with contributions from the scavengers who multiplied like roaches in the shadows of a so-called civilized society. A pusher here, a loan shark there; nobody who'd be missed for long or mourned by many. Call it wealth redistribution for the common good.

Waiting in line for takeoff, Bolan went back over what he knew about the targets at his second destination. Wah Ching business was conducted on behalf of Hong Kong by a thug named Tony Cheung, while one Arif Durrani

fronted for Khalil Nazari's syndicate. Things had been
tense between them, but they were not at each other's
throats.

Not yet.

France had been a key transshipment point for heroin
since the 1930s, when Paul Carbone's Corsican Mob set
up its first refineries in Marseille. During the cold war,
agents of the CIA had helped establish what would be the
"French Connection," in one of their harebrained schemes
to battle communism through collaboration with the underworld. Arrests during the 1970s had failed to shut the
network down. Long story short, the trade still flourished
in the hands of Corsicans, Sicilians and the new Afghan
practitioners. Most of the morphine processed in Marseille
these days came from Afghanistan instead of Turkey, but
the final product and its profits were unchanged.

Meanwhile the Wah Ching Triad had been staking
out French territory for itself, trying to undersell its Afghan competition on the streets of Paris, Nice, Lyons and
any other city where the trade was flourishing. A survey
from 2006 had identified 230,000 "problem" drug users
in France, roughly half of them full-time heroin addicts.
"Generous" dealers were constantly striving to broaden
that base with handouts to the young, the unemployed and
anyone else for whom self-medication seemed attractive.
If they moved against Arif Durrani's outfit—more specifically, against his Marseille labs—the net result would
be a shooting war.

And if they didn't move against Durrani, Bolan had a
plan to light the fuse himself.

"We're up next," Grimaldi said from the Dassault Falcon's flight deck. "Five minutes till we're in the air."

And seven hours, give or take, until they touched down
on the other side of the Atlantic, in another war zone. Bolan

settled back, sat-phone beside him, nothing to report until he touched base with Brognola at the end of their approach to Paris. He and Jack were on their own now; totally deniable if anything went wrong.

The warrior closed his eyes and waited for that sense of buoyancy, the stomach drop that signaled liftoff. Maybe he would sleep, and maybe dream of ghosts from other battles, other wars. Or, if his luck held, dream of nothing until he was on the ground and raising hell again.

Justice Building, Washington, D.C.

"YEAH, I'M WATCHING it right now," Brognola said. "I'll call you back in ten."

He dropped the telephone receiver back into its cradle, staring at the television on the stand against the west wall of his office overlooking Pennsylvania Avenue. He had it turned to CNN as usual, had been listening to a story from New York. There had been a hell of a shootout between Chinese gangsters and a group of Afghans on an island in the East River.

Twenty-three dead, apparently, and two in custody. Both had been wounded critically when they had turned their weapons on police. No injuries were reported inside a nearby hospital, which city spokesmen found to be miraculous. The mayor promised an investigation and a vigorous campaign against what he called "savages with no concept of what it is to live within a civilized society."

Round one, the big Fed thought, muting the sound with his remote control. He left the picture on—some soccer game from South America where fans had gone ape-shit and started killing one another. Over what? Who knew?

Sometimes he thought the world was going crazy. Other times, he knew it had already gone around the bend and wasn't coming back. His job, in either case, was to impose some sense of order—make that justice—when and where he could. And if it seemed as if he was merely amplifying chaos in the process, well, that was the price of doing business in the shadows, on the wrong side of the law.

Roosevelt Island, for example. Brognola might not have picked that spot to massacre a couple dozen gangsters, but he'd known Mack Bolan long enough to trust the warrior's instincts and abilities. True to form, there had been no collateral damage, and there'd be no blowback onto Stony Man from anything that might have happened in Manhattan.

Run it down: two drug cartels dismantled, more or less, and something like three million dollars' worth of heroin destroyed before it hit the streets. Brognola logged that as a win-win situation in his mental ledger, hoping Bolan's luck would hold and that he wouldn't stumble as he took the game further afield.

France was a problem. Always had been, really, with its prickly politicians making in-your-face decisions for the hell of it, apparently delighting in the chance to piss off anyone and everyone they could. For all of their contrariness, however—and the tons of wine they drank with every meal—Brognola knew the French could be efficient at suppressing crime when they were so inclined.

And face it, when he hit the field, Mack Bolan *was* a criminal.

Landing in France, he'd have to deal with two distinct and separate federal agencies. The Police Nationale, once called the Sûreté, consisted of 146,000 agents working under the Ministry of the Interior, conducting broadly defined security operations that ranged from traffic control to identity checks, while its "judicial" branch pursued criminal investigations, served warrants and pursued fugitives. Their other federal outfit, the Gendarmerie Nationale, was a branch of the French armed forces in charge of public safety, with police duties among the civilian population. At last count, it had about 102,000 operatives in the field.

Call it a quarter of a million coppers ranged against one man.

From personal research, Brognola knew the French police were armed with standard-issue SIG SAUER SP2022 sidearms chambered in 9 mm Parabellum. In tight spots, they also used the SG540 assault rifle in 5.56 mm NATO. Either piece could put a person down for good, and when you had a quarter million of them tracking you…

Brognola caught himself and snapped out of the drift toward negativity. He owed a callback to the Farm, where Barbara Price had also watched the news out of New York. He knew she would have subtle feelers out to One Police Plaza and the local FBI field office, sniffing for leads if they had any, giving a nudge as needed toward the theory of a gang war brewing without any outside intervention.

Which should be an easy sell, all things considered. When two voracious and volatile syndicates start grazing on the same turf, there was bound to be a conflict sooner rather than later. Manhattan had seen its fair share of such blow-ups, going back more than a century, and there was nothing new under the sun—except when Mack Bolan dropped into the mix.

The big Fed made the call and got Price on the second ring. Without preamble, he began, "I don't see anything to tip them off."

"Agreed," she said. "I know a guy who knows a guy who writes for the *New York Post*. If you want me to, I can arrange a leak to him about the triad–Afghan thing."

"Go for it. If that goes any further than New York, it might help stir the pot."

"Okay, I'm on it. Any other news?"

"Not yet. I'm standing by."

"You'll keep us posted?" Price asked.

"Never fear," Brognola said, and cut the link.

Shāre Naw, Kabul, Afghanistan

KHALIL NAZARI WATCHED the Caspian cobra glide slowly, sinuously, toward the mouse he had dropped into its glass terrarium. The mouse was plainly terrified. It sat and trembled, barely moving otherwise, as if in hope the snake might somehow overlook it. Obviously the rodent did not know that every time the cobra's tongue flicked out and back it read the mouse's scent as plainly as a hunting dog might track prey with its nose.

Nazari kept the cobra, and a host of other snakes, because it pleased him to observe them. He admired their total lack of visible emotion, something that he strived to mimic in his own life with, he admitted, only marginal success. Without exception, they were cold, implacable killers, focused absolutely on their quest for prey to the exclusion of all else. As *he* had learned to be, when he determined that his future lay in crime.

The cobra struck, released, then waited for the mouse to die. Its venom, as Nazari had discovered through research, included both a neurotoxin to paralyze its victim and a cytotoxin that caused necrosis in various cells. Left alone after being bitten, the mouse would decompose more rapidly than if it simply died without the cobra's intervention—but that would not happen, since its fate was to provide a meal as soon as it stopped twitching in its death throes.

Nazari wondered what his neighbors would think if they knew he kept venomous snakes in his home. Shāre Naw was one of Kabul's most expensive neighborhoods, the other being Wazir Akbar Khān, home to many embassies and Kabul International Airport. Nazari preferred the relative peace and quiet of Shāre Naw—"New Town," in its English translation—where he lived behind ten-foot walls with a private army keeping his enemies out.

And they were legion now, his enemies.

The Taliban despised him for collaborating with the government and the Americans; no small achievement since the two "allies" were constantly at odds. Within the U.S. government, while working closely with the CIA and army, he was subject to surveillance by the CIA and FBI, both operating from the embassy in Wazir Akbar Khān. If that were not enough, he had to pay off leaders of the Afghan National Police while ducking Interpol on rare occasions when he left the country to confer with Turkey, France or Spain. Britain was closed to him, by order of the Home Office, but what of that?

Nazari hated their cold, rainy weather, anyway.

The cobra had begun consumption of its meal, unhinging the elastic jaws that let it swallow rodents whole, its teeth unsuited to the act of chewing flesh. One mouse per week was adequate to keep the reptile sleek and happy. Or, at least, as happy as a snake could ever be.

Nazari, for his own part, was not happy. He felt calmer now, after the cobra had performed its lethal ritual, about the infuriating news he had received from the United States that morning. Wasef Kamran had been killed, more than a dozen of his men along with him, in some pathetic skirmish with the Chinese. The tabloid media was slavering over the prospect of more bloodshed, running "special" stories on the drug trade and demanding new restrictions on firearms.

Neither of those crusades concerned Nazari. Long experience had taught him that the flow of heroin would never be disrupted seriously, in the long term, if the necessary politicians, judges and policemen got their share of the proceeds. As for the gun control debate, what did it matter? If the Congress ever acted to restrict gun sales, Nazari would export arms to America as he exported heroin.

But first, his outpost in the States would have to be rebuilt.

And that would have to wait until he knew what had gone wrong.

No doubt, the Wah Ching Triad was involved. That much was evident from triad bodies at the latest shooting scene, and from reports Nazari had received before the massacre. He had instructed Kamran to put pressure on the Chinese, to steal their drugs and customers and generally make their lives unbearable. What he had *not* expected was a wild pitched battle making headlines, with the details broadcast hourly on every major network in the West.

Kamran was fortunate that he'd been killed the previous night. If he had managed to survive, Nazari would have been compelled to punish him, make an example of him for the other members of their crime family. Instead his task was now to fortify security on other outposts of his empire—and at home. If this was war with the Wah Ching Triad, he had to be ready for their next audacious move.

And if it turned out to be something else, Nazari needed fresh intelligence.

Frowning, he left the cobra to its meal and reached for the telephone.

Mid-Atlantic, Altitude 49,000 feet

THE SAT-PHONE purred at Bolan's side and roused him from a dream of falling. He retrieved it on the third ring, saw Brognola's coded number on the little screen and double-checked the automatic scrambler prior to speaking.

"What's up?" he asked.

"The media is eating up this East-meets-Farther-East scenario," the big Fed said. "They haven't been this hyped about a gang war in New York since Gotti went away to supermax."

"Too bad we can't tap into circulation," Bolan said.

"Funny you'd mention tapping, since it's why I'm calling, more or less."

"How's that?"

"You know we piggyback on NSA's data collection."

"Right."

The National Security Agency, unlike the CIA, was barred by law from doing fieldwork to collect intelligence. Its function was to collect and analyze foreign communications and SIGINT—signals intelligence—while simultaneously protecting U.S. government communications and information systems. Under several presidents, from Nixon to Obama, the NSA had overstepped its bounds by monitoring the communications of American citizens.

Stony Man had found a way to eavesdrop on the eavesdroppers and turn some of their product to the team's advantage on occasion.

"So now," Brognola said, "we've got a whisper out of Kabul. Someone at Khalil Nazari's place reached out to Paris. They were speaking Pashto, mind you, *and* using some kind of private code, but there was definitely mention of the Wah Chings and Manhattan. Wasef Kamran's name came up repeatedly. There seems to be concern about a blowup in Marseille."

"You think they're psychic?" Bolan asked.

"My money goes on paranoid," Brognola answered. "But they're likely not far wrong. We might be able to sit back and watch it go from here, now that the fuse is lit."

"Too uncontrolled," Bolan replied. "Both sides are prone to random drive-bys, and the Afghans like to play with IEDs."

"Agreed. Just thought I'd put it out there."

"Nothing more specific about mobilizing on the Western Front?" Bolan asked.

"If there was, the Puzzle Palace missed it."

That was common nomenclature for the NSA's headquarters at Fort Meade, outside Odenton, Maryland.

"And Hong Kong?" Bolan prodded.

"Quiet as the grave so far," the big Fed said. "If they're communicating, it's been slipping past our ears somehow."

"Maybe an ancient Chinese secret."

Brognola gave that the second's worth of laughter it deserved, then said, "You know they've got about a quarter of a million coppers waiting where you're going, not counting the locals. Add another twenty thousand municipal uniforms that roll out on calls but don't conduct investigations."

"That's a lot of law," Bolan agreed.

"My point is, whether most of them are straight or in somebody's pocket, they won't want a war in their backyard. You might run short of targets in a hurry."

"Which would mean the cops have done their job," Bolan replied. "And I move on."

"About that. Have you given any thought to where this all ends up?"

"Not much," Bolan replied. "They'll want something

approximating neutral ground, with full security in place. I'll do whatever's possible to help them pick a spot where I can operate."

There was a brief silence on the other end before Brognola said, "You know I'm not about to second-guess you."

"I appreciate it."

"But." He dropped the other shoe. "If this gets too damned hairy, we could always think about a drone."

"No good," Bolan declared. "It wouldn't just be one, for starters, and you know the heat that's come from using them in Pakistan and Yemen. Who'd approve a rocket strike in France, much less Hong Kong?"

He could almost see his old friend's shrug. "Could be an accident," the man from Justice said.

"Could be an accidental war," Bolan reminded him. "Forget about deniability if things start falling from the sky."

A sigh came through from Washington. "You're right again, damn it. No birds."

"Don't worry," Bolan said. "If all else fails, I've got my secret weapon."

"What would that be?"

"Human nature," he explained. "Nazari hates the triad, and it's mutual. They never learned to share."

"Like kids," Brognola said. "But bear in mind that you'll be playing in their sandbox once you land."

"And I'll be bringing all my toys," the Executioner replied.

Victoria Peak, Hong Kong

GAZING FROM HIS office window over Kowloon and Victoria Harbour, Ma Lam Chan mused that geography sometimes reflected a person's station in life. Victoria Peak was the highest point in Hong Kong, and the most expensive neighborhood. A few doors from his home on Barker Road, another house had sold for HK$68,228 per square foot, officially ranked as the most expensive mansion in the world.

Chan, who had paid a mere HK$40,000 per square foot for his fifteen-room mansion, disdained such wasteful displays. He rarely entertained at home, not counting visits from expensive prostitutes, and had not seen the inside of a nightclub for at least five years. A man in his position must be circumspect, conservative. Above reproach.

For that reason precisely, Ma Lam Chan found the reports from New York City most disturbing. He had trusted Paul Mei-Lun—a young man, sometimes rash but clearly capable—to keep the Wah Ching outpost in Manhattan's Chinatown discreet and profitable. Now, instead, Mei-Lun was dead, together with a dozen of his men, and the survivors of his cadre were scattered to the winds, fleeing from the authorities.

Chaos.

Chan stood in darkness, barely conscious of the neon landscape spread below him or the sheen of moonlight on the bay beyond. Though he was nude, the tattoos covering his flesh from neck to wrists and ankles made it seem as if he wore a brightly colored unitard. Closer inspection would reveal a host of dragons, tigers, serpents, toads and other creatures that appeared to writhe and flex their muscles anytime Chan moved.

The story of his life and dedication to the Wah Ching Family was written on his skin. He was the tiger that devoured and the dragon that left devastation in his wake. He soared on wings of power earned by taking lives, too many for a bookkeeper to count. Nothing that Chan possessed had ever been given to him; he had taken it by guile or pure brute force.

Eyes cold and fixed, Chan stared into the night as if he could see all the way around the world to where his current trouble had begun—the arid, blighted landscape of Afghanistan. He pictured Kabul as the center of a spiderweb, and crouching at its heart, Khalil Nazari. Chan had peered into Nazari's fortress compound, courtesy of Google Earth, and wondered whether it was possible to kill him there, perhaps obliterate him in his sleep.

Of course it was, if he had been director of the CIA, perhaps a Coalition general on the scene. But for all his wealth, and all the men at his disposal, Chan did not possess an air force or a team of Navy SEALs. A Chinese face would stand out in Kabul as obviously as if it were painted blue.

Nazari, he'd decided, was invulnerable at his home— but that did not preclude Chan from attacking other portions of the Afghan warlord's empire. Something might be done about his poppy fields—an accidental overflight with herbicides perhaps—if certain palms were greased. Outside Afghanistan, drug routes were fraught with peril, and Nazari's representatives abroad were not as well protected as their master. Chan had soldiers in Los Angeles, in London, Paris. If Nazari wanted war, Chan could accommodate him.

But he wanted to collect more information first.

Acting rashly went against his nature, even when he was insulted and had suffered a substantial loss. Hasty responses often went awry, rebounding to the detriment of those who failed to plan for all contingencies.

Chan thought he could afford to wait a little longer, try to find out what his enemy intended to do next. A greedy man such as Nazari might extend himself too far, too fast, and thereby place his own neck in a noose. And when that happened, Chan would pull the lever that propelled his adversary into everlasting darkness.

The air-conditioner kicked on, its cool breath a caress on Chan's expanse of naked, illustrated flesh. He suddenly desired a woman, something to distract him from his thoughts of war and carnage, even though the hour was late. Chan owned a hundred of the city's finest courtesans, who would be pleased to service him at any time of day or night, but calling one of them at this hour seemed inconsiderate.

And rudeness, Chan understood, was a weak man's imitation of strength.

He would forgo the pleasure for this night and rest instead. If sleep eluded him, he had a fair variety of chemicals to aid in its pursuit. Perhaps a clever resolution to the problem of Khalil Nazari would come to him in a dream.

Ma Lam Chan did not believe in Hell, per se, but he would introduce his adversary to the next best thing.

CHAPTER SEVEN

Charles de Gaulle Airport, Paris

Jack Grimaldi landed the jet on Runway 3 without a hiccup, an east-west touchdown, rolling over 2,700 meters of asphalt toward Terminal 1. The terminal looked like an injured octopus from on high, with its circular central part housing check-in and baggage claim, food courts and various shops, while seven arms extended from the body, rather than the normal eight, their satellite departure gates accessed by underground walkways.

The Falcon, as a private charter flight, and miniscule beside the giant airliners of Air France, Air Europa and the like, would not be nosing in to any of the standard jetways built for Boeing 737s and their larger kin. Instead, Grimaldi taxied toward the hangars and expanse of tarmac set aside for smaller aircraft, well removed from the commercial traffic.

When he'd reached the designated spot and powered down, Grimaldi came back to retrieve his bag and to exit with his only passenger. They had to clear Customs and Passport Control before proceeding to the rental agency that had their cars on standby. Choosing different lines deliberately, both of them passed through without a second glance from their respective customs agents, passports duly stamped, and they were on their way.

Their rides, selected in advance, were a Renault Mégane for Grimaldi and a Citröen C4 sedan for Bolan, both small family cars, both four-doors with fairly spacious trunks. The Citröen had a five-speed manual transmission, while the Renault featured a four-speed automatic. As usual, Bolan had taken full insurance out on both cars, just in case.

Their first stop, after clearing Charles de Gaulle, was Montparnasse, on the left bank of the Seine. Specifically, their destination was a shop on Rue Daguerre, south of the district's famous cemetery. Its owner, a septuagenarian veteran of the long-defunct *Organisation de l'armée secrète,* now supported himself by selling antique furniture and weapons that were anything but obsolete.

The aged gnome greeted his latest customers with admirable bonhomie, once Bolan had pronounced the password fed to him from Stony Man. The old man introduced himself as Jacques and asked no names. Hanging a sign that read *Fermé* on his front door, he led them to a storeroom in the back, down a flight of stairs and into a basement that was evidently both soundproofed and climate controlled.

It was, in fact, an arsenal, the weapons on display ranging from handguns through assault rifles and shotguns to light machine guns, RPGs and other more exotic items. Bolan and Grimaldi separated, browsing, picking out what suited them. A Steyr AUG caught Bolan's eye immediately, backed up by a Beretta 8000 in 9 mm Parabellum, its muzzle extended and threaded to accept a sound suppressor, plus spare magazines and ammunition for both weapons. In case he needed something heavier, he also chose a Milkor MGL grenade launcher, the South African creation whose revolving cylinder held six 40 mm rounds. Jacques offered him a choice of high-explosive, buckshot or incendiary rounds, and Bolan scooped up six of each.

Grimaldi liked to travel light where hardware was concerned. He chose a Heckler & Koch HK416 carbine, with an Aimpoint CompM4 red dot sight and a vertical foregrip. For his sidearm, he went Austrian, picking a Glock 22 chambered in .40 S&W, with 15-round magazines and its muzzle threaded to accept the sound suppressor he picked out as an afterthought.

"All done?" Bolan asked.

"Good to go if you are," Jack replied.

Bolan settled the tab and helped Grimaldi pack their new toys into duffel bags, after they'd slipped their pistols into fast-draw shoulder rigs beneath their windbreakers. As they passed out into the street, Jacques changed his sign from *Fermé* to *Ouvert*.

"You think he'll rat us out?" Grimaldi asked after they'd turned a corner and the shop was out of sight.

"There's no percentage in it for him," Bolan said, "but it's just as well we didn't let him see the cars."

"You want to check the flat?" Grimaldi asked.

Hotels were out, as far as Bolan was concerned. In France, the law required all foreigners to fill out registration forms and have them verified by hotel staff from passports or national identity cards in the case of European Union citizens. Police made daily rounds, collecting the forms and comparing them to documents completed on arrival, prior to stamping of a subject's passport by an immigration officer, or checking them against the database for EU citizens. Instead of leaving more tracks at the start of his campaign, Bolan had made arrangements for a crash pad in advance, through Stony Man.

"You go ahead," Bolan replied. "I want take a look at Chinatown, first thing."

Grimaldi frowned. "I can tag along with you, no problem."

"Better if you check the flat and see if it needs anything," Bolan replied. He didn't plan on spending much time there, but it should have some food, first-aid supplies and so on.

"If you're sure," Grimaldi said.

"We're good. Something pops, you'll be the first to know."

"How come I doubt that?" Grimaldi asked, but he didn't wait for Bolan's answer as he stowed his bag in the Renault Mégane and slid in behind the steering wheel.

Because you know me, Bolan thought, watching his good friend pull away.

Little Asia, Paris

THE DISTRICT KNOWN as *Petite Asie,* located in the 13th arrondissement of Paris, differed from Chinese immigrant communities in other major cities of the world, from London to New York, Toronto, Los Angeles and San Francisco. Parisian "Chinatown" was the largest in Europe, and it harbored ethnic Chinese refugees from the former colony of French Indochina—now Vietnam, Laos and Cambodia—together with ethnic Laotians and others from French Guiana, French Polynesia and New Caledonia. Common languages within the community of some fifty thousand residents included French, Cantonese, Vietnamese and Khmer.

As large as it was, *Petite Asie* was not the only Asiatic settlement found within the City of Lights. Three others were found in the 3rd arrondissement near Rue au Maire, where immigrants from Wenzhou settled in 1900; in Belleville, established in the early 1980s; and around the crossroads of Rue Sainte-Anne and Rue des Petits-Champs, home to Japanese and Koreans. All three areas attracted tourists, making white faces familiar, but Mack Bolan had his sights focused on Little Asia, also known as *Triangle de Choisy*.

Going where the action was.

Wah Ching Triad headquarters in Paris was a so-called social club—the Lau Hu Shao, or Tiger's Lair—on Rue Toussaint-Féron, near the Parc de Choisy. High-rise apartment buildings lined surrounding streets, while ground-floor offerings mixed East and West: a Buddhist temple sat beside a fast-food restaurant; traditional apothecaries offered ancient remedies next door to legal offices; a kung-fu school shared space with a studio for modern dance.

Bolan had parked his Citröen C4 on Avenue de Choisy and walked into Little Asia, window-shopping, sampling street food as he went, proceeding inexorably toward his target. He was traveling light, just the Beretta 8000 in its armpit holster, with a couple of spare magazines in his jacket pocket. A soft probe for the moment, unless he was favored with a target that proved irresistible. Fortune favored the bold, and he had never been afraid of taking risks.

The Tiger's Lair was nothing much to look at from the outside. Other than the street number above its door, the place was perfectly anonymous; no invitation offered even inadvertently to tourists passing on the street. Bolan crossed to the south side of Rue Toussaint-Féron before he reached the club, dawdling along in the same direction as the street's one-way traffic, roughly northeast to southwest.

A shop directly opposite the Tiger's Lair caught Bolan's eye, its window filled with items of exotic cutlery ranging from swords to shaving razors. He paused there, used the polished window as a mirror to observe the building at his back and count the triad soldiers drifting in and out through the Tiger Lair's unmarked front door.

Some entered bearing satchels and reappeared empty-handed moments later. Others spent a little longer in the club, came out checking the street in both directions, then moved off with quick, determined strides on some appointed errand for the Family.

When Bolan thought he'd spent as much time standing on the sidewalk as he could afford, he picked one of the earnest triad soldiers and trailed him toward Avenue d'Italie, where he crossed again and followed on the same side of the street as his selected mark.

A wild-goose chase? Maybe. But he was angling for a first move in the new offensive, something that would rattle Tony Cheung a little without putting him on red alert. More than a feint, but nothing that would be mistaken for a knockout.

Watch and wait.

The soldier he was trailing stopped at restaurants and shops along the avenue, went in and out, five minutes tops at any one establishment. The sixth stop was a grocery store with ducks and chickens hanging in its window like the victims of a barnyard lynch mob. Bolan glanced beyond the dangling carcasses and saw the store's proprietor handing an envelope across the register. It disappeared into the Wah Ching soldier's pocket while the grocer pulled a sour face.

Collections, no doubt for the tried and true protection racket run by thugs in every ethnic ghetto on the planet from the dawn of urban living. Pay to keep your home or business standing, unmolested, buying fragile peace of mind. Some gangs might offer true protection of a sort, from an incursion by their rivals, but the main threat always came from them directly.

It was perfect.

Bolan passed the grocery store, betting his pigeon

would continue in the same direction on his rounds, rather than turn back or cross to the far side of the street. Ahead and on his right, a narrow alley beckoned, running east–west in the gap between a laundry and a trendy clothing store. He ducked in there and waited, the sniper's stillness settling over him.

LOUIE SHUMIN LIKED making collections. He enjoyed seeing the trace of fear in older people's faces as he made his rounds, appreciated recognition as a man with weight behind him that could crush them if they gave him any attitude or held back on the tribute they owed the Wah Ching Family. He liked it best of all, though, when some of the younger ones thought they could get away with showing him a hint of arrogance—or better yet, refusing payment in a foolish fit of pique.

Shumin liked breaking things. It didn't matter whether they were windows, bits of furniture or faces. No, on second thought, that wasn't true. He liked breaking the faces best of all.

Six stops down and seven remained before he turned back toward the Tiger's Lair. Shumin did not open the envelopes as he received them, knew by feel if they were light and there was any cause to vent his anger. So far, all the places on his route had paid in full, without complaint.

The way it was supposed to be.

He passed the alley on his right, the same one he'd passed countless times before, and gave it no thought until a strong hand clutched his nape and dragged him back into the shadows, spinning him through a blurred one-eighty and propelling him face-first into the brick wall of a shop that peddled women's clothes. The impact stunned him, driving spikes of pain into his eyes and forehead as it cracked his nose.

"Chee lun seen! Dieu lei lo mo!"

The rough hand spun him back to face a tall white man. Before Shumin could make another move, he felt the muzzle of a handgun wedged under his chin and biting deep.

"I'm hoping you speak English," Bolan said. "Otherwise you're useless to me."

Shumin glared into a pair of ice-blue eyes, trying not to tremble. "Man," he said, "you don't know who you're messing with."

The white man cocked his pistol, grinding it a little deeper into Shumin's throat. "I'm messing with a flunky from the Wah Ching Triad," he replied. "Is that about the size of it?"

Speaking around his pain, snuffling through blood, Shumin said, "If you figured that much out, you know that it's a bad mistake."

"I've made a few," Bolan said. "This isn't one of them."

He held the gun in place, using his free hand to retrieve the envelopes of cash from Shumin's pockets, tucking them into his own, one at a time.

"Hold on you son of a bitch!"

The pistol moved so quickly Shumin never saw it coming as it cracked into his forehead, bounced his skull off the brick wall behind him and then resumed its place under his chin.

"You need to learn some manners," Bolan said. "Maybe you'd do better without kneecaps."

When the pistol moved again, Shumin was terrified that he might wet himself. "Don't do it!"

"Nice and quiet, then."

The hand resumed its rummaging, relieving Shumin of the remaining envelopes. He stood and let it happen, praying that he would survive the moment. If he did, then he would still have to survive reporting back to Tony Cheung.

One problem at a time.

When all the cash had made its way into the gunman's pockets, he stepped back and checked the alley left and right. They were alone, screened by a garbage bin from the sight line of pedestrians passing on the avenue.

"When you see Tony Cheung," Bolan said, "tell him this is his first down payment."

"What? Are you—?"

"From now on, he pays tribute to Arif Durrani. Do you think you can remember that?"

"Remember it? Hell, yes. But if you think—"

Bolan slashed a kick into his groin and Louie Shumin's world went red. He did not feel his knees strike pavement as he fell, clutching himself and gasping in a vain attempt to breathe. A heartbeat later he was vomiting his lunch onto the asphalt.

The gunman stood above him, waited for him to recover just a bit, then asked, "Can you hear me?"

"Uh…huh."

"Good. Repeat the message you were given."

"Tribute. Arif. Dur…Dur…"

"Close enough. As soon as you can walk, get back to Tony and deliver it. I won't be gentle if you let me down."

Shumin thought he was nodding in agreement, felt his aching cheek scrape blacktop as his head bobbed. When his tear-filled eyes opened again, he was alone behind the garbage bin, shuddering in pain, humiliation and the first heat of ferocious anger.

Through the fog, he realized that he was lucky. Nearly crippled, sure, but that could work to his advantage when he limped back to the Tiger's Lair. Let Tony see that he had fought to save the money, that he'd suffered on the Family's behalf.

With any luck at all, it just might save his life.

Quartier Pigalle, Paris

THE ACTION NEVER ended in Pigalle, which straddled the border between the 9th and 18th arrondissement of Paris. For generations it had been the city's hot, erotic heart, notorious for sex clubs and the prostitutes who worked the streets around its public square. American servicemen stationed in Paris during World War II nicknamed the district "Pig Alley," and while it had undergone various facelifts, its flavor remained. The Grand Guignol Theater, specializing in gruesome horror shows, may have shut down in 1962, but in its place had risen the Museum of Eroticism and the Sexodrome.

The beat goes on.

Arif Durrani loved the action in Pigalle and owned a fair piece of it, thanks to wise investments and the application of a little muscle, both his specialties. Encroachment on the French sex trade had not diverted him from his primary occupation, which was still and always would be trafficking in heroin, but it kept him amused while putting extra money in his pocket.

The best of both worlds.

This afternoon he was preparing to review a group of nubile applicants who sought positions at his flagship club, Le Monde du Sexe, already looking forward to the different positions they might fill—or pose in, while he took stock of their assets.

What was it clerics said about the wages of sin? Durrani banked them every day.

The girls were waiting for him when the phone rang in his outer office. Durrani ignored it to let Mahmud Zabuli take the call, and was about to slip out through the side door to the area where dressing—and *un*dressing—rooms were located, when Zabuli called to him.

"You'd better take this, boss."

"What is it?"

"Says he's Tony Cheung."

"Oh, does he?"

"He could be lying, could be crazy. One thing's for sure, he's hopping mad. Line two."

Intrigued, Durrani lifted the receiver, pressed the lighted button and inquired, "Who's this?"

"Your *bat po* told you who it was!" an Asian-sounding voice replied.

"Remind me."

"Tony Cheung, *nan yeung!*"

"That's quite a mouthful," Durrani said, smiling at the obvious insults he couldn't translate. "I know the name by reputation."

"Yet you test me? You demand tribute? *Ngoh jau yim lei! Ham ka chan, chee lun see!*"

"That all sounds very serious. Unfortunately, I don't understand a word you're saying. If you want to tell me something—"

"*D'iu lay, hai yeung! D'iu ne lo mo!* You will get the message!"

And *click,* the line went dead.

Durrani frowned at the receiver for a moment, then replaced it in its cradle. Most of what he'd heard was gibberish, but he was puzzled by the reference to tribute. What had Cheung—if it *was* Cheung—been talking about?

No matter.

He had been at odds with the Wah Ching Triad since setting up his Paris operation, wondering when they would clash at last over the trade in heroin. If Tony Cheung had lost his mind—

The building shuddered, echoing with the sound of an explosion coming from the general direction of Rue

Deperré. Framed posters of Durrani's favorite porn stars leaped from his office walls, their glass fronts shattering on impact with the floor.

Durrani bolted from behind his desk and through the open door into his outer office, where Zabuli stood with a pistol in his hand. "What was that, boss?" his gatekeeper demanded.

"How should I know? Put that thing away and come with me."

They passed a gaggle of excited, frightened girls, no longer foremost in Durrani's mind, skirted the showroom and in moments reached the lobby of Le Monde du Sexe. It didn't look like Sex World now—more like Demolition World. A blast, albeit not a large one, had removed the double front doors from their hinges, flinging them aside, and pocked the lobby walls with shrapnel. Over all hung smoke, and in Durrani's nostrils was a scent he recognized. Like marzipan.

"Semtex," Zabuli announced before Durrani had a chance to voice the same thought. "Someone bombed us."

"Not just someone," Durrani said through clenched teeth. "That bastard on the telephone."

"The Chinese?" Now Zabuli looked confused. "Why him?"

Durrani pulled the man aside and lowered his voice. "He said something about our Family demanding tribute from him."

"What is that supposed to mean?"

"I have no idea," Durrani answered. "But I'm going to find out."

Two possibilities occurred to him as he surveyed the damage and awaited the arrival of police. The first: someone within his circle might be poaching on the Wah Ching Triad's turf without Durrani's knowledge or permission.

If that proved to be the case, Durrani would be forced to choose between swift punishment and calculating how to turn the situation to his own advantage.

On the other hand, he thought it might be possible that Tony Cheung was seeking an excuse for war, using a fabricated incident to make the bombing and whatever followed after it resemble acts of self-defense. Durrani knew he should not underestimate the deviousness of his new adversary's mind.

But Cheung was not invincible, by any means.

BOLAN DROVE PAST Le Monde du Sexe in his Citröen C4 and saw police swarming around the club, which looked as if its front doors had been struck by lightning. It surprised him that the triad had responded to his goad so quickly—if, in fact, this was their handiwork.

Who else could be responsible?

Bolan moved on, considering his next move. He'd been planning something for Durrani, point and counterpoint to stir the pot in Paris to a rolling boil, but now he'd have to pick another target. Let the cops pick over Sex World, ask their questions, poke into the outfit's shady corners while he found another pressure point.

No problem.

Bolan had not spent his whole time sleeping on the seven-hour transatlantic flight. He'd linked to Stony Man's computers and run through the lists of enterprises owned or dominated by the Wah Ching Triad and Durrani's gang in Paris. He'd logged the addresses, phone numbers, names of managers and so-called owners who controlled the properties on paper, kicking back the lion's share of profits to their hidden partners.

Bolan was as ready as he'd ever be to play this game, without letting a glitch or two along the way distract him.

As for the explosion at Le Monde du Sexe, he wouldn't even count that as a glitch. Call it a bonus, if the triad had been quicker off the mark than he'd anticipated. That told Bolan the triad was in the game to win it and was ready to extend itself—to stick its neck out…while he stood ready with his ax.

His next stop, if he wanted to increase Durrani's paranoia, ought to be the Afghan's home. Durrani occupied the penthouse of a posh apartment block on Rue Condorcet, midway between the Grand Hotel de Turin and the Hotel St. Georges Lafayette. The cops would have Durrani tied up for an hour or so, at least, but in the meantime Bolan could arrange a little housewarming.

Something to ramp the Afghan drug lord's anger up another notch or two and start him plotting a response.

To that end, Bolan had acquired a can of purple spray paint and had memorized some Chinese characters from the internet, accessed on his laptop. Durrani would not understand them at first glance, but he would find someone to tell him what they meant. And once the insult had sunk in, there would be no doubt in Durrani's mind as to its source.

Psy-war in spades.

From there, he could shift back to Tony Cheung and turn the heat up on the Wah Ching side, if any further heat was needed. Cheung might be prepared for battle now, ready to drive Durrani out of Paris with support from cohorts in the Asian underworld who owed him favors—the Vietnamese, Laotians, even Yakuza. But Bolan had not started this to leave one drug cartel triumphant when the smoke cleared. He was bent on wrecking both.

Or leaving them to wreck each other, with a little help.

After his house call on Durrani he would try to work out something similar for Tony Cheung, more difficult in

Chinatown, but not impossible. If Bolan needed any help, he had Grimaldi standing by.

Paris tried to confuse him with her one-way streets, but Bolan knew the route he had to follow. Kamikaze drivers kept him on his toes as he headed toward his target, whipping past on either side of Bolan's Citröen with shrill horns bleating insults or apologies, hands flailing when their fingers should have been locked tight on steering wheels. The mopeds, mostly Peugeot models, added spice and danger to the mix, darting erratically from lane to lane and leaning into sudden turns as if their drivers thought themselves impervious to harm.

Bolan relaxed, went with the flow. He had time, thanks to the explosion at Le Monde du Sexe, and if he ran into security where he was going, he would deal with it. His message would be emphasized, in fact, if blood were spilled.

It had to start somewhere, and he supposed Durrani's doorstep was as good a place as any.

Give the dealer something else to think about, another reason to retaliate against the Wah Ching Triad in his rage. As long as innocent civilians were not dumped into the mix, Bolan was satisfied.

The predators could watch out for themselves.

CHAPTER EIGHT

Quartier Pigalle

Standing amid the ruins of the lobby at Le Monde du Sexe, Captain Claude Aubert frowned at the swarthy owner's blank expression. "You have no idea who may have wished to bomb this fine establishment?" he asked, making no effort to conceal his sarcasm.

"It is a mystery to me," Durrani said, almost straight-faced.

"Is it a common part of life for you, to have explosives detonated on your doorstep?"

"Common? No, sir. I would not say common."

"But it's happened in the past?"

"I am originally from Afghanistan," Durrani said, as if that answered everything.

Aubert considered that perhaps it did. The Russians had invaded this suspicious fellow's homeland, followed by a civil war between the Communists and Taliban, before America had occupied the country to pursue its longest war. A battle against "terror," as if anyone could ever hope to crush a primal feeling.

"Now," Aubert observed, "you've come to France and brought your war along with you?"

Durrani shrugged and said, "I am a simple business-man."

Another lie. Aubert knew this man was involved in

drugs, along with dabbling in the sex trade, but he had yet to be caught at it. Rumors that Durrani dealt in child pornography and had a hand in human trafficking were also unsubstantiated at the present time.

"No one has threatened you in any way that you recall?" Aubert inquired.

"No, sir. This comes as a complete surprise."

"That must be very distressing, yes?"

"Very," Durrani agreed.

"And there's nothing you can offer that might lead us to the individuals responsible?"

"Nothing. I'm sorry."

"No doubt. But you will be more sorry, I suspect, if they return and try again.

"You own this club yourself?" Aubert added.

"Of course."

"No silent partners? Someone back at home, perhaps?"

"I wish that were the case," Durrani said. "Alas, the whole investment and expense is mine."

"You've done well here, since your arrival. Making others envious, perhaps?"

"I cannot say how others feel."

"Not psychic, eh? What a pity."

"Too bad. Yes, I agree. If I knew magic, possibly I could repair all this for free," Durrani said, a slight smile on his face.

"Someone has cost you time and money," Aubert pointed out unnecessarily. "You understand that it is not your role to pay them back in kind."

"Yes, sir. As I've explained—"

"You're just a simple businessman. Well, I suppose that's all for now. If more questions arise, you'll hear from me again."

"And if you find the guilty parties?" Durrani asked.

It was Aubert's turn to shrug. "It's possible. Who knows? We have so little to proceed with, as it is."

"Forensic evidence, perhaps?"

Durrani might have known that most modern explosives came with taggants—microscopic bits of colored plastic—used to let investigators trace the manufacturer of an explosive substance after it had detonated. If he did not know, there was no reason to enlighten him, so Aubert merely shrugged again, replying, "Don't believe all that you see on television."

Aubert was pleased to leave the Afghan frowning as he stepped out through the gaping doorway to the street. His sergeant, Alain Pradon, stood on the sidewalk, surveying the outer damage with a vague expression of disdain.

"He knows nothing," Aubert reported.

"Naturally. He's a pimp."

"More than that, I think," Aubert replied.

"Shall we arrest him?"

"Because someone bombed his sex club? I don't think so."

"It could be insurance fraud," Pradon suggested.

"That's a novel thought, but unsupportable."

"I would enjoy running him in."

"No doubt," Aubert replied.

"Perhaps there's something in his background. We could find it and deport the problem."

"That's better," Aubert said. "While you pursue that avenue, I need to speak with my informants and determine who might wish to harm this sterling citizen."

"Must we protect him now?"

"Not for his sake, Pradon, but for our own. I will not have it said that we stood back and let a war begin in Pigalle."

"War, sir? It's only one explosion, and a rather small one."

"Every war starts somewhere, doesn't it? It's bad for business. Bad for any plans that you may have to rise above your present rank."

"And bad for captains, eh?"

"Most especially for captains," Aubert said, already moving toward their blue-and-white police car parked at the curb.

ARIF DURRANI'S HIGH-RISE building was nothing special on the outside: pink stucco, with a film on the windows reflecting late-afternoon sunlight, but its neighborhood was trendy, which suggested luxury inside. The north-facing penthouse windows would provide a view of Montmartre, the 130-meter hill that lent its name to the larger 18th arrondissement, topped by the white-domed Sacred Heart Basilica and an older church, lesser known among tourists, Saint-Pierre de Montmartre.

Montmartre owed its name to Latin—*Mons Martis,* the Mount of Mars—in dedication to the Roman god of war, and it had lived up to its name. In 1590, during the French Wars of Religion, King Henry IV had laid siege to Paris, placing his artillery atop the high ground to bombard the city. Russians occupied Montmartre in 1814, while invading Paris, with Cossacks erecting the city's first bistro. Even the Sacred Heart Basilica was a monument to war, commemorating lives lost in the Paris Commune turmoil and the Franco-Prussian War of 1871.

Now war was coming back to Montmartre, but the district didn't know it yet.

Bolan considered his approach while winding through the maze of one-way streets. Scouting the target would have meant another time-consuming circuit of the neighborhood, so Bolan let it go, presuming that Durrani would not have a team of gunmen loitering around outside the building where he lived to agitate the other residents and attract attention from police. Granted, that might change since the bombing of his club, but there had been no time for him to station troops around the high-rise yet.

So, the direct approach.

Bolan left his vehicle in the parking lot of a medical complex next door to the apartment tower, checked for signs threatening tow-aways and found none. Before going EVA, he attached the Beretta 8000's sound suppressor and snugged the pistol away in its holster beneath his lightweight raincoat that was de rigueur for most pedestrians he'd spotted on the streets so far. Beside him on the shotgun seat, the can of spray paint nestled in a canvas shopping bag he'd picked up at the same hardware store, printed as a joke of sorts with a Cartier logo.

At a glance, he could be anyone: an office worker headed home after a long day crunching numbers, or a plainclothes cop fresh off pursuit of pickpockets and burglars. Handsome in a way, well dressed but far from flashy. Not exactly memorable.

Bolan passed by the apartment building on foot, noting its doorman in the lobby, moving on until he reached an alley to the west. There, he ducked in and hurried past a row of garbage bins to the building's rear and found the service entrance, slipping in with no one to observe him. He thought about the service elevator, didn't like his odds of meeting someone from the building's staff and opted for the fire stairs.

Fifteen floors meant thirty flights of concrete steps. A decent workout, and he paced himself, not jogging, slowing as he came to each successive landing, ready if someone came bulling through the doors. No one appeared, but moments later Bolan heard a seeming echo of footsteps above him. They were not descending, rather climbing, and he paused until a distant door opened and closed.

What floor? It was impossible to say.

He was more cautious after that, keeping one hand inside his open raincoat, close to the Beretta in its armpit holster. He could draw and fire within a second if required to, and the concrete walls surrounding him should keep the muffled sound of any shots within the stairwell, passing without notice from the building's residents. Unfortunately, Bolan couldn't say the same for any weapon that an adversary might be carrying, if he allowed said enemy a shot.

He paused on twelve to listen once again, heard nothing but the grumble of an elevator rising on the far side of a nearby wall. His watch told him that it was still too soon for the police to wrap their business with Durrani at Le Monde du Sexe, but what if he was wrong? What if the Afghan had eluded them and left a flunky in his place to deal with the inquiry? Might he be at home already, plotting strategy, when Bolan reached his doorstep?

Doubtful, but it could be interesting.

And it could require a change in Bolan's master plan.

Rue Toussaint-Féron, Little Asia

"Repeat that," Tony Cheung demanded, scowling at the smartphone in his hand.

"A bomb," said Armand Chiang, his man in Pigalle. "It took the front doors down. Looks like some damage to the lobby, too."

"Police are there?"

"Like roaches," Chiang confirmed.

"Goddamn it! Keep an eye out for the police," Cheung

said, "but carefully. Don't let them see you under any circumstances."

"Got it."

Cheung cut off the call and turned to face his chief lieutenant, Danny Lam, seated in a chair facing Cheung's desk. "You heard it. Somebody bombed Sex World."

"So? Durrani has a thousand enemies."

"But only one of them called up to threaten him before the bomb went off," Cheung said.

"Look on the bright side. Now he'll take you seriously."

"And he'll think it came from us."

"Again, so what? It had to happen sometime. He's been stepping on our toes for months now."

"I had ways in mind to deal with that," Cheung said. "You knew the plan."

"Until he made the move on Louie."

Cheung felt the scowl forming on his face at the mention of his bungling courier. He'd waited long enough to settle that account with Louie Shumin. The selected tools of retribution were arranged neatly on a side table, with a painter's plastic drop cloth spread beneath it.

"Bring him in," Cheung ordered.

Lam passed through a doorway in the office's west wall, returning seconds later from a holding room with Shumin trailing him. The runner's broken nose was bandaged, and he still walked slowly, favoring his battered genitals. Stopping at a point in front of Cheung's desk, he stood with eyes downcast, ashamed and rightly so.

"You understand that you have failed us," Cheung declared, not asking.

"Yes, sir." No argument.

"Surrendering the take without a fight is inexcusable."

Shumin seemed on the verge of saying something, possibly a plea for sympathy, but wisely reconsidered it and simply nodded.

"Now you are required to make amends," said Cheung.

His soldier knew the drill. Looked toward the side table and winced in grim anticipation of the pain to come.

"Yes, sir."

Cheung rose and said, "Proceed."

Shumin crossed to the table, studied the implements arranged there. In the middle of the table lay a wooden chopping block, its inlaid surface deeply scarred. Beside it, to the right, lay an Asian bone cleaver with an eleven-inch blade. Farther to the right, beside the cleaver, stood a butane torch. Coiled to the left side of the chopping block, a rubber tourniquet lay like the flaccid carcass of a snake.

After a moment's hesitation on Shumin's part, Danny Lam prodded him. "Thumb or hand. Your choice."

Shumin removed his jacket, looked around for someplace to put it, and seemed grateful when Cheung accepted the garment. Next, he rolled his left shirtsleeve above his elbow and retrieved the tourniquet, gripping one end in his teeth while he tied the band tightly around his forearm, just below the elbow.

Breathing slowly, deeply, he made a fist of his left hand and placed its knuckles on the chopping block, his thumb extended like a hitchhiker's. He grasped the cleaver in his right hand, hefting it to judge the weight and balance, closed his eyes and muttered an apology in Cantonese, head bowed. Beside him, Lam picked up the butane torch and pressed its trigger, sending out a thin blue jet of flame.

Shumin's eyes opened once more. He raised the cleaver overhead, then slammed it down onto the chopping block before he had a chance to hesitate. A gout of blood sprayed from the stump where he'd once had a thumb, as Lam leaned in to clutch his wrist, the blue flame finding flesh and sizzling as it cauterized the wound.

Shumin slumped to his knees, gasping in agony. Standing above him, breathing in the odor of seared flesh, Cheung placed a hand upon the young man's trembling shoulder.

"Now you're one of us again," he said. "See Dr. Chow. And next time—if there is a next time—bear in mind your duty to the Family."

Rue Condorcet, Montmartre

"WE NEED TO get some women up here, eh?" Mamnoon Qahar said.

Khushal Maqsooti looked at him askance. "You think so? What would Arif do if he came back and found us with them?"

"I don't know. Join in, maybe? My point is that it's boring here."

"Be thankful for it. Better to be bored than bombed, I say."

The phone call from Durrani at Le Monde du Sexe had put them both on edge at first, thinking about the bomb and who might be responsible for planting it, but after they had checked around the penthouse and found nothing out of place, the time began to drag. No updates to the first report were offered, and Maqsooti pictured Durrani in his mind, perhaps being detained by the police for questioning while they dug through his past and looked for reasons to expel him from the country.

To expel Maqsooti, too, if they looked far and deep enough.

Khushal Maqsooti liked living in Paris. It was infinitely better, more amusing than Kabul—unless you counted daily bombings, sniper fire and drone attacks as entertainment. He had no real desire to ever see Afghanistan again, if truth be told, though he supposed that choice would not be his.

Durrani's hasty call had blamed the Wah Ching Triad for the bombing, and Maqsooti had no reason to dispute his master's judgment. They were tough, those Chinese, and he had known the two cartels were set on a collision course over the trade in heroin. What set them off just now he could not say, but he'd been ordered to remain alert and guard Durrani's penthouse with his life, if it should come to that.

At the moment that meant sitting on Durrani's leather-covered sofa, watching porn on his flat-screen TV and getting paid for it. The boss had said he'd phone before returning home so there were no mistakes—meaning he did not want his watchdogs shooting him by accident.

It was a good plan. Stranger things had happened.

"Now I'm hungry," Qahar said, his eyes still following the sweaty action on the giant screen.

"Go get something from the freezer."

"You want anything?"

Maqsooti shook his head, then realized Qahar would not have seen it and said, "No."

Qahar was up and moving toward the kitchen, filled with all of the equipment needed by a gourmet chef but rarely used, when he stopped dead. "Khushal!" he hissed, his voice almost a whisper. "The alarm!"

Maqsooti turned, frowning, and saw a red light blinking on the security panel beside the front door. It was a silent alarm, designed to let Durrani and his soldiers surprise any prowlers who tried to take *them* by surprise. The flashing red light meant that someone was approaching on the stairs that served the building as a fire escape.

Maqsooti picked up his PM-84 Glauberyt machine pistol, chambered in 9 mm Parabellum, fed from a 25-round box magazine in its pistol grip. Qahar, already moving toward the master bedroom with its secret exit to the outer hallway, clutched a Heckler & Koch USP Tactical pistol fitted with a chunky sound suppressor.

The hidden exit let Durrani play his little games, sneaking young women into his boudoir without parading them in front of his leering soldiers, and it offered an escape hatch from the penthouse in the case of an emergency. This afternoon, Maqsooti hoped that it would serve its *other* purpose, and allow them to bag the intruder who dared to trespass on Durrani's domain. Maqsooti hoped, more to the point, that they could capture him—or them—alive, for later questioning.

It would be quite a feather in his cap, if he possessed one.

They reached the hidden door in Durrani's master suite, Maqsooti in the lead now, opening the door a crack and peering out into the corridor between the penthouse entrance and the elevator that delivered guests who were invited. Kneeling by the door, his back turned toward Maqsooti, a lone man was doing something with some object in a canvas bag.

Maqsooti eased into the hallway, creeping up behind the stranger until he was almost close enough to touch him with the muzzle of his weapon. "All right," he said, gruff-voiced from tension. "Let me see your hands."

BOLAN CLEARED THE final flight of stairs and paused a moment at the steel fire door, first listening, then peering through the little window pane, two layers of glass with wire mesh in between. He heard nothing and pushed the door open an inch, then six, thankful for well-oiled hinges.

He heard a man's voice then, muffled but audible and coming from his right. Drawing his pistol, he shouldered the door open far enough to clear it, stepped into the corridor and eyed the strange tableau downrange.

Two men were standing with their backs to Bolan, spaced about six feet apart, one carrying a silenced pistol, while the other held a compact submachine gun. They were covering a third man who was down on one knee, looking up at them, his hands hovering above an open canvas shopping bag. All three appeared to be of similar complexion, with the same dark hair, but one was clearly an outsider, caught while doing something he was not supposed to do, somewhere that he was not supposed to be.

Bolan began his slow approach, taking his time to close the gap of sixty feet or so that separated him from the two gunmen and their prisoner. The shooters, he presumed, had to be a couple of Durrani's men. As for the third man, it was anybody's guess, a question mark that interested Bolan but would not be a determinant of his next move.

In fact, that move was dictated by circumstance. The kneeling man saw Bolan moving toward him, just as he was asked a question by the watchman with the submachine gun. Staring past his captors, frowning at the new arrival, he ignored the question long enough for number two—the *pistolero*—to glance over his shoulder, seeking whatever it was that had the prisoner distracted from his plight.

The swarthy soldier blinked at Bolan, snapped a warning to his pal in Pashto, and was swiveling to use his pistol when a silenced round from the Beretta 8000 opened a keyhole in his forehead. He went down without a fuss, the other gunman spinning now and squeezing off a short burst from his SMG before he managed to acquire a target. Bolan shot him twice, in chest and throat, then had the kneeling figure covered by the time the second gunman hit the floor.

"Speak English?" he inquired.

The third man bobbed his head. "Yes."

"Stand slowly," Bolan ordered. "Step back from the bag. If you have a weapon, here's your one and only chance to let it drop."

The man obeyed with no argument. The pistol he retrieved left-handed, from beneath his jacket, was a SIG SAUER P226. He set it beside the shopping bag and then backed away as Bolan moved in closer. Peering into the open bag, he saw a block of claylike substance that could only be plastic explosive, with battery and timer fastened to it by a strip of duct tape.

"Let me guess," Bolan said. "You're behind the fireworks at the sex club?"

"Who are you?" the would-be bomber asked.

"Maybe a friend. Depends on who *you* are."

The other man stalled for a second, thinking, then replied, "Lieutenant Heydar Bizhani, MISIRI."

Bolan translated that to the Ministry of Intelligence and National Security of the Islamic Republic of Iran. "You're a long way from home," he observed. "We should talk."

"We should go," Bizhani countered.

"In a minute." Bolan took a major gamble, holstered his Beretta and reached into his own bag. "I need to leave a message first."

They left the bomb, Bolan's idea, after Bizhani had deactivated it. Another message, coupled with his own to ramp up the confusion without jeopardizing any innocents, be they police, custodians or neighbors in the apartments below the penthouse. They left the leaking corpses and the message he'd spray-painted on the wall beside Durrani's door and exited the way they'd both come in, via the stairs.

At the rear of the apartment building, Bizhani nodded toward a black moped standing with half a dozen others. "This is mine," he said.

"I'm parked next door. You want to meet me somewhere for a talk, or go our separate ways?"

"To talk, I think," Bizhani answered. "You know the Square Louise-Michel, below the Sacred Heart Basilica?"

"I'll find it," Bolan said.

"Shall we say half an hour?"

"See you there."

Or not, if the bomber was lying and had no intention of showing. In that case, Bolan would wait, but only briefly, moving on before a trap could close around him, and he would report the strange encounter to Brognola. It wasn't much to go on, just a name that could be false and an alleged association with Iran's primary intelligence agency, also variously known as VAJA, VEVAK and MOIS. Bolan knew the outfit by reputation, including public charges that its agents—or "rogue elements" within the agency—had killed dozens of Iranian political dissidents both inside and outside the country. Still, he didn't have a clue as to why a MISIRI operative would be planting bombs in Paris, targeting an Afghan drug lord.

But if possible, he wanted to find out.

THE SQUARE LOUISE-MICHEL, he soon found out, was less than half a mile from where he'd parked the Citröen C4. The square itself sprawled over some twenty-four thousand square meters at the foot of Sacred Heart Basilica, accessed by a double grand stairway.

It was another tourist draw, and brightly lit as dusk fell over Paris. Bolan found a place to park his rental, locked and left it, strolling casually toward the square with couples, families and lone sightseers all around him, watching for the man whose life he'd saved without counting the cost. Their meeting, he'd decided, could go one of four ways.

First, the man who called himself Heydar Bizhani might turn out to be a no-show. Second, he could keep their date and try to make a move on Bolan, silence him for good to minimize his own exposure. Third, he might send someone else to deal with Bolan, whether the police, other MISIRI agents or a firing squad from whatever outfit he actually represented. The fourth option—a simple talk, perhaps to mutual advantage—was the one Bolan preferred, but he would have to wait to see what happened next.

Five minutes in, just getting ready to depart, Bolan spotted Bizhani coming toward him from the east side of the square. He moved with confidence, seeming at ease, clearly aware of everyone and everything around him. Bolan scanned the meeting ground, saw no one who appeared to be tracking Bizhani or walking in parallel to him, closing a noose. Leaving his raincoat open, the Beretta close at hand, Bolan moved on an interception course.

"You are American," Bizhani said when they were close enough to speak without raising their voices.

"Yes," Bolan agreed.

"Our countries are not friendly."

"No." An epic understatement, if in fact Bizhani was Iranian.

"Yet," Bizhani said, "it seems that we may have a common cause."

"Arif Durrani."

"And the drugs he sells, perhaps?"

This time, Bolan was satisfied to simply nod.

"I will be frank with you," Bizhani said. "I wish him dead, along with those he serves."

"We're on the same page," Bolan replied. "Let's take a walk."

CHAPTER NINE

Rue Condorcet, Montmartre

On most days Arif Durrani enjoyed coming home. His penthouse, with its sweeping views of Sacred Heart Basilica and Pigalle was several cuts above any other residence that he had ever occupied. It was his sanctuary, his retreat and his playground. But this night, after the bombing at Le Monde du Sexe, it would be his armed command post for reprisal against mortal enemies.

Durrani brought six soldiers home with him—enough, he calculated, in addition to the pair he'd left on-site, to guard the penthouse without crowding it beyond endurance. He would plot his strategy against the people who thought they could humiliate him without any consequences. By this time the following night, the Wah Ching Triad would bitterly regret attacking him.

Durrani still had no idea what Tony Cheung had meant when he was ranting about tribute payments. Was the man insane? Had he been smoking opium before he placed the call? It seemed unlikely, given the intensity of anger he had vented on the telephone. It made no sense, and senseless things confused Durrani. He did not enjoy confusion, doubt or any other feeling that suggested he had lost control.

The high-rise had an underground garage. Two elevators served the upper floors, one for the other tenants and one, with a special key required, that served the penthouse. Ringed by soldiers, feeling perfectly secure, Durrani made the short walk from his limo to the elevator, used his key and let himself relax inside the car with walls of burnished copper as they rose past fourteen floors to reach his private aerie.

Relaxation vanished in a heartbeat as the elevator door slid open and Durrani stepped into the hall.

The men he'd left behind to guard his home while he was off at work lay dead outside the entrance to the penthouse. Both had suffered ghastly wounds, spilling quarts of blood across the marble floor. Above them, on the wall left of his door, someone had sprayed a string of Chinese characters in purple paint.

"Can anyone read that?" Durrani asked. "Well, can you?"

Standing with their guns drawn, staring at the corpses and graffiti, none of his selected guards responded verbally. A couple of them shrugged; one shook his head. Another moved around the corpses, toward a canvas shopping bag that stood beside them, soaking up some of their blood. He peered into the open bag, then stepped back hastily.

"A bomb," the soldier said.

Durrani almost bolted, but he caught himself in time to ward off that embarrassment. "Is there a timer?" he inquired, pleased that he heard no tremor in his own voice.

"Yes, sir."

"It's deactivated, then."

The soldier nearest to the bag frowned back at him. "How can you tell?" he asked.

The answer's simple logic pleased Durrani. "No one knew when I was coming home. They couldn't set the timer for a blast to kill me. Plus, the guards disturbed them."

"But they still took time to paint the wall," another of his soldiers said.

"Part of their plan to frighten me," Durrani answered.

"So, why leave the bomb?"

"How should I know what they're thinking?" Durrani snapped.

Chastened by his anger, no one asked him any further questions. One soldier went off to check the stairwell while the others milled around, guarding their boss and the dead.

Durrani's mind was clicking, making plans. "I want the bodies out of here," he ordered. "Take them to the scrap yard. Put them in the furnace. All this blood must be mopped up before the building's maintenance crew arrives. Sahar and Fahran stay with me. The rest of you, get busy!"

"What about the bomb, sir?" someone asked him.

"I'll hold on to that," Durrani said. He had experience with IEDs and reckoned he could deal with it. "Maybe I'll send it back to them," he added with a bitter smile.

But first he had riddles to solve—one psychological, one practical. Before he struck back at the triad, he wished to know why they had chosen this approach and this time to attack him. What had so infuriated Tony Cheung that he felt driven to begin an all-out war?

As for the practical, he had to find someone who could translate the message painted on his wall. It might be nothing but profanity. And then again...

Durrani stepped around the bloody corpses of his men and stooped to check the bomb himself. He confirmed its timer was not counting down to detonation, then picked up the bag and let himself into the penthouse. While his troops cleaned up the mess outside, Durrani would begin to sketch a blueprint for revenge, plotting his campaign one step at a time.

Square Louise-Michel

"IT'S NOT WHAT I'd expect from a MISIRI operation," Bolan said. "Hunting an Afghan narco-trafficker in France."

"You think we're only spies?" Bizhani asked.

"Not necessarily. I just don't see the angle."

"Angle?"

"Interest," Bolan explained.

"Ah. You are partially correct. Drug sales in France would not concern us, normally. The French are no friends of Iran. If they wish to destroy themselves with heroin, we leave them to it."

"So?"

Bizhani shrugged. "What is *your* angle?" he asked Bolan. "Why are *you* in France?"

"Because Durrani's part of something bigger."

"Yes! He serves a master who is not content to merely poison Europe—or America, for that matter. You may not know it, but my country has the world's worst plague of drugs. At last account, eight percent of the population was addicted to illegal drugs, seventy percent of those on heroin. Each year, another thirteen thousand souls become addicted. Thanks to sharing needles, one in every three of those has AIDS. Ninety percent have hepatitis B. Consider also that Iran is the main transportation route for Afghan heroin as it moves westward. We seize thirty-odd tons per year and miss another hundred tons, at least, by the most conservative estimates. It must be stopped."

"And you can't reach Khalil Nazari in Kabul?" Bolan asked.

"The matter is considered...sensitive," Bizhani said. "Their president pretends to sympathize with our dilemma and then accuses us of 'interfering' in his country, while he lobbies for your troops to camp next door indefinitely.

Our bilateral trade has increased, but alas, that includes hashish and opium."

"So, Paris?" Bolan said.

"It is a start. Have you considered targeting Nazari with a drone?"

"That's not my end of things," Bolan replied. He weighed how much he should reveal, then said, "Besides, we have another problem."

"Ah. The Chinese script."

"The Wah Ching Triad," Bolan replied, specifying the enemy.

"They are in competition with Nazari, I presume?"

"Big-time. Two birds, one stone, you know?"

"We say you cannot hold two melons in one hand."

"But you can juggle them," Bolan said. "Do it right, maybe they crack each other open."

"Ah. We at MISIRI have no quarrel with the Chinese," Bizhani said. "The People's Republic buys ten percent of its oil from Iran, with a contract in place to purchase 110 million metric tons of liquefied natural gas from us. Disturbing that relationship would be…impolitic."

"The Wah Ching thugs don't have anything to do with that," Bolan replied.

"Or with the drugs that blight my country," Bizhani added.

"No. But they could be a tool—a weapon—to remove Khalil Nazari."

"You propose to escalate their war?"

"By any means available," Bolan admitted.

"Why should I involve myself?"

"I haven't asked you to, although we seem to have a common goal. You want to run an operation on your own, it's fine with me, as long as we aren't tripping over each other every time we turn around."

Bizhani frowned, thinking. "You understand that I have no resources to contribute, if we should collaborate. I am, as you would say it, on my own."

"Same here, plus one," Bolan replied. And thought of Jack Grimaldi; how he might react to working with an agent from Iran.

"If I sought counsel from my agency," Bizhani said, "they would insist that I avoid all contact with Americans."

"About what I'd expect. It's easier to get forgiveness than permission."

"Not where I come from." Bizhani walked in silence for another moment and then said, "Which means that Tehran must never know."

"Think you can manage that?" Bolan inquired.

"Why not? I am a secret agent, after all."

Rue Toussaint-Féron, Little Asia

TONY CHEUNG WAS not the sort to fret, but he was worried now. Since Louie Shumin had been robbed, and more particularly since the bombing at Le Monde du Sexe, he'd felt as if he was a character in a Polanski film. One of those stories where the world around you seems as normal as can be until you look a little closer and discover that the whole damned thing is skewed somehow, off-kilter, and that nothing really fit the way it should.

All right. The normal part of it—if any bit was normal—was Arif Durrani stealing his collections. That made sense, assuming that the Afghan wanted war with the triad. But then had come the Sex World bombing, moments after Cheung had phoned Durrani, raging at him, and Durrani had to think that it was the triad's doing, although he was innocent for once.

And there was nothing he could do about it. He couldn't

call Durrani back and tell him that he hadn't bombed the club, couldn't convince him of it, even if he said it nicely and abased himself by pleading for Durrani to believe him—which was not about to happen.

If their positions were reversed, Cheung would not swallow anything Durrani had to say. He'd recognize the lie for what it was: a stall, maybe a bid to set a meeting to discuss the problem, where he'd be assassinated on arrival. They were well and truly past the point of talking now.

And Tony Cheung still wondered how they'd got there.

Who had bombed Durrani's club?

Three possibilities came instantly to mind. First, he'd considered that some member of his own clan might have taken the initiative, in the hope of pleasing Cheung, then seen his furious reaction and was now afraid to claim the deed. It was a possibility, but after grilling all his soldiers at the Tiger's Lair, Cheung had effectively dismissed it from his mind.

Another thought: if someone from Durrani's crew had robbed Louie Shumin without Durrani's blessing—say a rogue within the Afghan's gang—that same person or persons could have set the bomb, hoping a war would give them opportunity to knock Durrani off his throne and seize control. The world of crime had seen a thousand palace coups, with unsuspecting bosses slain or driven into exile by a younger generation on the rise. It was a fact of life, almost expected, something that every leader had to guard against.

The final possibility that came to mind involved third parties, neither Wah Ching nor Afghan: someone from the outside who would hope to profit if the members of rival cartels fell to killing one another in the streets. Someone who reckoned he could come along behind, pick up the pieces and declare himself a king.

And who might that be?

There, he hit another wall, because there were too many suspects. French police and crime reporters commonly described their country's underworld as the *Milieu,* a polyglot collection of Italians, Corsicans, Albanians, Maghrebis from Tunisia and Algeria, *gitans*—the ethnic Sinti and Yeniche people, sometimes tagged as Gypsies— and Tamil Tiger–affiliated clans. Toss in the motorcycle gangs with roots in the United States, constantly at each other's throats, and Cheung thought he could lose his mind trying to sort them out.

Particularly now that time was short.

Arif Durrani would not let the Sex World bombing stand. Retaliation would be his priority, the only questions being when and where the blow would fall. Cheung could not prove his innocence, and truthfully no longer cared to try. War seemed inevitable, and he meant to win it.

To that end, he had his soldiers armed and on the prowl, watching for any opportunity to strike Durrani, his associates or any of their operations in the city. Someone else might have provoked the fight, but that would not prevent Cheung from ending it on his own terms.

And when he'd finished with Durrani, he would find the individuals who'd lit the fuse.

He would enjoy making them pay. In blood.

Champs-Élysées, Paris

BOLAN WAS NOT prepared to let Heydar Bizhani see the "safehouse" Jack Grimaldi had been prepping while he'd made his run to Chinatown. Instead he phoned Grimaldi for a meeting in the city's teeming tourist district centered on the Avenue des Champs-Élysées—French for Elysian Fields, the heaven set aside for blessed souls in Greek mythology. Some travel writers called it the most beautiful avenue in the world, and while Bolan wasn't sure he'd go along with that, he couldn't argue with the fact that it displayed an epic slice of history, from the Arc de Triomphe to the Place de la Concorde. Landmarks aside, the broad avenue was also one of the world's most famous streets for upscale shopping, with shops including Cartier, Louis Vuitton, Hugo Bass, Lacoste, Guerlain and continental Europe's largest Gap outlet.

Something for everyone. But Bolan knew Grimaldi would be less than thrilled to meet the unexpected maybe-member of their team.

They met outside the Hôtel de la Païva, once renowned for a solid silver bathtub that featured three taps: the traditional two for hot and cold water, plus one that spewed milk or champagne on demand.

Grimaldi turned up wearing a windbreaker to conceal his Glock 22, plus a rigid expression he made no real effort to hide.

"MISIRI, is it?" he remarked after his introduction to Bizhani.

Putting on a bland half smile, Bizhani said, "No doubt you've heard distorted stories of our operations from your media."

"I've heard about Saeed Emami," the Stony Man pilot replied.

"The so-called 'chain murders,' of course," Bizhani said. "That was regrettable."

"Funny, the way it took ten years and eighty-some-odd dead before your people pinned it on a deputy minister of intelligence," Grimaldi observed.

"Who killed himself in custody," Bizhani said, "thereby proving his guilt."

"Which makes me wonder where he got that poison, locked in maximum security."

"I dare say we shall never know."

"And now we're buddies?"

"Allies for the moment," Bizhani replied, "in a common cause."

Grimaldi turned to Bolan, asking him, "Has you-know-who signed off on this?"

"I'll fill him in tonight," Bolan replied. "That's if we're all on board with it."

"No problem here," Grimaldi said. "I'm good to go if you are."

Bolan understood his old friend's difficulty, working with an agent of a longtime adversary. The soldier wasn't sure about Bizhani's motives for cooperating with him, either, but he knew he'd rather have Bizhani where he could observe him, rather than at large in Paris, waging a campaign that might prove detrimental to the plan he'd hatched with Stony Man.

"You bombed Durrani's club?" Grimaldi asked Bizhani as they strolled along the avenue.

"A first step toward unsettling him," Bizhani said.

"And what about civilians?"

"As I understand it, none were harmed."

"Sounds more like luck than planning, with a street-side IED."

"I have experience with such devices."

"Figures."

"We're beyond that," Bolan interjected. "We're sticking to the game plan with a minor variation, since Durrani thinks the Wah Chings made the hit on Sex World. Now we've tagged his penthouse, he'll be thinking overtime on ways to pay them back."

"So, what's up for the triad?" Jack inquired. "Do they get equal time?"

"It's next in line," Bolan assured him. "We'll be heading back to Chinatown later tonight."

Grimaldi frowned. "When you say *we…*"

"I'll take it with Bizhani. You're still in reserve."

Grimaldi nodded, showing no surprise. If he was disappointed, he concealed it well. "Phone duty. I can handle it."

"And the arrangements for Marseille, when we wrap up the local end."

"I'm on it."

Solid and convincing. Bolan knew his longtime friend would play the hand that he was dealt and see it through.

"Do you have to talk with anyone on your end?" he asked.

"Better that I leave them in the dark for now," Bizhani said. "Forgiveness rather than permission, yes?"

"And that's my cue," Grimaldi said, stepping away. "If you need me for anything, you know where you can find me."

"Thank you," Bizhani replied, as if the comment had been meant for him.

"Don't mention it," Grimaldi answered, already retreating down the avenue.

Justice Building, Washington, D.C.

"You heard me right the first time," Hal Brognola said. "Iran. An agent from MISIRI."

Barbara Price was quiet for a second, then replied, "He has to have a reason, Hal. I wouldn't second-guess him."

"Neither would I, ordinarily. And, yes, he explained it. Same goals, more or less. Enemy of my enemy and all that. In the service they used to say we rather have 'em in the tent and peeing outside, not the other way around."

"Okay. So what's the worry?"

"It's MISIRI," the big Fed repeated. "Since they started up in 1984 they've been involved in hundreds of murders worldwide and God knows how many cases of state-sponsored terrorism. We know they work with the Revolutionary Guard's Quds Force on 'extraterritorial operations' from Afghanistan to the States. You remember Adel al-Jubeir."

"They missed him," Price replied, "and the bureau caught one of them."

"Caught one and lost one," Brognola said sourly.

Adel al-Jubeir had been Saudi Arabia's ambassador to the United States in 2011, when a couple of Iranians planned to kill him with a bomb in Washington. Someone had leaked the plan, and FBI agents had nabbed one of the plotters, Manssor Arbabsiar, at JFK International Airport, minutes short of escape from the States. His partner, Gholam Shakuri, *had* escaped to parts unknown. As usual, Iranian officials had denied involvement in the scheme, while friendly reporters pushed the blame off onto "rogue elements" of MISIRI and the Republican Guard. But Brognola didn't buy it. Neither did the White House, which had slapped more sanctions on Iran after exposure of the incident.

As if the ayatollahs in Tehran gave a tinker's damn about global opinions.

"So...what? You want to call it off?" Price asked.

"Too late for that, as you well know."

"Okay, then. Wait and see what happens. Trust him."

"Not a problem," Brognola assured her. "It's the new guy on the team who's got me worried. Can you check him out?"

"Give me a name. I'll do my best."

"Heydar Bizhani," the big Fed replied, and spelled it out as best he could, phonetically. "Try any variation you can think of."

"Will do."

He already knew that data on MISIRI agents would be slim at best in the computer database at Stony Man. They'd have a file on the ministry's director, naturally, and his leading deputies, but profiles on individual agents would be scarce. Aside from normal security precautions, MISIRI effectively controlled Iran's national media through its Islamic Ideology Dissemination Organization, otherwise known as the Organization for Islamic Propaganda. The ministry owned Tehran's Mehr News Agency outright, and dictated editorial policy to the country's largest "independent" newspaper, the *Tehran Times*. Outside Iran, MISIRI and Mehr News made its influence felt through various far-right, anti-U.S. and anti-Israeli fringe publications and websites.

The bottom line: no matter what a person heard or read about MISIRI's plots and actions in the West, there was a good chance he or she had been fed a heaping helping of disinformation by the ministry itself. As far as names and backgrounds on its operatives in the field, little or nothing in the public venue could be trusted.

Heydar Bizhani? He could be a straw man or a stalking horse, a phantom or *agent provocateur*. Was he even Iranian, in fact? Brognola didn't know and wasn't sure if they could ever sort it out. Bolan had chosen to adopt the guy, rather than leave him running wild in Paris unrestrained, but if he proved to be a Judas goat, where would it lead?

"Okay," he said. "Send me whatever you can find, ASAP. If something's out of whack and we can pin it down, I'll need to get in touch with Striker."

"Roger that."

He cut the link without goodbyes and left her to it, trusting Price to find whatever was available, if anything. It was the *if* that worried Brognola, the risk of finding nothing out until it was too late.

Trust Bolan and Grimaldi? Absolutely. But the game had just taken an unexpected turn and Brognola could not help thinking that it might lead two of his best men to a dead end.

Little Asia, Paris

BOLAN DROVE Heydar Bizhani past the Tiger's Lair, spotting a group of nervous-looking Wah Ching soldiers on the street outside the club. A couple of them watched the Citröen C4 roll past in traffic with a white man in the driver's seat, but there was nothing to distinguish Bolan from the other tourists passing by.

"They seem quite young for master criminals," Bizhani said. "In my country, the narco-traffickers are generally older men."

"That bunch is more like cannon fodder," Bolan said. "Expendable."

"You have not told me what you painted on Durrani's wall."

"I was trying for 'Your days are numbered,' but I can't swear that the characters were properly arranged."

Bizhani laughed at that. "It doesn't matter, I suppose. Whether or not he's able to translate it, I suspect he will get the message."

"Meanwhile," Bolan said, "I need to do some rattling on the other side. You up for that?"

"Indeed. It seems a fine idea, which I regret had not occurred to me."

"No reason why it should, unless you're dealing with the triads."

"Thankfully, that is one blight we have been spared."

"Are you all right with just the SIG?" Bolan asked.

"That depends on what we plan to do," Bizhani said.

"I have some targets marked in Chinatown," Bolan replied. "The kinds of places we can grab some cash and raise a little hell."

"And blame it on Arif Durrani?"

"That's the ticket."

"Possibly I should pick up another weapon, in that case."

"Where is it?"

"Not too far. A flat on Rue de Domrémy. I can direct you, if you like, or go alone and meet you afterward. Perhaps at Place Jeanne d'Arc?"

"Driving you over's not a problem," Bolan said. "What are you picking up, exactly?"

"Nothing ostentatious," the Iranian replied. "A small Kalashnikov."

"Okay."

Bolan allowed Bizhani to direct him to a picturesque B and B where the Executioner parked and Bizhani ducked inside. He was back moments later with a black gym bag that didn't sound like it was filled with sports equipment. From its size, Bolan surmised that it contained an AKS-74U, the smallest Kalashnikov carbine manufactured in Russia. The "U" stood for *Ukorochenniy,* or "shortened," and so it was, with its 8.3-inch barrel, barely nineteen inches overall with its skeletal stock folded. Chambered in 5.45 mm, the carbine included a conical flash hider combined with a cylindrical muzzle booster featuring an internal expansion chamber to compensate for the ultra-short barrel and increase the weapon's efficiency. Its U-shaped flip sight also deviated from the standard Kalashnikov format, with settings for 350, 400 and 500 meters.

"All set?" Bolan inquired before he pulled into traffic.

"I brought the works, as I believe you say?"

"That's what we say," Bolan agreed.

"If I may ask, what is your plan for duping the Chinese?"

"Same deal as with Durrani," Bolan answered. "Do a switch-up. Make the Wah Chings think the Afghans are retaliating."

"I may be of help in that regard," Bizhani said. "To the Chinese, I would suspect, all people from my part of the world look alike."

"You could be onto something there," Bolan allowed.

"And as a bonus," Bizhani added, "I speak Pashto. Let the games begin."

CHAPTER TEN

Rue Charles Moureu, Little Asia

Eddie Tam opened his top desk drawer, stared for a moment at the pistol he kept hidden there, then shut the drawer again. His job as overseer of the Smiling Dragon rarely involved resorting to violence. That was the job of younger men whom he employed as bouncers, but this night he had received a warning of potential danger to himself and to the gambling club. The runner had brought the message to him from the Tiger's Lair, talking about attacks by Arabs, leaving Tam worried and confused.

For starters, nearly all his customers were Asian, 90-odd percent of them Chinese, the rest Laotian or Vietnamese. They liked to play mahjong, fan-tan and pai gow poker, games of skill approved under French gambling laws that permitted games of skill, along with slot machines, while banning games where players bet against the house. In simple terms, that meant the roulette wheel, craps table and the blackjack games were kept behind close doors and out of sight.

Tam could not remember the last time an Arab walked into the Smiling Dragon—if, indeed, one ever had. White tourists wandered in from time to time, seeking "exotic" entertainment, and their money was as good as anyone's, but normally they only lingered for a short time, obviously feeling out of place.

Tam's upstairs office was soundproofed, but he had a bank of closed-circuit TV monitors that let him watch the action in the front and back rooms if he chose to. An identical set of screens was installed in the basement, where his security personnel paid close attention to the players, watching for cheaters who deserved a beating. But Tam only watched for amusement. The clothes some of his patrons wore were curious, to say the least, their hair sometimes outlandish. Also, with the CCTV screens, he was forewarned of surprise inspections by the Française des Jeux, charged with supervision of all betting games and lotteries. The FDJ employed no Asian officers, so the appearance of suspicious-looking Frenchmen on the club's main floor alerted backroom operators to keep still behind the false wall that concealed them.

Simple.

Except now he had a war to think about, and no idea what had provoked it. Tam had tried to ask the messenger who'd warned him, but he'd gotten the brush-off, nothing more than the alert to be on watch for Arabs.

Tam glanced up from his paperwork, his eyes bleary from the numbers he was crunching—good for business, bad for headaches—and froze at the sight of two men passing through the front door. One was white and roughly six feet tall; the other was shorter, with a dark complexion and a hint of stubble on his cheeks.

An Arab, possibly?

Tam leaned in closer to the monitor and then jerked back as the men drew pistols and began to clear the gaming room, waving his players toward the exit. Tam could see their lips moving but heard no voices, since the CCTV link broadcast no sound. It was for watching only, not eavesdropping.

Tam hit the backroom's panic button, shifted toward

that monitor and saw his dealers scooping up the latest bets, shoving cash and chips into canvas bags they all kept ready for emergencies, preparing to escape. Down in the main room, muzzle-flashes marked the passing of Daniel Lu, the only armed guard Tam had on duty at the club this night.

So it was down to him.

If he ran out with no attempt to save the club or the day's take, he'd have to keep on running, praying Tony Cheung could never find him. Louie Shumin's punishment, already known throughout the Family, would be a wrist-slap by comparison to what Tam could expect.

Dismemberment? At least.

He took the pistol from his desk drawer, made sure that the safety was not on, then bolted for the office door. He had no plan, but knew that rushing forward was the only way to keep himself from sprinting out the back door and away.

A flight of stairs led to the ground floor, and Tam smelled gun smoke immediately on emerging from his office. As he started down the stairs, clutching his gun so tightly that his knuckles ached, the trembling in his legs made descent a perilous endeavor. Halfway down, he saw the two men staring up at him, the taller of them barking at him. "Drop it!"

Tam fired, had time to see his wasted bullet strike a wall before their slugs ripped through his legs and sent him tumbling head-first down the stairs. Somehow, he failed to break his neck and wound up lying at their feet in blood, his pistol lost, the pain eclipsing conscious thought.

The shorter, darker man leaned over him, smiling, and said, "Arif Durrani sends this message to the Wah Ching Family. You understand me?"

Tam didn't understand a thing, but he was happy to repeat the name upon command.

Arif Durrani. If he lived, he was unlikely to forget it.

Rue Aumont, Little Asia

THE KEY WAS SPEED, moving ahead to the next mark before alarms could circulate and rouse an army in pursuit. The target was a brothel, whose translated name, Bolan understood, was House of Relaxation. On the record, it was listed as a spa and massage parlor, since French law, while permitting prostitution, punished pimping, solicitation and owning or operating a whorehouse. Any bargain struck between employees and their customers was theoretically legitimate, as long as management was left out of the loop.

And if you swallowed that, Bolan thought, there was a bridge in Brooklyn going for a discount.

"In my country," Bizhani said as they neared the target, "prostitutes are flogged. Running bordellos is a serious offense—ten years in prison."

"How's that working for you?" Bolan asked.

"Poorly. Not so long ago, Tehran's police chief was arrested in a brothel with six prostitutes. Can you imagine? Six! Of course, he was a general."

"Rank hath its privileges."

"I've heard it said. But fortunately, under Sharia law, we recognize *Nikah al-Mut'ah.* Have you heard of this?"

"It isn't ringing any bells."

"A temporary marriage under contract, for a specified amount of time. The wife receives a dowry in advance. The union is dissolved according to the contract deadline, without the formality of a divorce."

"And what's the deadline?" Bolan asked.

Bizhani shrugged. "It's flexible. The shortest one that I'm aware of ran for fifteen minutes."

"Tricky."

"But *legitimate.* Appearances are vital, don't you find?"

"Some people seem to think so."

Personally, Bolan had no quarrel with prostitution, gambling or any other consensual crime, based on strict moral grounds. His objection was purely practical: the massive flow of cash that kept crime syndicates in business, armed with high-tech weaponry, corrupting cops, judges and politicians who had taken oaths to serve the public and uphold the rule of law. Unfortunately legalizing gambling in the States—and prostitution, in selected counties of Nevada— hadn't kept the predators from skimming untaxed profits off the top or from using licensed businesses as cover for a host of other crimes.

"What is our plan, then?" asked Bizhani as they neared the bordello.

"No whippings," Bolan said. "We'll roust the customers and working girls or boys, whatever, grab the cash and leave our message. Deal with any guards who interfere."

"And afterward?"

"I'm thinking switch back to Durrani for another change-up. Stay in motion. Keep the ball in play and hope they jump in on their own."

"And after that?" Bizhani pressed.

Bolan considered lying, but decided he would play it straight. "Marseille. I want to pay Durrani's labs a visit while I'm here."

"Rather than simply killing him?"

"Optimal damage," Bolan answered as he nosed his Citroën into a curbside parking space. "Ready?"

Bizhani reached under his raincoat to adjust the carbine hanging from a shoulder sling.

"Ready," he said.

They crossed the sidewalk, passed beneath the bordello's distinctly modest sign—no neon, just a pair of small wall-mounted spotlights to illuminate it—and pushed through the door to enter. In the lobby, a receptionist tried smiling at them, then gave up and pressed a button hidden underneath her desk. A door behind her opened for a bouncer who was sumo-size and holding a club Bolan recognized as a cricket bat.

Before he could approach and tee off on their heads, Bizhani swung his carbine from under cover, fired a round into the watchdog's massive chest and put him down. A shriek from the receptionist brought other soldiers on the run as Bolan drew his pistol, braced for anything.

Do it the hard way? Sure, why not.

They would leave their message, one way or another, scrawled in blood for Tony Cheung.

Tiger's Lair, Little Asia

"AND THEY GOT away with *how* much?" Tony Cheung demanded.

"Eddie thinks it must have been a quarter million euros, more or less," Danny Lam stated. "He hadn't done the final count."

"I want to see him," Cheung informed his number two.

"The doctor says he'll have to stay in hospital a few more days. They barely saved his legs."

"I don't care shit about his legs or how he feels. Could he at least describe the men who robbed him?"

"One looked like an Arab," Lam replied. "The other one, he couldn't tell. A white man's all he said. We would have had them both on tape, but they took out the video recorders after Joey Suen came up from the basement."

"So they knew what they were doing."

"Definitely," Lam agreed.

"A so-called Arab and a white man. Same description from the spa," Cheung said. No point in mentioning a brothel when a cell phone conversation could be plucked out of thin air. The gambling loss was one thing, with the club licensed and registered, but he didn't need a pimping bust on top of all his other problems at the moment.

"Has to be Durrani," Lam replied.

"Agreed. Get back here and we'll talk about what happens next."

"I'm on my way," Lam said, and broke the link.

Cheung knew what had to be done. The only question now was *how* to do it. When he killed Arif Durrani—preferably with his own hands, staring right into the bastard's eyes—Cheung wanted no loose ends, no possibility that the Afghan mobster's death or disappearance could be traced to him. It didn't matter what the police suspected; what could be proved in court was what counted.

France had abolished capital punishment around the time that Tony Cheung was born, so he had no fear of the guillotine, but he didn't fancy spending the rest of his life in La Santé Prison, where TV reports had described inhuman living conditions. Cheung knew, as a matter of curiosity, that French prisons had the highest suicide rate of any European penal system, and he didn't plan to share that grim experience.

Not for Durrani's sake.

Running numbers in his head, he calculated that he still had thirty-seven soldiers left in Paris and a dozen in Marseille. It wasn't much, but they were well armed, dedicated to the Wah Ching Family and obeyed his orders even if it came to laying down their lives. Cheung knew Durrani's home address and could post shooters there to take him if he showed himself, but Cheung supposed the lousy bastard had found a better place to hide by now.

A moment of uncertainty vexed Cheung. He took for granted that the two raids on his properties had been Durrani's work—three, if he counted Louie Shumin's robbery and beating. But he still had no idea who had bombed Le Monde du Sexe mere moments after he had phoned Durrani, threatening revenge. Was there another unseen hand at work in all of this?

Unseen. Unknown. It made no difference. Cheung had to deal with enemies whom he could see and punish. For the moment, that could only be Durrani and his men, wherever they were found.

War had begun, against Cheung's wishes, but he had to see it through. Retreat was not an option. Failure was unthinkable. Losing meant death and worse, the ultimate disgrace.

His men would find Durrani. Cheung would make the Afghan wish that he had never come to Paris.

And he would enjoy it.

Rive Gauche, Paris

"I HATE THIS PLACE," Arif Durrani said.

"It's only temporary," Siddiq Ghobar assured him. "Until we get a handle on this thing with the Chinese."

Durrani spit a curse at that and looked around the basement chamber with its walls and floor of stone. "It's like a tomb in here."

"Your new command post for a short time."

"Never mind. What's the news from Chinatown?"

"It's curious," Ghobar replied. "Our man with the Gendarmerie Nationale reports attacks on two Wah Ching establishments. One of their gambling clubs was robbed, also a brothel."

"All right, what's curious about it?"

"We were not responsible for either raid," Ghobar explained. "I've no idea who did it, but our contact says that your name was mentioned in each case."

"My name?"

"Specifically."

"Someone impersonated me?" Durrani asked.

"No, Arif. But they used your name as if you sent them."

"Who are they? What's their game?"

Ghobar could only shrug at that. "If we can find out who they are, the why explains itself."

"So find them!" Durrani snapped. "Spare no effort or expense."

"And the Chinese?"

"We'll deal with them, as well. I want all soldiers mobilized in Paris and Marseille. Double the guard on our refineries."

"It's done," Ghobar replied.

"Then leave me to my prison cell," Durrani said. "I need some time to think."

The raids in Chinatown disturbed him only insofar as he had been identified with them. Durrani had not ordered any strikes against the Wah Ching Triad yet; he was still collecting information to be sure the blows he struck would be effective, causing maximum disruption. Now he had to worry about who else was involved, besides himself and the Chinese.

First there had been the call from Tony Cheung, barely coherent, ranting about some demand for tribute, then the Sex World bombing and the vandalism at his home, with two men dead. He'd found a translator for the inscription painted on his wall, essentially an order for Durrani to get out of Paris, as if he would simply run away without a fight.

Ridiculous.

But now he had to wonder whether Tony Cheung had sent that message or had been responsible for the explosion at Durrani's club. The call before the blast *had* been legitimate. Siddiq Ghobar had bribed someone at Bouygues Telecom and traced it back to Cheung's cell phone. Beyond that, he knew nothing.

When Durrani tried to think of who might be responsible for the attacks, he drew a blank. The Gendarmerie Nationale, while as corrupt as any other law-enforcement agency he'd ever known, gained nothing by provoking bloodshed in the streets of Paris—and, in fact, had much to lose from an ongoing war. An intelligence agency, perhaps? France had the General Directorate for External Security and a Central Directorate of Interior Intelligence, either of which might take an interest in drug trafficking, but he had never heard of either practicing domestic terrorism.

The only other suspect he could think of would be RAAM—the Riyast-i-Amoor-o-Amanat-i-Milliyah, Afghanistan's own intelligence group, said to have financed certain terrorist actions against India, in collaboration with Pakistan's Directorate for Inter-Services Intelligence. But why would they pursue Durrani here, in Paris, when Khalil Nazari paid them very well to overlook the trade in opium?

Again, it made no sense.

Durrani thought his problems had to be linked somehow to the reports from New York City, where Wasef Kamran had died in battle with the Wah Ching Triad. That brought his thoughts immediately back to Tony Cheung, and yet he knew his men had not attacked the gambling club or the massage parlor in Little Asia.

Not unless Siddiq Ghobar was wrong somehow…or had been lying to him.

Shaken by that thought, Durrani dropped onto the couch set against one wall of his basement hideaway. He did not have to wonder why Ghobar might turn against him. It was always the same story: money, power, jealousy. Durrani had come up the same way, from the streets of Kabul, working for a man of influence until he'd seen and seized an opportunity for personal advancement. He could not feel angry at Ghobar, if that turned out to be the case.

But he would kill him, naturally, all the same.

As soon as he found out the bitter truth.

Boulevard Saint-Germain, Paris

"IF YOU WANT to find these guys," Bolan said, "sniff around for social clubs. It rarely fails."

"The name translates as 'Happy Times' in English," Bizhani replied as they motored past their target. "Do you think Durrani recognizes irony?"

"Maybe he'll get acquainted with it after this."

Bolan found a parking space downrange from Happy Times and nosed the Citröen C4 into it.

"You've got your mask?"

Bizhani reached to the floor between his feet and raised the plastic likeness of a snarling dragon, fitted with a thin elastic cord to hold the mask in place. "If only I could breathe the fire, eh?" he remarked.

At their last stop in Chinatown, Bolan had bought a smiling Buddha mask, while his companion had chosen the dragon. He'd imagined that the shop's proprietor regarded them with thinly veiled suspicion but it made no difference. The news of their attacks on Wah Ching properties had just begun to spread and there had been no general alarm as yet.

That was about to change.

They left the car, weapons and masks concealed beneath their raincoats as they walked back to the Afghan social club. The plan was simple: don the masks before they cleared the entrance and be ready for whatever happened next. If they found no one in the place, or if the customers saw fit to laugh it off, Bolan would leave a message for Durrani with the manager. But if the patrons reached for guns…

"Remember," Bolan told Bizhani. "One survivor, if it's possible."

"I'll do my best."

They reached the recessed doorway, Bolan glancing left and right along the street before he donned the Buddha mask. Bizhani's dragon face was gold and green with blood-red fangs. Though made of lightweight plastic, almost paper-thin, Bolan's disguise produced the same odd, claustrophobic feeling that he'd felt in childhood dressing up for Halloween. Pretending he was something that he wasn't—which, in some respects, had turned into a way of life.

The club was air-conditioned, almost chilly as they entered, with a jukebox pumping out a whiny song with some stringed instrument playing in the background. As they stepped into the smoky club, a dozen men stood frozen at the bar or seated around small square tables, all gaping in wonderment at the intruders.

It was make-or-break time, based on how Durrani's goons decided to react. One reckless move and it would all go straight to Hell.

It started with a shooter at the bar. A short guy, curly hair and thick mustache, broad shoulders, barrel chest. He grinned at Bolan and Bizhani as he thrust a hairy hand under his jacket, dragging out a pistol, stainless steel with satin finish. Bolan let him see the Steyr AUG and ripped a 3-round burst across the smiling soldier's chest before the room exploded into chaos.

The trick in close range combat, when someone was needed left alive to tell the tale, was stopping short of wholesale slaughter. There'd be no help from the opposition, since they didn't understand the plan and hadn't drawn straws to decide who would survive. A dozen men were bent on killing Bolan and Bizhani where they stood, and simply getting through it was a challenge, much less picking out a lucky winner from the pack.

With close spaces, point-blank fire, the good news was that it didn't take long. Bolan's Steyr and Bizhani's AKS sprayed death around the room, their bullets mangling flesh and bursting skulls, spoiling the aim of shooters they had taken by surprise. When it was finished, all of thirty seconds later, Bolan scanned the room and found one guy still breathing, bleeding from a ragged shoulder wound.

The Executioner stood over the survivor, kicked his piece away, then knelt beside him, just outside a spreading pool of blood, and asked, "Can you hear me?"

"Uh."

"I've got a message for Arif Durrani. If you make it, tell him that the Wah Ching Triad will not tolerate his insults. Got it?"

"Help...me."

"Answer first, before I call an ambulance."

"Wah Ching," the wounded gunman muttered. "Tell Durrani."

"There you go," Bolan said, reaching for his cell phone as he trailed Bizhani toward the street. He punched number

112 to reach emergency assistance, rattling off the club's address before they reached the Citröen.

He hoped the wounded gunman would survive. If not, the Buddha mask he'd left behind should do the trick.

Directorate-General of the Gendarmerie Nationale

"ANOTHER SHOOTING? MORE CHINESE?" Sergeant Pradon inquired, trailing his captain toward the parking lot behind headquarters.

"Yes and no," Captain Aubert replied. "There *has* been a shooting, but it's Afghans this time. On boulevard Saint-Germain, no less. But with a Chinese mask found at the scene."

"So it's a war, then."

"It appears so."

"You are doubtful, Captain?" Pradon asked as they reached the car they'd been assigned.

"I have no fixed opinion yet. We certainly have two cartels in play, neither averse to bloodshed. Whether they are truly killing one another still remains to be determined."

Aubert slid into the cruiser's passenger seat, leaving Pradon to drive. As they pulled out of the parking lot, rolling southeastward toward the Seine and the Place de l'Alma crossing, Pradon asked, "We have the Chinese message from Arif Durrani's penthouse, now the Chinese mask. You think that someone else may be involved?"

"I try to keep an open mind," Aubert answered. "But not so open that my brains fall out."

Pradon supplied the short laugh that his captain expected, switching on the cruiser's flashing lights and siren as the traffic thickened up ahead. "It still seems like a gang war to me," he said.

"But *which* gangs?" Aubert countered. "Might another we have not considered profit from a war between the Afghans and Chinese?"

"Ah. A conspiracy?"

"By definition, everything Durrani's people and the triad do is a conspiracy. The same is true of every other crime gang. All live by their wits, and any one of them might see advantages in such a conflict."

"Must we question all of them?"

"Not yet," Aubert replied. "Only if all else fails."

The captain pondered his problem as they wove through traffic, other cars and motorcycles yielding with reluctance to their lights and whooping siren. Soon he saw more cruisers and a veritable fleet of ambulances parked outside the drab and unremarkable façade of the massacre site. The ambulances, Aubert noted, were in no rush to depart.

"All dead?" Pradon inquired.

"There's one survivor," Aubert replied. "Or was, at least. I don't know if he made it to the hospital alive. We'll check there next."

"For all the good that it will do. These bastards never talk."

"You won't mind if I ask him, anyway?"

"Of course not."

"Park over there," Aubert instructed, pointing to the left.

It had begun to rain again as Aubert stepped out of the cruiser. Normal weather for this time of year, coincidentally in sync with his dark mood. Crossing the sidewalk with Pradon a step behind him, Aubert met the first cop who had responded to the shooting call.

"How bad?" he asked.

"See for yourself," the officer replied, remembering in time to add the "sir."

Aubert moved past him, reached the door and stepped into the slaughterhouse.

CHAPTER ELEVEN

Avenue Victor-Hugo, Paris

Not every enterprise conducted by a crime cartel was criminal. It paid to have legitimate investments as a front, a source of reportable income and as a repository for cash from sources best left unmentioned. One such operation owned by Arif Durrani was Automobiles Royales, a luxury car dealership located within sight of the Arc de Triomphe. The shop specialized in high-end exotic rides, the more expensive the better, crowding its showroom with the latest models from Aston Martin, Lamborghini, Koenigsegg, Bugatti and Pagani, among others.

Closed now, the dealership still blazed with lights, its sleek products on permanent display. The window glass, Bolan surmised, was both ballistic in defense against vandals or thieves, and tinted to prevent sunlight from fading custom paint, assuming that the vehicles on show remained in stock that long.

"You have no mask to leave this time," Bizhani noted as they circled once around the Arc de Triomphe on Place Charles de Gaulle.

"Won't matter," Bolan answered. "This is strictly hit and run."

"No more Chinese graffiti?"

"Just a poke to get Durrani moving."

"And to cost him many euros."

"Hit them where they live," Bolan replied.

The cheapest car displayed in the Automobiles Royales showroom cost about a quarter of a million dollars, and the rest went up from there. Figure a dozen on display, together with the building whose designer had spared no expense, and any major damage meant a price tag in the millions. Money was a normal mobster's prime directive, and a hit that size would resonate from Paris back to Kabul, where Khalil Nazari kept an eye on every penny spent on his behalf.

Bizhani had the wheel as they came off the circle, slowing as they passed the auto dealership, Bolan manning the Milkor MGL. The grenade launcher weighed twelve pounds and measured just twenty-two inches with its stock folded, resembling nothing so much as an old-fashioned Tommy gun on steroids. Its double-action trigger would let Bolan fire three rounds per second, launching the 40 mm projectiles four hundred meters downrange, but he didn't need rapid fire or the MGL's M2A1 reflex sight for the slow-motion drive-by that he had in mind.

Point and squeeze from thirty feet. Keep it simple.

His first high-explosive round breached the bulletproof windows, no problem. The second round turned an electric-blue Bugatti Veyron Super Sport into a pile of flaming scrap with a $1.5 million price tag, smoke rising up to cloud the showroom's vaulted ceiling.

Round three stood a Lamborghini Aventador 700-4 Roadster on its tail, riding a ball of fire that cost Arif Durrani $441,000 at base sticker price. Its lake of burning gasoline spread underneath a Koenigsegg Agera R, lighting another bonfire worth a minimum $1.6 million.

Round four punched through the windshield of an Aston Martin One-77, $1.85 million manufacturer's suggested retail price, and peeled the roof back like the lid of a sardine can, shrapnel flying on to mutilate a Maybach Landaulet valued at $1.38 million.

Round five took out a Ferrari Enzo, a virtual steal at $677,000, now worth a couple of grand to the neighborhood scrap metal dealer. Part of its engine block landed on top of an SSC Ultimate Aero, billed as the fastest street legal car in the world with a sales price of $654,000.

Round six, his parting shot, ripped through a Zenvo ST1 from Denmark, $1.23 million on the sticker, hurling what was left of it across the showroom and into the manager's office, leaving a large jagged hole in the wall. Bizhani had been counting and accelerated then, smiling from ear to ear as they rolled out of there, with bright flames leaping in the rearview mirror.

"What a waste of fine machinery," he said.

"I want Durrani mad enough to make mistakes," Bolan replied. As he spoke he released the Milkor's cylinder axis pin and broke the weapon open, then removed the spent cartridge casings. That done, he inserted his fingers into the empty chambers and wound the cylinder against its driving spring before reloading it with six fresh rounds.

"Where next?" Bizhani asked.

"Head back to Chinatown," Bolan advised. "They should be having fireworks pretty soon."

Rive Gauche, Paris

ARIF DURRANI WATCHED the fire on television, broadcast live over NRJ Paris. The reporter, blonde and bundled in a raincoat with a hood to keep her hair dry, seemed to find the blaze exhilarating, though she naturally wore a mask of grave concern. Damages in the millions, she declared, with sabotage expected, possibly an act of terrorism.

"Terrorists!" Durrani snarled, as if the blonde could

hear him. Anyone who thought the bombing was political had to be a raving idiot. It had to be the damned Chinese, unless—

His cell phone rang. Durrani checked before he answered it and recognized Siddiq Ghobar's number. "I'm watching it now," he declared without wasting his breath on a greeting.

"We have a witness," Ghobar stated. "She told the police that she saw two men in a car, one with a 'big gun' causing the explosions."

"Chinese?"

"That, she could not say," Ghobar replied. "The car was possibly a Citröen, silver, maybe gray or white. It's difficult to tell at night, under the neon, with explosions going off."

"Will cash improve her memory?"

"I doubt it, Arif. She was taken by surprise, then badly frightened."

"So we know nothing."

"As instructed," Ghobar said, "I looked into the other thing." Not mentioning the massacre at Happy Times specifically. "Hakim was conscious when I called on him."

"And?"

"You already know about the masks."

"What else is there?"

"One of the visitors told him to say the Wah Ching tolerate no insults."

Staring at the flaming ruin of his auto dealership on television, minus any sound since he had muted it, Durrani felt his stomach tighten, bitter acid rising in his throat. Despite misgivings, he could only see one clear-cut course of action open to him now.

"Drop whatever else you're doing," he commanded. "Get back here at once."

"Of course. I'll see you soon."

The line went dead. Durrani laid his phone aside and picked up the TV remote, pressing the Mute button to reactivate the sound. The blonde was speaking to a policeman now, one of their plainclothes detectives, asking him about her terrorist hypothesis.

"There is no reason to suppose that this crime is political," he said.

"What, then?" she asked him, almost challenging.

The middle-aged policeman shrugged. "It's early yet to say. In such a case, we normally investigate competitors, insurance policies, unhappy customers or ex-employees."

"You believe there is no cause for public apprehension, then?"

"That is a different question, obviously," the detective said. "With this level of violence, concern is clearly justified. No effort will be spared to find the perpetrators of this deed before they strike again."

"So, you are worried that this crime might be repeated."

"Worried for myself, no. If I were the owner of this property…well, that's another matter altogether." And he smiled, a mocking gesture for the camera.

With a sharp jab of his thumb, Durrani switched off the television and glared around the basement room that had become his prison cell. He hated everything about it, hiding underground as if he were a rodent fleeing predators. He should be on the street, hunting the enemies who had embarrassed him and cost him so much money.

The damned Chinese? Or someone else?

His choice was obvious. Retaliation could not be delayed a moment longer if he meant to salvage any portion of his reputation. Barring any other likely suspects, he could only strike at the Wah Ching Triad, whose leader had overtly threatened him before the shooting started. If it later proved that he had been mistaken...well, at least one group of rivals would have been eliminated in the process.

And if, during the course of wiping out the triad, he discovered that his enemy was actually someone else, Durrani would enjoy eradicating them, as well. One battle at a time, to minimize confusion, concentrate his strength and get the most good out of each successive move.

Siddiq Ghobar might still bear watching. If he proved to be disloyal, although he was a nephew of Khalil Nazari, he could be eliminated safely, with the Chinese blamed. How fitting if, in fact, Ghobar was at the root of all Durrani's troubles to begin with. And if he proved to be innocent, so what?

A periodic change in personnel was often good for business.

Rue George Eastman, Little Asia

TONY CHEUNG HAD cabin fever. He was sick and tired of living undercover, and it made no difference that he'd been hiding out for only half a day. He was accustomed to the high life, being seen around the streets of his domain with or without an entourage of Wah Ching soldiers, and his sudden disappearance sent the wrong message to people who relied on him for strength—and paid him for protection from prospective adversaries.

How could he control a neighborhood, much less the drug trade in a country, if he was afraid to go outside?

Near midnight, he decided that had to change. Arming himself with a matched pair of Walther PPS semiauto pistols and a balisong knife, he set out to walk a circuit of the Parc de Choisy, checking in at all his normal stops, glad-handing regulars and simply being seen. More to the point, he would be doing it alone.

A man did what he had to do.

Cheung started off walking southeastward, against traffic on Avenue De Choisy, checking in along his route at various clubs and shops that stayed open all night. From there, he turned northeastward on the next street, repeating his visits. At three different places, he let fawning bartenders give him free drinks, which he sipped, then left unfinished as he moved on toward his next appointed destination.

Was he nervous? Absolutely. But the trick was to hide it so well behind a mask of smiling arrogance that no one realized his guts were twisted in a knot. Put on a brave face and command the whole damned world to kiss his ass.

By one o'clock, he had finished roughly half his circuit of the large park. More stops, more idle conversation, nothing he'd remember in the morning, but the people would remember seeing *him,* and any doubts they might have had about who ran the show in Chinatown would disappear.

Coming out of a massage parlor where he'd declined a hand job on the house, Cheung heard a man's voice shout his name, somewhere behind him.

"Tony Cheung! Hey, Tony!"

It was not an Asian voice. That much Cheung knew before he turned to face oncoming traffic, where a black sedan was pacing him, traveling slow enough that drivers trapped behind it would soon be laying on their horns. Cheung saw a bearded face behind the steering wheel, another grinning at him from the open left-rear window.

Jacket hanging open, pistols close at hand, Cheung waited for an instant, not about to run if there was no threat there. A heartbeat later, when the backseat passenger produced a short machine pistol, Cheung drew one of his Walthers, squeezing off two shots right-handed with the pistol's "QuickSafe" double-action trigger, then turned on his heel and bolted for the trees without assessing any damage he'd inflicted on the enemy.

Whether he'd drawn first blood or simply startled them, the shooters let him reach the trees before they opened fire, sending a swarm of slugs after him in the darkness there. Ducking and dodging, running for his life, Cheung gave no thought to facing them with odds of three or four to one. His men were waiting for him at the Tiger's Lair.

And Cheung needed all the help that he could get.

A mad sprint through the night, and he could hear someone behind him—make that at least two men, calling to each other in language that reminded him of Arabic. Durrani's men; they had to be. He had a good head start, but far to go, expecting to be cut down from behind at any moment.

When the trees cleared in another fifty yards or so, he'd have no cover for his run across the park toward his sanctuary. There'd be nothing to prevent them stopping at the tree line, sniping at him as he sprinted over open ground.

Unless...

Changing his plan, Cheung stopped and drew his second pistol, crouching behind the largest tree that he could find. When his pursuers passed him—*if* they passed him— he could shoot them in the back. And what was wrong with that? This wasn't some old-fashioned Western movie, where everyone played fair and let the other man draw first.

This was his life. And Tony Cheung was not prepared to die just yet.

A sound of labored breathing reached his ears. Cheung held his own breath, clutched his matching guns in sweaty hands, immobile as the shooters rustled past him, one on each side of his hiding place. When they were clear, he chopped them down with rapid fire, no mercy, and then lurched forward, running past their slumped, still-twitching forms. He stopped along enough to snatch up one of their machine pistols, then ran for all that he was worth into the night.

Rue Toussaint-Féron, Little Asia

"HERE HE COMES," Heydar Bizhani said a slivered second after Bolan spotted Tony Cheung approaching the Tiger's Lair alone.

"Looks frazzled," Bolan noted, watching Cheung glance nervously over his shoulder, keeping one hand tucked inside his jacket as if holding injured ribs—or maybe clinging to a hidden weapon. Cheung was sweating, his hair mussed, limping slightly on his left leg.

"I would say that he has run a marathon, but he's not dressed for it," Bizhani said.

Cheung reached the Wah Ching hideout, where two guards were covering the door, spoke briefly to his men, then ducked inside while they remained on watch.

"Some kind of rumble," Bolan said. "It shook him up."

"Durrani joins the game, eh?"

"If he hasn't, we've been doing something wrong."

Five minutes passed before a black four-door sedan pulled up and double-parked outside the Tiger's Lair. A moment after that, five men rushed from the club, four soldiers covering their boss until he'd ducked inside the car, then filling in around him, leaving no great space to spare. Two motorcycles growled out of an alley on the west side of the club and fell in just behind the black car as it pulled away.

Bolan gave them half a block's head start, then followed in his Citröen C4. The one-way flow of vehicles on Rue Toussaint-Féron took them to Avenue d'Italie, where Cheung's little motorcade turned north. Bolan trailed his quarry to a seven-story building he took for an apartment building. He read the address as the car and motorcycles pulled away, his mind flashing back to what he'd gleaned from Hal Brognola's files at Stony Man.

"The Wah Chings own this building," he informed Bizhani. "If I had to guess, I'd say that Cheung is going to the mattresses."

"Which means...?"

"He's hiding out, on lockdown."

"And presumably he has more men inside," Bizhani said.

"Bet on it."

"But we cannot let him rest in peace, I take it."

"I can't," Bolan said. "You're free to take a pass on this."

"I think not," the MISIRI agent said. "You have a plan in mind?"

"It's basic," Bolan told him. "Get inside, confirm we only have Wah Chings on site, then raise some hell. Removing Tony Cheung's job one. Beyond that, it's all gravy."

"You have decided not to pit his force against Durrani's, then?"

"I've got another angle on Durrani," Bolan said. "Smart money says he'll trail me to Marseille once he starts losing labs there."

"Ah, yes, Marseille."

"It's not a problem if you want to sit it out. Try for Durrani on your own, if that's the way you want to go."

"Your way appears more promising," Bizhani said. "And after that?"

"I like your optimism," Bolan told him. "After that, I'm out of France and on to someplace else."

"We part ways, then?"

"Depends on how you feel about it, on the flip-side. Take it one step at a time."

"Of course."

"Going in here," Bolan advised, "bring everything you've got. Better to have it and not need it than be caught short when the chips are down."

THERE WAS A GUARD on the back door of the Wah Ching apartment building. Bolan took him down with a silenced round from his Beretta 8000 and dragged his body behind a large trash bin, field-stripping the dead man's pistol before it went into the garbage. Entering the place was easy after that; a moment with his lockpick set and they were in.

Beneath his raincoat, bulked out now, Bolan was carrying the Milkor MGL and Steyr AUG on shoulder slings. Bizhani had his AKS-74U out and ready as they reached the service stairs, Bolan advancing with his pistol still in hand. He hadn't checked to see if there were elevators in the place and didn't care. The last thing the Executioner planned to do was to telegraph their move to Cheung's guards waiting on the floors above.

He took it for granted that the boss would have a top-floor suite, well covered by his men to stop intruders from approaching him. That didn't make him safe, of course, but if it gave him the illusion of security so much the better. He'd be counting on a rush from street level, Durrani's men trying to fight their way upstairs, instead of infiltrating quietly to take Cheung when he least expected it.

Or so Bolan hoped, anyway.

They met a second lookout as they neared the seventh floor. The guy looked bored until he spotted them and then stooped to reach a carbine he had leaned against a nearby wall. Too late, as Bolan plugged his left eye socket with another muffled round and stood aside to let the body tumble past him on its way downstairs.

On seven, Bolan holstered his Beretta and removed the

Milkor from concealment. First up in the 6-shot cylinder, an M576 buckshot round containing twenty pellets roughly half the size of double-00 buck in a 12-gauge cartridge. The spray was devastating at close range, and the cartridge would place thirteen of those pellets inside a five-foot-diameter circle at forty yards out. The other five rounds in the cylinder were high explosive, primed for bringing down the house.

Three Wah Ching soldiers had the hallway covered, one armed with a FAMAS autorifle that was standard issue for French military forces, while the other two were packing Uzi submachine guns. Two of them were facing Bolan as he stepped out of the stairwell, number three with his back turned, but none of them had time to raise their weapons as he let fly with the Milkor, shredding them with buckshot from a range of thirty feet.

Three down; two of them obviously dead and their companion on the way. Bolan stayed where he was, Bizhani stepping out behind him, while the echo of his shot rang through the corridor. Another moment and the doors on either side began to open, spilling gunmen who'd been startled out of downtime by the shot.

He let the Milkor rip, firing a 40 mm high-explosive round off to his left, immediately followed by another to the right. Their detonations filled the corridor with smoke and dust, while short bursts from Bizhani's AKS ripped through the haze, dropping the Wah Ching gunners who weren't caught up in the twin explosions.

Bolan marked the one door that remained unopened when the shooting started, judged that Tony Cheung had to be somewhere behind it and moved forward to confirm it. From a range of twenty feet, he sent another HE round to take the door off its hinges with a clap of thunder, then charged through before whoever waited for him on the other side could bounce back from the blast.

The triad overlord of Chinatown was sprawled across a sofa, bleeding from a gash below his hairline, fumbling for the semiauto pistols he had dropped when he went down. He stared at Bolan, saw death in the stranger's face, and asked him, "Who in hell are you?"

"Your judgment," Bolan replied, letting the Milkor drop and whipping out his pistol, drilling Cheung with a 9 mm Parabellum round between his arched eyebrows. Cheung sagged and slithered off the couch, leaving his final thoughts spread over the upholstery.

"Back out the way we came," Bolan advised Bizhani, brushing past him on the short run toward the service stairs. He had the Steyr AUG in hand before he reached the landing, ready to greet any soldiers waiting on the flights below to bar his way.

Job done, and all that mattered now was getting out alive, to try his luck again the following day, in Marseille.

Charles de Gaulle Airport

JACK GRIMALDI HAD completed all the paperwork required for takeoff. All he needed now were passengers. Unfortunately, from his point of view, the last call he'd received from Bolan had informed him that there would be two of them.

The ace pilot had been worrying about the new addition to the team since he'd been introduced, no need to list the problems that he had with taking an Iranian on board. To him, MISIRI was a gang of murderers no better than SAVAK under the shah or DINA under General Pinochet in Chile. One thing that could be trusted about them: they were looking out for Number One around the clock, seven days a week.

The rub was that he trusted Bolan absolutely, owed the guy his life and knew that the man wouldn't risk a mission on a whim. There had to be something about this stranger from the other side—the enemy, in Grimaldi's view—that had prompted Bolan to invite him in.

Okay. But afterward, what then? Bizhani had already seen their faces, could describe them—Jesus, even had some kind of micro-camera in a button on his shirt, for all Grimaldi knew. The agent couldn't tell the mullahs back at home who they were working for, but he already knew enough to make the Stony Man pilot damned uncomfortable.

He was mulling over various solutions to that problem when the Citröen C4 rolled up and parked beside the hangar. Bolan and Bizhani stepped out of it, retrieved duffels from the trunk, and walked toward the jet.

"Everything okay downtown?" Grimaldi asked Bolan.

"We wrapped it up. All set on this end?"

"If you're sure about the excess baggage."

"Got it covered," Bolan said, patting Grimaldi on the shoulder. "Trust me."

"Always have," Grimaldi answered. "Always will."

And meant it, sure.

The aircraft's cockpit looked like something out of *Star Wars* to the uninitiated, with its console and heads-up display. Grimaldi took the right-hand pilot's chair, no more concerned about a solo takeoff than he would have been driving across town in a Volvo. If you broke it down statistically, his odds of dying in an auto crash were twenty thousand times greater than dropping from the sky.

He'd made it a point to look it up.

It wasn't taking off or landing that concerned him. It was Bolan's ride-along.

Grimaldi ran the checklist of his instruments and gauges, got his clearance from the tower and began to taxi out. "Four planes in line ahead of us," he told his passengers via the Falcon's intercom, then settled back to wait.

Marseille had the potential to get hairy. Bolan might have left the Wah Ching Triad's Paris outpost leaderless, in disarray, but there was still Arif Durrani to consider. In Marseille, the Afghan would be fighting for his drug labs, maybe teaming up with the Corsicans who'd been refining heroin in the vicinity for generations. Grimaldi would never think of second-guessing Bolan, much less underestimating his abilities, but on the other hand, he'd never seen the man go up against those kinds of odds, trusting an enemy to watch his back.

If anything went wrong...

Grimaldi told himself not to think like that, but couldn't help it. Bet your life and take it to the bank. If anything went wrong, the pilot would pursue Heydar Bizhani to the farthest corners of the earth—hunt him through stinking sewers in Tehran, if that was what he had to do. He wouldn't rest until that debt was paid in blood.

Enough!

He had to concentrate on flying now, the tower telling him that they were next in line for takeoff.

"Buckle up," he cautioned, keeping both eyes on the airliner in front of him as it sped down the runway toward escape velocity.

Then it was his turn, barreling along and lifting off, loving that moment when he lost touch with the ground and soared aloft. This was the good part, leaving all your troubles down below.

Grimaldi only wished that it could last.

CHAPTER TWELVE

Rive Gauche, Paris

"You're sure?" Arif Durrani asked, his hand trembling as he held his smartphone.

"Positive," Siddiq Ghobar replied. "It's definitely Cheung, with six or seven of his men."

"All dead?"

"Beyond a doubt. Others escaped, but they are being hunted by the police."

"And," Durrani pressed him, "we were not involved?"

"Unfortunately, no. We did not learn the address until it was done."

"Then who?"

He pictured Ghobar's shrug before his second in command said, "Who can say? Who even cares, so long as Cheung is gone?"

"It cannot be that easy," Durrani said.

"Arif, you suspected someone else might be involved. Now they've removed the triad. We should thank them."

"Find out who they are and I'll be happy to."

Ghobar chuckled, then said, "You're serious."

"Listen, Siddiq. You think these strangers killed Cheung and his soldiers as a favor to us? After blowing up the club and violating my own home? *Of course* I'm serious. We need to know their names and where to find them before they come back for us."

"All right. I'll keep the pressure on our police contacts for information. If they find out anything, you'll be the first to know."

"Not if," Durrani told him. "When."

"It's what I meant to say."

"No doubt."

Durrani killed the link and put the phone back in his pocket. Rising from the sofa, he began to pace the confines of his basement hiding place. The walls seemed to be closing in around him, but he did not dare go out. Not yet. Whoever had eliminated Tony Cheung was still at large in Paris, operating as he pleased with virtual impunity.

Durrani thought of letting the police deal with his problem, but he could not trust them. Truth be told, for all he knew, the police might be involved somehow. They had GIGN—the Groupe d'Intervention de la Gendarmerie Nationale—created as an elite counterterrorist force completely capable of using extralegal dirty tricks against selected targets. As was the DCRI, the Central Directorate of Interior Intelligence, with special branches dedicated to terrorism and violent subversion. If the attacks were officially sanctioned, Durrani knew that any police investigation would be mere sham, all for show.

And he might be next on the hit list.

Which left Durrani…where, exactly?

Troops depleted, routed from his home, under attack by enemies whom he could not identify. It struck him now that his mistake was lingering in Paris while Ghobar was sorting out the mess. If he got out, retreated to a safer place, he could regroup, lay plans and take steps to redeem himself.

But where to go?

The answer, once he'd posed the question, was immediately obvious. His second largest group of soldiers was assigned to guard the factories that processed Afghan morphine into heroin. He would be safer there, four hundred miles from Paris on the Côte d'Azur, where he could flee by plane or boat if matters went from bad to worse. And if Khalil Nazari questioned his retreat, Durrani had an explanation ready for him. He was merely going to protect the most important part of their investment personally.

Following the call of duty.

Durrani had a Learjet 40 standing by at Orly Airport, ready to depart on half an hour's notice. He could call the pilots now, make the arrangements and be in the air by— what? Two-thirty, maybe three o'clock. Less than an hour's flying time and he could leave the madness in the capital behind him. Let Ghobar use his initiative and take the fall for any failure that resulted.

Meanwhile, if their enemies turned toward Marseille, Durrani would be waiting for them, ready to take credit for their ultimate defeat. He'd called ahead already, doubling security on both morphine refineries, alerting all his people in the nation's second largest city to be on alert. Durrani almost hoped his unknown adversaries *would* try taking out the plants. It might, he reasoned, be his best chance to destroy them.

And with that done, how could he be criticized for small setbacks in Paris? So far, he had suffered relatively little damage by comparison with Tony Cheung and the Wah Ching clan. Indeed, once he'd eliminated those responsible for taking out the triad, he could claim that victory, as well. Who would be left among the living to dispute it?

Taking out his smartphone once again, Durrani set about waking his flight crew. They were paid to fly, not sleep. Now let them earn their salaries.

Over the Loire Valley, 40,000 feet

BOLAN PEERED FROM his window in the jet, surveying the long valley known as the Garden of France for its vineyards, fruit orchards, artichoke and asparagus fields. From Bolan's altitude it all seemed minuscule, the valley's classic Renaissance châteaux reduced to the size of Monopoly houses, boats moving along the river shrunken to specks of drifting flotsam. He thought about the centuries of toil and struggle that had made this place a garden spot and tourist attraction, then shrugged them off.

This day was all that mattered to the Executioner.

Marseille was waiting for him, branded in media reports as Europe's most dangerous place to be young. With a population barely one-tenth the size of New York City's, Marseille rivaled the Big Apple's record for drug-related murders, many of the victims being young men slain in turf wars over distribution of cocaine and cannabis. Police congratulated themselves on breaking up the "old gangs," then lamented a lack of "honor" and restraint among the hoods from low-income housing estates who replaced them, buying guns for next to nothing on the streets and using them on any pretext.

But were the old gangs really gone?

Based on Stony Man's intelligence, Bolan knew that members of the Unione Corse—Corsica's version of the Mafia—were still alive and kicking in Marseille, managing drug labs that had been their staple source of income since the 1930s. Leaders rose and fell, arrests and prosecutions cleared space in the ranks, but commerce churned along as usual, surviving the periodic attacks of virtue suffered by fickle politicians. Now, with Afghan opium replacing Turkish product, the refineries were running at full capacity once more.

Bolan planned on changing some of that.

He glanced across the aircraft's central aisle and found Heydar Bizhani dozing, or pretending to. Bolan had no idea if the Iranian had been in touch with his commanders at MISIRI, or if they were even cognizant of his cooperation with a pair of agents from the "Great Satan" of the United States. As long as no one else from Tehran got in Bolan's way, he wasn't overly concerned about Bizhani talking to his masters, but he would remain on full alert against the possibility of a betrayal down the line.

Bolan did not share Jack Grimaldi's thinly veiled hostility toward their companion, but he'd drop Bizhani in a heartbeat if it came to that, and take out anyone Bizhani might call in to sabotage the mission or threaten him and the Stony Man pilot. He'd saved Bizhani's life, but whether that meant anything to a committed agent of the other side, he couldn't say.

A glance at Bolan's watch told him they were twenty minutes out from Marseille Provence Airport, the fifth busiest in France for passenger traffic and third for cargo. As a domestic flight, they would not be subject to customs inspection or passport control, but the same rules applied as in Paris for registry at a hotel. Not that many rooms would be available this time of year, with tourists packing into Provence-Alpes-Côte d'Azur.

Grimaldi had accommodations lined up at the airport—which, Bolan surmised, meant sleeping on the plane—while Bolan and Bizhani would be on the move. They didn't plan to linger around Marseille or to spend too much time at any given site.

Two men against a syndicate—those were long odds, but Bolan saw them as another kind of opportunity.

People who said one man could never make a difference in the world were wrong. Those who believed they were too small to trouble "bigger" men had never tried to sleep with a mosquito in the room.

Mack Bolan was a different kind of pest: a grim, determined wasp that bore a lethal sting.

Within an hour, give or take, his enemies would start to feel the pain.

Victoria Peak, Hong Kong

THE CALLER WAS a lowly blue lantern, uninitiated and scarcely worthy of attention from the Mountain Master of the Wah Ching Triad, but he had delivered vital news. The second in what now appeared to be a series of disasters had befallen Ma Lam Chan and his extended Family, this time in France.

Chan did not mourn for Tony Cheung per se, although he would go through the motions at a suitably ritualized memorial service in two days' time, arranged by the Family's incense master. In truth, a red pole who could not control his territory meant no more to Chan than any other peasant on the street—except that his removal by an unknown enemy had to be avenged for Chan's sake, and the Family's.

A war was one thing. Chan had weathered many in his time and always managed to advance himself over the corpses of his foes. His latest enemy, it seemed, was the Afghan savage Khalil Nazari. His men had been responsible for the disruption of Chan's enterprise in New York City, and it now appeared as if they were behind the French fiasco. In New York, Chan had been mollified somewhat on learning that his red pole, Paul Mei-Lun, had slain Nazari's man in charge and many of his soldiers, even as Mei-Lun himself went down. No consolation of that sort would be forthcoming out of Paris, where it seemed Nazari's thugs had won the day.

Why had Nazari chosen this time to begin an all-out war? And where would he strike next? Immigration to Hong Kong was strictly controlled, and the officers in charge were well paid to alert Chan if any potential enemies passed through the screening process. Ninety-five percent of the island's population was Chinese, while Indians and Pakistanis—the ethnic groups most likely to be imitated by Afghan infiltrators—comprised only half of one percent. They were easily counted and monitored.

Still...

What would prevent Nazari from employing mercenaries to advance his cause? Nothing. First-rate assassins were a rare commodity, but killers with a military background were a dime a dozen in a world where wars dragged on for decades, major powers often hiring private armies to conduct their dirty business with a measure of impunity. Khalil Nazari had the cash on hand to hire Americans or Europeans, even members of a rival triad who would relish Chan's destruction for their own motives.

For all the loyalty built into any given triad clan, the larger world of Chinese syndicates was brutally competitive. Aside from the Wah Ching Triad, there were at least twenty-six other triad clans. Some of the larger triads had multiple clans beneath their global umbrella—eighteen for the 14K group, eleven for the Sun Yee On, and so on. Oaths and organization aside, the Mountain Master of a large triad might not know what his troops were doing at any given time in Singapore, Manila, Bangkok or Los Angeles, while he sat at home in Hong Kong or Macau.

Chan wondered now if he was any better off. Were traitors in his ranks conspiring with Khalil Nazari to bring him down? If so, he meant to root them out and execute them with his own two hands. The punishment for treason was declared in the sixth of thirty-six vows made by each new recruit: death by five thunderbolts.

Of course, since Chan could not control the weather, he would think of something suitable to take the place of lightning. Perhaps he would employ electrocution, or make due with five shots to the head. The end result was all that mattered, finally: swift death for anyone who challenged Ma Lam Chan.

But first he had to determine *who* to kill, then make arrangements for a suitable demise that would impart his message to the world without legally implicating Chan. Revenge was of no use to him if he wound up in prison while achieving it. Hong Kong had abolished capital punishment in 1983, clinging to that principle since the 1997 handover, even though China maintained the death penalty and presently executed more prisoners than any other nation on earth.

Given a choice of death or decades in a cage, Chan knew which he would pick.

But his first choice was life, with time to celebrate the slaughter of his enemies.

Stony Man Farm, Virginia

BARBARA PRICE PICKED up the red phone on its second ring. It was Brognola's private line into the Farm, demanding her immediate attention.

"Price."

"What's new from over there?" Brognola asked.

The line was clean and permanently scrambled. "They got out of Paris, headed south," she said.

"Still three of them?"

She heard concern in Brognola's voice and replied, "So far."

"Okay," he said, half muttering, as if it were a curse. And then he said it again, with somewhat greater confidence. "Okay."

"You know he always has a plan," Price said.

"I hope so. Once they finish in Marseille, it just gets worse."

"He'll handle it."

"You're right. That other thing, with Able Team…?"

"It's still on track."

"All right, that's good. I've gotta run. Call me whenever, if you hear something."

"Will do."

Brognola cut the call at his end, leaving Price with a dial tone buzzing in her ear. She set her phone down, swiveled through a quick one-eighty in her desk chair to face a large map of the world mounted on her office wall. It wasn't anything spectacular, no flashing lights or interactive features, just a portrait of earth spread out in the classic Mercator projection that made Greenland look twice the size of the United States.

Rising, she approached the map and spotted Paris, then charted the course Bolan would follow to Marseille. It didn't seem that close to Corsica, but mobsters from the outlaw island had infested France's second-largest city for generations. Its members reportedly included certain elected officials, along with members of the Gendarmerie Nationale, the Directorate-General for External Security and the Central Directorate of Interior Intelligence. Whether they would involve themselves in thwarting Bolan's move against Arif Durrani was an open question, but it stood to reason that they wouldn't let a multimillion-dollar heroin connection go to hell without a fight.

And beyond France, what?

She was not privy to the plan Bolan was following, but knew that circumstances altered cases and his final course of action might bear small resemblance to the scheme he'd had in mind that last night they had seen each other at the Farm. Each time Bolan left, Price knew it might be the *true* last time that she would see him. It was something she accepted as a fact of life, doing her job in spite of constant apprehension that the man she cared so much about would always be in harm's way, by his own choice, until someday he ran out of luck and time.

Because she cared for him deeply.

There was no desire to settle down behind a picket fence and raise a brood of children. That was never in the cards for Bolan—nor for Price, she'd realized after she'd taken the job as Stony Man's mission controller. She was not controlled by a maternal urge, much less the nagging of a family to hurry up and procreate. Price knew that there were other ways to make a contribution in the world than simply adding to its population.

Bolan's life was focused on the battlefield. And Price's, the one that offered her the most fulfillment, was exactly where she found herself right now. Backing whatever play he made from Stony Man, with every resource at her disposal.

Until something went awry and it was time to let him go.

Directorate-General of the Gendarmerie Nationale

"MARSEILLE? WHEN DID he leave?" Captain Aubert asked.

"Within the hour," Sergeant Pradon replied. "A private jet from Orly."

"So he's nearly there by now."

The sergeant nodded in agreement.

"It is curious, would you agree, that our Mr. Durrani chooses this precise time to leave Paris, when his enemies are dropping dead like flies and we are bound to question him?"

"Hardly coincidence," Pradon observed.

"He leaves me no choice, then, but to go after him."

"You're going to Marseille?"

"We are," Aubert corrected him.

"Is it approved?"

"It will be. Contact Squadron Leader Marcel Beaudry at the Air Transport Gendarmerie. Tell him I need the first flight that he has available, no later than an hour from now."

"And if the squadron leader does not wish to take his orders from a sergeant, sir?"

"Mention Suzette in Boulogne-Billancourt."

"Suzette?" Sergeant Pradon was frowning mightily by now.

"In the event of a misunderstanding, mention File 1793-A."

"Sir, I'm not sure—"

"We're wasting time, Pradon."

"Yes, sir. Just as you say, sir."

The truth be told, Aubert was not concerned about the deaths of Tony Cheung or any of his lackeys. They were criminals, and Paris would not miss them. On the other hand, if he could find sufficient evidence to prosecute Arif Durrani for their killings, Aubert reckoned that the Afghan would receive a life term as a drug kingpin accused of aggravated murder. For a first offender under French law, that meant eighteen years before he would be eligible for parole. Call that a lifetime in the hellhole of La Santé Prison, and if there were any Chinese gangsters in the lockup with Durrani…well, let nature take its course.

Aubert had been assigned to Marseille once upon a

time. He still had contacts there, like Squadron Leader Beaudry, who would assist him if required to prevent their precious secrets from becoming public property. He had refined coercion to an art form over twenty-seven years of service with the Gendarmerie Nationale. Close to retirement now, Aubert no longer worried about stepping on important toes if it was necessary to resolve a major case.

And something told him he would never see another case as big as this.

Sergeant Pradon was back within ten minutes, a bemused expression on his face. "We have the flight, sir," he reported. "Leaving Charles de Gaulle in forty minutes, if we make it."

"We'll be there," Aubert assured him. "There's no need for any luggage. If you need a toothbrush or a razor, we can get it in Marseille."

As they were walking to the motor pool, Pradon spoke up again. "If I may ask you, Captain, who is Suzette?"

"Sometimes it's best not to be too inquisitive," Aubert replied. "Even for a detective like yourself."

Aubert kept track of indiscretions—both his own and those of others—but he did not share them lightly, and on no account for the amusement of subordinates. Knowledge was power. Used correctly it could change a stubborn mind or even move the world, perhaps, and once a threat was made it had to be carried out. But only in the last extremity.

Aubert knew he had made an enemy this day, but that was less important than succeeding in his mission. If he could bring down Durrani and the rest of his cartel, there would be praise enough to go around and Marcel Beaudry would be welcome to his share of it.

Results came first.

Aubert had everything he would need upon his person:

his credentials and his SIG SAUER SP 2022 sidearm. A cruiser would be waiting for him on arrival, and whatever else he might require could be obtained by one means or another in Marseille.

First, information on Durrani's whereabouts. And after that?

Aubert suspected the bloodshed was not finished yet, and that it would direct him to his proper targets. Failing that, he would be forced to make the rules up as he went along.

Marseille Provence Airport

THE RENTAL CAR waiting for Bolan was a Renault Clio IV with a five-speed manual transmission. He loaded their duffel bags into the baggage compartment and, leaving Grimaldi at the airport, rolled out with Heydar Bizhani in the shotgun seat.

Marseille Provence Airport was located in Marignane, the largest suburb of Marseille, lying northwest of the city proper, with runways protruding over a lagoon called Étang de Berre. To reach Marseille, Bolan drove south, then east, to catch the Autoroute du Soleil, winding its way southeastward to his destination. Despite the highway's name promising sunshine, the sky was overcast and threatened rain.

"Does this gray weather always follow you?" Bizhani asked.

"I don't pay much attention to it," Bolan said.

In fact, while he was well versed in the hazards of exposure to the elements, Bolan was trained to fight in any climate. Rain, in the amounts he had experienced so far in France, was nothing by comparison with a monsoon. At worst, it plastered down his hair; at best, the drizzle would provide a cover for the raincoat that concealed his weapons.

Bolan had a list of targets in Marseille, provided courtesy of Stony Man. The roster included three drug labs that refined morphine into heroin, a deep-cover brothel that catered to the sick set and assorted other properties owned or leased by Arif Durrani. For good measure, the Farm had tossed in some Corsican marks, in case Bolan wanted to stir things up on a broader scale, without discriminating between scavengers.

He knew enough about Marseille to realize it wouldn't be an easy ride. The town was struggling back from dark days, known for crime and poverty, trying to reinvent itself as a European Capital of Culture, investing $135 million in public and private funds to rejuvenate the tourist industry. New editions to the cityscape included a huge, mostly glass Museum of Civilizations from Europe and the Mediterranean and the Villa Méditerranée, a center for dialogue concerning the region and its peoples. Bolan wasn't sure if his campaign would be a setback to those plans or not.

Frankly, he didn't give a damn.

He'd called Durrani from the jet while they were airborne, but had missed him. When he'd tried again on landing, one of his goons offered to take a message. It was simple. *Tell him he's invited to a party in Marseille.*

Whether the goon would pass it on was anybody's guess. Bolan wasn't concerned about delivery. If necessary, he could always try again once things were popping, calculating that Durrani was, at most, an hour away. They would be meeting soon, even if Bolan had to double back to Paris, track Durrani down and drag him from his hideyhole into the light of day.

The last light he would ever see.

"Where first?" Bizhani asked.

"I thought we'd try the clinic."

"Ah."

It was a clinic in name only, located on Rue Samatan, pretending to offer drug counseling and help with kicking the habit. In fact, the front *did* furnish some addicts with Methadone and Subutex to help them get the monkey off their backs—though some reports claimed that the medicines prescribed were as addictive as the smack they were designed to beat. Others who ventured through the clinic's doors got heroin to go, and that was profitable, too, but the real money-maker was a backroom lab that ran around the clock producing heroin from morphine manufactured in Afghanistan.

He had to give Durrani credit for the one-stop-shopping angle. Where else could a junkie either feed or kick his habit, while the same technicians tasked with running drug tests on their clients churned out bricks of uncut heroin for sale throughout the Western Hemisphere?

It was a classic business model. And the Executioner was on his way to shut it down.

Step one in what was promising to be a brutal dance of death across Marseille.

CHAPTER THIRTEEN

Rue Samatan, Marseille

Jami Baba enjoyed his job at the Clinique de Saint Germain. It hardly felt like working, really. Seven hours a day, on average, he hung around the clinic, making sure none of the so-called "clients" tried to rip off any drugs without either paying cash or signing all the proper forms for reimbursement required under the Social Security Funding Act. More importantly, he oversaw security for the drug lab that patients never saw, sometimes escorting shipments to and from the airport as required.

Easy.

There'd been no major problems since he'd taken the job, thanks to Arif Durrani's contract with the Unione Corse. Once every other week or so, Baba was called upon to kick a rowdy client's ass and toss him out into the street, but that was just a bit of exercise he treated as routine. Most of the users knew him now and caused no trouble when they heard that he was on the premises. The medics seldom spoke to him, and that was fine, since Baba had no use for over-educated types.

The nurses, now…well, they were something else entirely.

Since yesterday, however, his routine had been disrupted by alarms from Paris, where it seemed that war had broken out between his people and a triad faction operating out of Chinatown. Baba had volunteered to come and join the action, but his orders were specific: stay in place and guard the lab. Lay down his life, if necessary, to protect it.

To that end, hardly believing that it might be necessary, he had dusted off the hardware. Sitting in his small office next door to the lab, he finished cleaning his FN P90 submachine gun. If that wasn't enough to discourage trespassers, Baba also had a Swiss-made Brügger & Thomet MP9 machine pistol chambered in 9 mm Parabellum for backup, *and* a Heckler & Koch HK45 semiauto for last-ditch defense, if neither of the full-auto weapons proved adequate.

All that and two more boys out front, with sawed-off shotguns underneath their jackets.

Baba believed that he had covered all his options—was convinced of it, in fact, up to the very moment when he heard shots echo from the clinic's lobby, junkies squealing as they bolted for the nearest exit in a panic.

Baba froze, his weapons lined up on the desktop, hairy hands fidgeting around them like a pair of nervous tarantulas. What to do? He could rush out and join the firefight—but no, it was already finished. Most of the screaming had subsided, and he heard footsteps advancing toward his office. Toward the laboratory he was duty-bound to guard.

He scooped up the P90 submachine gun, snapped a fully loaded magazine into place atop the receiver and pulled back the ambidextrous cocking knob to chamber the first round. He was about to circle the desk—or, rather, was considering it—when the footsteps hesitated in the corridor outside.

Seizing the moment, Baba ripped a burst across the hollow-core door, splintering its cheap veneer with nine or ten of his mag's fifty rounds. Instead of crying out in pain or simply dropping dead, however, his opponents started firing back with automatic weapons of their own, drove Baba under cover, then kicked through the riddled door and pumped more rounds into his desk. It slowed their velocity somewhat, but couldn't stop the slugs from drilling through and ripping into Baba's flesh. Too late, he tried to squirm away from them, firing a wild burst from his SMG that ripped across two metal filing cabinets, scarring them with shiny divots.

More rounds hammered through the desk and Baba heard more screaming now. It seemed to come from far away, yet left his throat feeling as though he'd gargled razor blades. Was that his own voice, sharp and high-pitched? When a bullet struck the P-90 and ripped it from his grasp, he knew he was finished.

Footsteps came around the desk. Two men peered down at him as he lay wallowing in blood. A part of Baba's mind worried they might mock him for his screams, but neither said a word. The shorter man aimed an assault rifle at his face, one-handed, no real need to aim at point-blank range.

Baba bared his teeth in an approximation of a snarl and waited for the muzzle-flash.

THE LAB TECHNICIANS had evacuated through a back door by the time Bolan and Bizhani finished mopping up security at the clinic. Three shooters hadn't done the place much good. All that remained now was to trash the place beyond repair and make sure that its present stock of heroin would never reach the streets.

Bolan let his Steyr AUG hang from its shoulder sling, switching to the Milkor MGL grenade launcher. He hung back in the laboratory's doorway and fired off a buckshot round to sweep the nearest worktable of beakers and retorts. A cloud of morphine base, dull brown, hung in the air like smog beneath fluorescent ceiling lights as Bolan fired a second 40 mm round—incendiary, this time—toward the back wall of the chamber. Detonation sent a fireball rushing toward Bolan as he cleared the entryway and slammed the door behind him. He saw Heydar Bizhani already retreating toward the main street exit and trailed in his wake.

Both men had their weapons fairly well concealed beneath their raincoats as they reached the street. Bolan's burden was bulkier, the AUG hanging below one arm, grenade launcher beneath the other, but he kept them covered on the rapid walk to the waiting Clio IV. Behind them, someone saw smoke rising from a skylight at the clinic and shouted an alarm. Bolan glanced back, as anybody might under the circumstances, and confirmed that no one seemed to be connecting them with noise that may have echoed from the building moments earlier. The smoke now served as a diversion, covering their hurried hike back to the car.

When they were on the move, Bizhani said, "I do not think Durrani takes us seriously. Only three guards on the property, and one hides underneath his desk?"

"Don't take it personally," Bolan said.

"You told him we were coming to Marseille, yes?"

"There's a chance he didn't get the message," Bolan answered. "Or he may have thought it was a setup for another round of hits in Paris, drawing him away. This ought to wake him up."

A red fire truck with yellow side panels came barreling toward Bolan, southbound, its blue lights flashing, siren *bing-bong*ing to warn the drivers and pedestrians ahead. Bolan slowed and edged their rental to the side, in full compliance with the traffic laws, then rolled on when the way was clear.

After another block or so, Bizhani said, "It will be difficult for me when I explain this deviation from my mission."

"There's still time to bail," Bolan advised him. "Leave us to it. You can catch a flight to Tehran as easily from here as if you were in Paris."

"We're not finished yet," Bizhani said. "I cannot leave until Durrani is disposed of. It is probably the closest I will come to injuring Khalil Nazari."

"Possibly," Bolan replied.

"You have another plan in mind?"

"I'm working on it as I go along."

Bizhani frowned. "I would not recommend a trip into Afghanistan."

"Let's call that one a last resort."

Bizhani lapsed into another momentary silence and then asked, "Where shall we go next? The other lab?"

"I'm saving that one for dessert," Bolan replied. "First, I'd like to drop in on some Corsicans, then maybe see a man about some slaves."

"The Maison de Merveilles?"

"A little change-up," Bolan stated. "I hate to be predictable."

Marseille Provence Airport

BAD NEWS WAS waiting for Arif Durrani when his Learjet taxied to a stop outside a hangar on the west side of the airport. A Rolls-Royce limousine was standing by—that was the *good* news—but the rest immediately sent Durrani's mood from dark to seething rage.

First up, a message from a caller who refused to give his name: *Tell him he's invited to a party in Marseille.* The call had come while he was airborne, and the idiot who'd answered it in Paris thought it best to phone ahead and leave the message with Durrani's front man in the port town, Majid Akbari, rather than disturb the boss while he was flying. Punishment would be imposed when he returned to Paris. For now, this moment, there was worse in store.

"They hit one of the labs," Akbari told him when Durrani's feet were barely back on solid ground.

"*They?* Who's *they,* Majid?"

The shrug Akbari gave him made Durrani want to smash his face. He might have done so, if they were not in a public place with witnesses and police loitering around the several airport terminals.

"The same one's who invited you to party, I suppose," Akbari said after the shrug, seeing the snarl form on his master's face. "The same bastards from Paris, perhaps. I don't know them. Do you?"

"If I knew them, Majid, they would be screaming out their final breaths right now," Durrani said. "Which lab?"

"Sorry?"

"Which did they attack, Majid?"

"Ah. The Clinique de Saint Germain."

"What damage did we suffer?"

"Three men dead. The place is gone."

"Gone?"

"Torched with some kind of incendiary. I don't have the details yet. The police and fire marshal are still investigating."

"What is our exposure?" Durrani asked.

"Well, there's nothing left to speak of, possibly some melted glass or other lab equipment. You know that the clinic dealt in Methadone and Subutex, so there's an explanation for the gear. It's thin, I grant you, but if all the heroin and morphine were consumed, they likely can't disprove it."

"And the property? Refresh my memory."

"Your name doesn't appear on anything," Akbari said. "The clinic's owned—*was* owned—by a shell company in Luxembourg. Owners of record on the paperwork are three old men who don't know anything about the operation past the dividends they bank each quarter. If the DCRI tries to trace it any further back, they hit a firewall. Nothing leads to you or back to Kabul."

"And you say police are still working the scene?"

"For hours yet, I should imagine. Going there would be a *very* bad idea, Arif."

"I worked that out myself, thank you. Where are we going?"

"I supposed to your apartment—or the office?"

"The apartment," Durrani said. "All the business done today will be transacted on the streets. You have the soldiers ready?"

"Every man accounted for."

"And can we put our fingers on the Chinese?"

"They've gone to ground, but we know all the places where they operate. None of them will stray far out of Chinatown."

"I want none of them left when we are finished," Durrani stated. "It is better if they disappear, but barring that, corpses will do."

"It shouldn't be a problem if the police leave us alone. There's one more thing."

"What else?"

"I asked about your caller when the message came from Paris. I was told he sounded like a white man, not Chinese."

Durrani thought about it. He wasn't sure the idiot who'd been afraid to call him in the air could tell the difference without a face in front of him to look at. Still...

"I'll think about it," he replied. "Meanwhile, deal with

the enemies we know. I want the Wah Chings out of Chinatown—out of Marseille—before another sun goes down."

Quai Marcel Pagnol, Marseille

"YOU HEARD THE news?" Lucien Rossi inquired.

"Calvi lost to Cameroon again," César Cardini said.
"Their goalkeepers are shit."

"Not soccer, stupid," Rossi replied. "The other thing."

"What other thing?"

"I mean the Afghan's lab."

"Oh, that. What of it?"

Rossi marveled at Cardini's seeming density, sometimes. "You know about the trouble up in Paris, eh? So
now it's hitting close to home."

"Not *our* home. Let Durrani take care of himself. He
bought a license to do business in Marseille. No one said
anything to me about protection."

"It could still affect us if the trouble spreads," Rossi
observed.

"Let's wait and see. I don't like Afghans well enough
to bleed for them."

Rossi could not dispute that logic. He took another sip of
his single-malt whiskey, savoring its smoky flavor. Lighting was dim inside the Club Ajaccio, no windows to distract serious drinkers with thoughts of time slipping away.
The half-dozen customers were all brothers of the Unione
Corse, grim life-takers who seldom smiled except at the
misfortune of their fellow man, and only then when there
was profit in it for themselves. Their violence was legendary on the Côte d'Azur, but no vendettas crossed the
threshold of the Club Ajaccio, on orders from their ruling boss.

Rossi finished his drink, set down the glass and said, "I have to go. There are collections to be made."

Cardini nodded, raised his hand to signal for another beer, then hesitated as the front door opened, spilling light into the murky barroom. Rossi glanced in that direction, frowning at a pair of strangers who had clearly mistaken the club for a public tavern. Then again, they had the look about them, making Rossi think they might fit in, except that neither of them wore the Moor's Head watch fob of the Unione Corse.

And was the shorter of the pair Arab?

Cardini saw the guns first, shouting, "*Pistolets! Attention!*" Rossi was diving for the floor by that time, groping for his Beretta 92G-SD as he hit the tiles and rolled to his left. He cleared it from his holster as the two intruders opened fire, raking the bar first with converging streams of bullets from their automatic weapons.

Rossi fired a wild shot toward the door, knowing that it was wasted in his haste. Behind the bar, Jérôme Ferraci had his shotgun up and angling toward the doorway when a bullet caught him in the throat and slammed him back against the shelves of liquor ranked against the mirrored wall. His weight collapsed one of the shelves, glass shattering around him as he dropped from sight, firing a blast into the ceiling as he hit the floor.

Cursing the shooters, Rossi flipped a table over on its side—poor cover, but the best available—and struggled to his knees, firing a double-tap in the direction of the doorway without aiming. Twelve rounds remained in the Beretta's magazine, and he had one spare in his pocket if he needed it.

Or if he lived that long.

As if in answer to that thought, one of the gunmen strafed his capsized table, hot slugs drilling through it.

Rossi bolted, firing as he ran, but it was hopeless. Both of them were tracking him, his brothers dead or dying all around him, sprawling in their own blood, as another burst of gunfire took him down. The pistol tumbled from his hand and slid across the floor, out of his reach.

Rossi heard them approach him, discovered that he could not move his legs. One of the strangers stooped to grab his jacket, rolled him over onto his back through waves of sudden agony and left him staring upward at the ceiling.

"If you live," the taller of them said in English, "take a message to Carlo Paoli."

Rossi wondered vaguely how they knew the name of his boss, but could not find his voice to ask the question. It was better to stay silent, anyway. An iron-clad rule within the Unione Corse. Say nothing, and you cannot say the *wrong* thing.

Barely noticing his silence, if at all, the gunman said, "Tell him it's open season on Arif Durrani and his friends. No one who deals with him is safe. Got that?"

"Nique ta mère," Rossi replied, breaking the rule to offer one last insult and be done with it. He waited for the bullet, but the shooters turned and left him there, wishing that he could simply die.

"THIS WAS A REHABILITATION clinic for drug addicts?" Captain Aubert inquired as he surveyed the ruins of a recent fire. Above charred timbers and the twisted, blackened siding, wisps of acrid smoke still rose.

"Yes. At least, ostensibly," Lieutenant Isabel Caron replied.

"But you think otherwise?"

She shrugged; an exercise worth watching in Aubert's

opinion. "The fire was started in a backroom laboratory. Quite a large one, actually."

"Is that unusual?" Sergeant Pradon asked.

"Not in itself. These clinics test their clients' blood and urine, as you know, for drug traces. A lab on site provides immediate results in most cases. The size of it, however, was unusual."

"Narcotics?" Aubert queried.

"We've found no traces yet," Caron replied. "The fire was very hot. A military-grade accelerant, the fire marshal believes, combined with chemicals already on the premises."

Aubert searched his knowledge of what was employed to refine heroin. "Acetic anhydride?"

"And ethyl alcohol. Both are highly combustible. The anhydride smells like pickles," Caron said.

"I don't smell anything but smoke," Pradon observed.

"Because it's burned," the lieutenant said. "If, in fact, they had it here."

"How long has this place been in business?" Aubert asked.

"Seven, perhaps eight years."

He turned to face Caron. "And you believe they were producing heroin throughout that time?"

Another pretty shrug. "Who knows?"

"If you suspected it—"

"I don't know how you operate in Paris, Captain," she interrupted him. "But in Marseille, we follow orders. If reports are filed and our superiors refuse to act on them, we don't go off on personal crusades."

"Which superiors received this information and declined to act?"

"It's not for me to say."

"And if I should insist? Make it an order?"

"Then I would direct you to the general of the division," Caron replied. "You'll find him at headquarters with his feet up on a desk, unless he's golfing."

"A sportsman, is he?"

"I have no opinion on how generals spend their leisure time," she answered diplomatically.

"In that case, can you name the clinic's owners for me?"

"Not specifically. The deed is held by a consortium from Luxembourg. We're talking to their lawyers."

"Ah. Good luck."

"We'll need a good deal more than luck, I think," Caron replied.

"Would anything suggest an Afghan silent partner in the clinic?"

"You're referring to Khalil Nazari?"

"Or his monkey here in France, Arif Durrani," Aubert said.

"Not yet. Perhaps when we identify the three men who were killed inside. They're badly burned. Unless we find their dental records, I can't promise anything."

"I don't suppose you could check the dentists in Kabul?"

She laughed at that. "So, they sent us a comedian."

"It's just a sideline. If I wanted to locate Durrani in Marseille, where should I go?" Aubert asked.

"He's here," Caron confirmed. "We checked him through the airport earlier today."

"And shadowed him?"

"Of course. But lost him in the 5th arrondissement."

"No small accomplishment, Lieutenant."

"It will be investigated, Captain, for all the good that does."

Aubert switched gears. "What can you tell me about triads in the city?"

"We ship some ninety million tons of cargo in and out

per annum, so they're here, of course. The main port is at Fos-sur-Mer, which is thirty miles northwest. At least three triad clans have people in Marseille. The 14K, Sio Sam Ong—"

"And the Wah Ching." Aubert finished the sentence for her. "They're the ones that interest me."

"Because of the trouble in Paris?"

"And now in Marseille."

"We've spoken to four patients who were in the clinic when the shooting started," Caron said. "None of them say the gunmen were Chinese."

"Did they take time to notice?"

"They were frightened, certainly. But it's a rehab clinic, not a center for the blind."

"And they described these killers…how?"

"One European. One of Arabic appearance."

"Arabic?"

"Dark-skinned."

"So, anyone from a Sicilian to a Tartar."

"Not Chinese," she stressed.

"I need to speak with your Wah Ching gang members, in any case."

"If we can find them, certainly."

"And are there more such clinics in Marseille?"

"I'm not aware of any, Captain. Perhaps you should consult the squadron leader for narcotics."

So that he can send me on a wild-goose chase, Aubert thought to himself. And said, "Perhaps I should, at that."

Maison de Merveilles, Avenue du Prado

THE SIGN TRANSLATED to "House of Wonders," vague enough to seem fairly sedate in the midst of Marseille's red-light district. A person didn't need to guess about the street's other establishments—massage parlors and "saunas," strip clubs and grind houses. Given the reputation of the Maison de Merveilles, Bolan wasn't surprised to note its understated advertising.

Every major city in the world had neighborhoods where everything was for sale, prevailing law and human decency be damned. Sometimes those districts generated disturbing headlines, but more often they were ignored by politicians, ministers and the police who let them operate as long as cash kept flowing up the ladder of command. This day, Bolan was bent on turning over one particularly nasty rock, to reach the maggots underneath.

"I never understood the urge to rape a youth," Heydar Bizhani said as Bolan drove them south along the Avenue du Prado, past the street girls showing off their wares. "And all the bondage, torture—it's disgusting."

"Nothing like that in Tehran?" Bolan inquired.

"Oh, yes. But when the individuals responsible are caught, we hang them. That makes everything all right."

Parking the car a half block from their target, Bolan said, "We'll have to watch it once we get inside. The youngsters and all."

"Shooting through walls. I understand. And for the customers?"

Bolan considered it and said, "To hell with them."

All brothels dealt in sex for hire. Some offered kinky twists for extra pay, ensuring that a scheme of "safe" words and signals prevailed, commonly with the sex workers dominating their johns or janes. Only a few took rank depravity to its ultimate depths without thought for the consequences, and one of those was the Maison de Merveilles.

About to go out of business for good.

Bolan left his Milkor MGL in the car, made sure he was packing extra magazines for the Steyr AUG and led Bizhani toward the beige façade of the hellhouse. One hand on his holstered Beretta 8000, he rang the doorbell and waited, smiling blandly for the fisheye lens of its peephole. When the door opened a moment later, they were faced with a bald behemoth stuffed into a gray suit, some three hundred pounds on the hoof.

"What do you want?" the giant demanded in French.

Bolan shot him in the face and stepped around his carcass, dragging it clear of the doorway with Bizhani's help. They heard footsteps approaching and another man's voice asking what was going on.

The second bouncer took a silenced slug while he gaped at the dead whale in the foyer, dropping to his knees and tumbling facedown to the floor. Bolan holstered his pistol and revealed the AUG. Bizhani, at his side, stood ready with his AKS carbine.

Beyond the entryway they found a parlor where, presumably, the customers selected their companions for a journey into madness. On a couch to Bolan's left, two dead-eyed youths, male and female, sat together, taking in the new arrivals and their guns as if nothing surprised them anymore.

"Get out of here," Bolan advised them, getting blank stares in return.

"Sortez!" Bizhani snapped, to get them moving.

They bolted for the exit and were gone. Bolan triggered a burst into the floor, rousing the house, and started up a flight of curving stairs to reach the second story while Bizhani started on the ground floor. By the time he'd reached the landing, three men had emerged from different doors along the balcony, two carrying their clothes, one bare-chested, grappling with the zipper on his slacks. They all looked prosperous and badly frightened as he herded them along the landing, Bolan pausing at each open doorway while he glanced inside, his anger growing colder by the second.

The three men were babbling at him, all trying to explain themselves, one holding out a crumpled wad of cash, when Bolan cut them down. He left them sprawled together, leaking on the carpet, as he cleared the other rooms, then doubled back to make his way downstairs. More shots from that direction let him track Bizhani's progress on the ground floor.

As they left that house of death, Bolan was on his cell phone, dialing the local France 3 television station. He had done his research in advance and didn't bother calling the police who'd let the Maison de Merveilles run with impunity for years on end. Maybe a special feature on the nightly news would help. If not, at least the keepers of the prison and their latest crop of customers were gone.

As for the youths, he could only hope they caught a better break and wished them well.

CHAPTER FOURTEEN

Kabul, Afghanistan

Khalil Nazari took the call from Hong Kong with a mixed sense of surprise and curiosity. He was surprised that Ma Lam Chan would try to reach him in the first place, curious to find out how the Dragon Head of the Wah Ching Triad would justify himself. Since both of them spoke English, they were able to communicate without interpreters. As far as trust went, that was something else entirely.

After an exchange of stiff and formal salutations, Chan said, "It appears we have a problem to discuss."

"You are referring to the actions of your soldiers in New York and Paris, I assume?" Nazari asked.

"Self-defense requires no explanation or apology," Chan answered.

"Self-defense? The murder of my men? Destruction of my property?"

"Reports I have received describe your men as the aggressors in both cities," Chan replied.

"My information says the very opposite."

"Then clearly we have grounds for a discussion to resolve the matter."

"Resolution normally implies concessions," Nazari said warily.

"A compromise, perhaps. Even collaboration, if you deem it possible."

"On what terms?" Nazari asked.

"Once again, a matter for discussion."

"I do not propose to speak about such matters on the telephone."

"Nor I. A meeting would be beneficial to us both, I think."

Nazari frowned at that, considering a trap. "And where would such a meeting be convened?"

Chan's smile was almost audible. "I can't imagine being welcomed to Afghanistan under the current leadership."

"Unlikely," Nazari conceded. "Nor I, in the People's Republic."

"Sadly true. I think, however, you might find the atmosphere in Hong Kong more conducive to a free exchange of views."

Nazari understood that Hong Kong, once controlled by Britain as his own homeland had been for eighty years, remained an island of thriving capitalism despite imposition of communist rule in 1997. With the former Portuguese colony of Macau, it was designated as a Special Administrative Region of the People's Republic of China, granted full autonomy in all affairs except those regarding diplomatic relations and national defense, with an independent judiciary operating under common law and a multi-party political system. Nazari also knew that Hong Kong's economy had been ranked as the freest on earth every year since 1995, by the *Wall Street Journal*'s Index of Economic Freedom.

In this case "free" meant "pay as you go," a philosophy that any drug lord understood.

"I would require your personal assurance of safe passage," Nazari said, knowing that Chan's word meant no more than his own, when treachery might turn a tidy profit.

"You shall have it," Chan replied without delay, "if you should deign to visit us."

"With an allowance for my staff," Nazari said, both of them recognizing that he meant an armed security detail.

"Of course. Important guests routinely travel with an entourage. I personally have some small influence with our own Hong Kong police force. The commissioner enjoys a round of golf with me from time to time."

"And firearms?"

"Licenses for our respected visitors are easily arranged."

"It would be beneficial if we could resolve our differences peacefully," Nazari granted.

"Beneficial, certainly," Chan said. "And profitable."

"Did you have a date in mind?" Nazari asked.

"Your earliest convenience. Every day our difficulties are protracted, we lose money."

"I will see to the arrangements, then, and send you the itinerary."

"Excellent. Give no thought to accommodations. All shall be arranged at our expense."

"Most gracious."

"Merely a small gesture of respect. Until we meet, then."

"I look forward to it," Nazari said earnestly.

And so he did. If he could strike a deal with Chan and the Wah Ching Triad, foregoing further bloodshed, it was worth a flight halfway around the world. And if no compromise was reached on terms he found agreeable, well, Ma Lam Chan would be within his reach. On hostile ground, of course, but there were ways around that minor obstacle.

Nazari gave no further thought to how he would reach Hong Kong. He owned two super midsize jets that he kept on standby for vacations and emergencies. Either one could transport him from Kabul to Hong Kong without refueling en route, while carrying enough armed men to make Nazari feel reasonably safe on arrival. And if he acted swiftly, certain others could precede him, settling in to be prepared if they were needed.

Certain specialists whose stock in trade was sudden death.

Avenue d'Antibes, Marseille

THE SECOND LAB on Bolan's hit list was not disguised as a clinic. Instead it occupied what once had been a four-bedroom apartment on the top floor of a five-story apartment building. With a couple of the walls knocked out, the windows barred and painted over, an exhaust fan venting to the roof and soundproofing installed, it had become a workshop for Durrani's backup team of chemists.

Cooking down the morphine base required about five hours, followed by some time for it to cool, then twenty minutes while a dose of chloroform dissolved colored impurities. Another twenty minutes, give or take, while activated charcoal finished clearing up the mix, then soda ash was added to precipitate solid heroin base, which was laid aside and heated to dry. The net result—seven hundred grams of heroin base per kilo of morphine—was then further refined into heroin hydrochloride by adding ethyl alcohol and ether, wrapped in clean filter paper and dried on wooden racks under heat lamps, commonly over lime rock, until it was ready for packaging and shipping.

Depending on the quantity of product presently on hand, busting the lab could cost Arif Durrani two, maybe three million dollars. Not much in the grand scheme of things, for a drug cartel that shipped cash in forty-foot cargo containers, but the public exposure would put a sharp crimp in his style, maybe get certain cops off their backsides and into the game.

The trouble, this time, would be getting to the lab itself.

A drive-by showed two guards on duty, covering the main street entrance. They were both presentable enough, wouldn't alarm the neighbors just by being there, but Bolan knew the enemy would be armed and ready to defend the place. There was no way to take them cleanly on a public street, with traffic passing constantly, and one of them was also carrying a walkie-talkie, ready to alert his counterparts upstairs at the first hint of trouble.

"Maybe from the rear?" Bizhani suggested as they rolled past the target. Neither lookout seemed to pay their Clio any more attention than the other passing cars. Watchful, but not particularly worried, even with the news they had to have heard by now about the other lab.

"Maybe," Bolan agreed as he boxed the block, coming around looking for a place to park. He found one distant from the nearest streetlight, pulled into the curb and killed the engine.

"Up that alley, there," Bolan directed. "It should put us out two doors from where we need to be. If that's covered too well, we'll improvise."

He wasn't shy about trouble, didn't mind a fight to get inside the building, but a skirmish in the alley would alert the other men Durrani almost certainly had waiting for intruders on the inside. Bolan was prepared to deal with them, as well, but every second wasted gave the enemy more time to clear the upstairs lab, specifically to move—and maybe hide—the drugs that were his primary concern.

Another option, though he hated to consider it, would be bombardment from a distance. With the Milkor MGL, Bolan could deposit 40 mm rounds four hundred yards downrange from anyplace he stood. Add the M2A1 reflex sight, and he could drop them through an upper-story window from street level if it came to that. The trouble was, he didn't know *which apartment* housed the refinery, and taking out the whole fifth floor with an incendiary storm would needlessly endanger innocents.

They reached the alley's southern end, laden with weapons, and peered around the corner to their left—and saw another pair of sentries standing watch at the apartment building's back door. The fire escape, their next best option, was within plain sight from where the sentries stood, smoking and talking quietly.

Whatever happened next, the lookouts had to go.

"Okay, we'll have to make this quick and quiet," Bolan said, easing his pistol from its shoulder rig. "I'll take them out and we can toss them in that garbage bin over by the fire escape."

"And then?" Bizhani asked.

"In through the back door, find the stairs or elevator. Get to five and find the lab."

"Agreed."

Standing in shadow, Bolan lifted his Beretta, muzzle-heavy with its sound suppressor, and sighted on his targets. Thirty feet was pushing it for pistol work, but he'd made longer shots in worse conditions. Dragging in a breath, he held it, framed a round face in the gun's iron sights, and fired.

"You can feel the misery in here," Captain Aubert remarked, moving from one pathetic bedroom cell to the next.

"The bouncers felt it, too," Sergeant Pradon observed, then pointed. "And this garbage. The customers, no doubt."

Staring at the bullet-riddled corpses on the landing, Aubert felt nothing but a sense of general depression that such places could endure and prosper. Six youths and five young women had been waiting in this house of horrors when the television crew arrived, with the police close behind them. Two more youths had been picked up on the street, identified as fugitives from the Maison de Merveilles. Thus far, none of the captives had been formally identified. That would be work for the detectives, maybe the counselors. Aubert was more concerned with who had pulled the triggers here and left the mess behind.

Heroes? Madmen? Or a rival syndicate intent on punishing Arif Durrani?

"They were scum, I grant you," Aubert said. "But in the law's eyes, these are also victims of a murder. It is our job to discover who has killed them. Celebrate their dying on your on time."

"Yes, sir." Pradon peered down into the brothel's parlor and inquired, "What has become of the lieutenant?"

"She's still looking for Durrani. I've advised her not to trouble us again until she has an address."

"She means well," the sergeant said.

"No doubt. And yet, this house of horrors has thrived under her very nose. How is that possible, I wonder?"

"Well—"

"It was rhetorical, Pradon."

"Of course."

"I want to see the other place," Aubert announced. "What was it? Club Ajaccio?"

"The Corsicans won't tell us anything," Pradon replied. "They never do."

"I don't expect it. The ballistics evidence may tell us if the same men were responsible for all of these attacks. That's something, you'd agree?"

"I would," Pradon conceded.

"And the weapons, if discovered, may identify the killers," Aubert added.

"*If* discovered."

"Now you are a parrot, eh?"

"I'm sorry, Captain."

"Don't be sorry, Pradon. Just get us to the next crime scene."

"And after that?"

"This is supposed to be a war between Durrani and the Wah Ching Triad. Where else should we go but Chinatown?"

DURRANI WASN'T TAKING any chances with the second lab. Another pair of guards covered the third-floor landing of the fire stairs, puffing cigarettes beneath a sign in French that ordered No Smoking, their open jackets bulging out of shape from hardware barely hidden underneath. Bolan was moving quietly, no warning to the bored, distracted watchmen until he suddenly appeared with gun in hand and dropped them both, spraying the cinder blocks behind them with a pair of dripping crimson Rorschach blots.

Bolan picked up the pace, ready for any further opposition waiting on the way, but they were clear until they reached the fifth floor, pausing to listen at a door marked Sortie de Secours—Laisser Déverouillé. As ordered by the sign, the fire door was not locked.

Now all they had to do was to find the drug lab. Durrani made it easy for them, with a soldier planted in a folding chair outside the door, a magazine in one hand and a cup of coffee in the other. He glanced up as grim death emerged from the stairwell, and took a Parabellum shocker in the face, its impact spilling him onto the carpet, coffee steaming as it mingled with his blood.

Stealth had allowed them to proceed this far; now it

was time for blood and thunder. Bolan holstered the Beretta, brought up the grenade launcher as he approached the now unguarded door, and slammed an HE round into the middle of it from a range of twenty feet. The door blew inward, driven on a rolling fireball, and they followed through into the lab.

The front room was a place for personnel to hang out while their potions cooked or cooled in the main lab. It had a television and a DVD player, a sofa and reclining chairs, a kitchenette with fridge and microwave. There were no beds per se, but one guy had been lying on the sofa when the door blew in and landed on him, opening his scalp. Others were frozen where they sat or stood, unless the blast had knocked them to the floor.

Five bolted from a room off to Bolan's left, but only two of them were armed. Bizhani stitched them with a burst of 5.45 mm rounds before they had a chance to reach their weapons, and the others hit the carpet, cringing, maybe hoping they'd be spared if they adopted prayerful attitudes.

Too late.

Still standing near the open doorway, Bolan triggered two more HE rounds in quick succession, firing across the parlor toward the lab behind it, shattering the walls back there, destroying tables lined with glassware, burners, drying racks and shrink-wrapped bricks of China white. The atmosphere would be unbreathable in seconds flat, but Bolan wasn't finished. One final round—this one incendiary—turned the apartment lab into a blazing crematorium.

He left the cringing lab rats to it, moving toward the exit while Bizhani gave the room another hosing with his automatic carbine. Bolan didn't bother looking back to see if he had finished off Durrani's crew or simply added to the damage in the ruined apartment. The fate of those he left behind meant less than nothing to him, either way.

Back in the fifth-floor hallway, Bolan paused to trip a fire alarm that set a Klaxon blaring through the building, rousing anyone who might have dozed through the explosions and the gunfire. As a bonus, it increased confusion, tenants spilling out of doors and rushing toward the stairs or elevator, barely glancing twice at Bolan and Bizhani on their way down to ground level.

The air was fresh and cool outside; no obstacles in front of them on the brisk walk back to their car. As they rolled out of there, Bizhani asked, "What next?"

"Imagine you're Durrani," Bolan said. "Where would you go now?"

"Back to Kabul."

"If you didn't have that option?"

"Then, I think, to find my enemies. In Chinatown."

"So THEY WANT open season, eh?" Arif Durrani raged. "I'll give the Chinese bastards open season!"

"I have told you," Michel Mariani said, "that the men were not Chinese."

"So they sent mercenaries. It was just the same in Paris. What's the difference, if they're afraid to fight the battle by themselves? The Wah Ching bear responsibility, and when I have one of them in my hands, he'll name the triggermen, I promise you."

"I hope you're right," the Corsican replied. "If not…"

"You'll see. We settle this today, once and for all."

Their caravan, five cars in all, moved on a southwest course toward Chinatown, mere blocks to go before they reached the heart of Wah Ching territory in Marseille. Durrani knew the triad forces were depleted, and was counting on an easy victory after the losses he had suffered. All he needed was a sole survivor with enough strength left to answer certain questions and to direct him to the gunmen Tony Cheung had hired to take down Durrani.

"And what about your boss?" Mariani asked.

"Never mind. He'll thank me when it's over."

"While he's sitting down to tea in Hong Kong?"

Silently, Durrani cursed himself for mentioning the phone call from Kabul. He thought Nazari had to have gone insane, agreeing to a meeting on the triad's turf while Ma Lam Chan's trained monkeys were attacking them on every front.

"I think he'll find the trip to China disappointing," Durrani said, adding silently, *If he survives.*

The good news: if Nazari died in Hong Kong, it would leave Durrani in position to advance himself. He could go home to Kabul, claim the cartel's leadership and rule the global empire on his own—or whatever was left of it.

Durrani's war party was thirty men strong, armed with every weapon he and Mariani's Corsicans could gather on short notice.

"This place we're going to first pretends to be a temple," Mariani told him, "but the Wah Chings run it as a cover. They've got gambling in the back and peddle opium for addicts with more traditional taste."

"Security?"

"I hope so," Mariani answered cheerfully. "It's no fun shooting triad gunmen who don't fight back."

"I like it just as well," one of the Corsican's companions muttered, staring out the limo's tinted window as they rolled through Chinatown.

"You never were a sportsman, Petru," Mariani chided.

"Whatever."

"No sense of adventure."

"How much farther is it?" Durrani asked.

"Henry?" Mariani called out to their driver.

"Two more blocks, boss."

Around Durrani, everybody started cocking weapons. He drew back his Czech-made submachine gun's top-mounted bolt to chamber a cartridge, being careful not to let his finger nudge the trigger yet. With its stock folded away to the right side, the little weapon measured less than fifteen inches overall and weighed about five pounds. He'd have to watch the muzzle climbing in full-auto mode, but otherwise it seemed to be a handy killing tool.

"And here we are," Mariani announced as the limo coasted to a stop. "No second thoughts?"

"I want this done," Durrani said.

"Of course," Mariani said, beaming as he stepped out of the car.

Durrani followed closely, making no attempt to hide his submachine gun as they crossed the pavement toward the ornate doorway of what seemed to be a Buddhist temple. At the doorway, soldiers all around them, Mariani told him, "Don't mind if you find some people praying."

"Open season," Durrani replied as they pushed in through the heavy door.

A cloying wave of incense hit his nostrils first and then a tinkling sound of bells assailed Durrani's ears. An old man in a saffron robe approached them, his empty hands raised, an alarmed expression on his face, and Mariani shot him in the chest before he had a chance to speak. The single shot hammered Durrani's ears, then everyone was firing, charging through the entryway, past statues of fat smiling Buddhas, into the main Bodhisattva chamber. Kneeling worshipers, rising too late to save themselves, went down in a raging storm of automatic fire.

The first shots brought a group of armed men running from a room behind the temple's altar, frightened gamblers peering through the open doorway as the guards cleared it. Durrani fired off half a magazine of Parabellum rounds, then scooped a fragmentation grenade out of his jacket pocket, yanked its pin and lobbed the bomb in the general direction of the altar. It exploded in a seated Buddha's lap, cracking the round bronze belly, and the statue toppled backward with a ringing crash, pinning one of the Wah Ching hardmen underneath it.

"Open season!" Durrani crowed. "On you all, and on your god!"

BOLAN FOLLOWED THE SOUND of wailing sirens into Chinatown, slowing a little as he overtook a cruiser with its blue and white lights flashing, weaving in and out of traffic.

"I'm taking a shortcut," he told Bizhani, and the agent grunted in reply, seating a fresh magazine in his carbine's receiver.

They were two blocks from the Wah Ching gambling club and headquarters that masqueraded as a house of worship. Bolan wondered if that set some kind of record for hypocrisy, and then dismissed the thought, preoccupied with tactics as he motored toward the battleground.

"We'll go in through the back," he told Bizhani. "Watch out for police."

"I *always* watch out for police," Bizhani said.

"I mean, don't shoot them."

"Oh, that. Very well."

They skidded to a halt a moment later, near the back of a building with a red pagoda roof and bright blue walls. As Bolan leaped from the Renault, a twenty-something Chinese man came out the back door of the temple with a pistol in one hand and a roulette wheel tucked under his other arm. Before he had a chance to fire, Bolan squeezed

off a double tap from his assault rifle and dropped the fleeing triad member where he stood.

They rushed the joint's back door, the sirens sound-
ing closer now, and reached it just as an explosion rocked
the building from within. It sounded like an antipersonnel grenade to Bolan, smaller than the standard IED but
just as deadly at close quarters. At the threshold, he could
smell the chemical tang of explosives, distinct and separate
from burned gunpowder, as he ducked inside a small but
well-stocked gambling den, complete with slot machines,
a craps table and a chuck-a-luck cage. The Wah Ching
Triad members who were fighting to defend it didn't notice Bolan and Bizhani coming in behind them, caught up
as they were in dueling with a strike force that had come
in from the street.

There was no chivalry in mortal combat. Bolan and Bizhani shot the triad gunners from behind without a second
thought, taking advantage of their terminal distraction.
Most of them were young men, one or two approaching
middle age, and none of them invincible. They dropped
where bullets found them, some stone-dead before they hit
the floor, while others thrashed and squealed their lives
away. A couple of them turned in time to squeeze off shots,
but they were wasted, pocking walls and ceiling as the men
behind the guns went down.

Bolan moved past the dead and dying toward the other
exit from the gaming room into the temple. Firing had
slacked off there for the moment, and he risked a glance
around the open doorframe, picking out Arif Durrani's
face among a group of swarthy gunmen edging closer,
poised to spray the altar and whatever lay beyond it with
another gale of automatic fire. He switched the Steyr for
his Milkor MGL and leaned into the doorway once again,

not aiming, simply firing the six rounds from its cylinder in rapid succession.

The temple's sanctuary went to hell with smoky thunder, razor-edged shrapnel from the grenade launcher's HE rounds slicing through flesh, plaster and furniture. A wooden rack of bells collapsed, adding its clamor to the din, a counterpoint to cries of sudden pain. As Bolan switched back to his AUG, peering through acrid smoke into the slaughterhouse, he heard fresh voices shouting from the entryway.

"Police! Drop your weapons!"

Bolan wasn't about to comply, but he didn't plan to duel with the cops, either. He doubled out the back, passing Bizhani on the way, prepared to take down the MISIRI agent if he seemed about to fire on the police. Instead, Bizhani followed him, a mad sprint down the alley to their waiting rental car, leaving the police to pick over bodies, sort the living from the dead and try to make sense out of bloody chaos. There was still no sign of uniforms behind them as they scrambled into the Renault and Bolan took them out of there.

"What now?" Bizhani asked when he'd had time to catch his breath.

"Durrani's either dead or busted," Bolan told him, "and he took the local Wah Chings with him. That's a wrap for France, as far as I'm concerned."

"And for Khalil Nazari?"

"That's another story."

"If you have some means to reach him…"

"Shouldn't you be heading home?" Bolan asked.

"I regret leaving a job unfinished," Bizhani said.

"Let me make some calls," the Executioner replied. "No promises. As far as travel documents—"

"I'm well supplied," Bizhani said, "for most emergencies."

Bolan considered how Grimaldi might react and almost smiled.

Almost.

Already airport bound, he told his passenger, "I'll see what I can do."

CHAPTER FIFTEEN

Justice Building, Washington, D.C.

The sat-phone hummed at Hal Brognola's elbow and he scooped it up before it had a chance to sound again. The call was right on time, no need to check the LED display and get the callback number.

"Any luck?" the deep, familiar voice inquired as soon as the big Fed was on the line.

"We caught a break," Brognola said, trusting in the scrambled link's security. If NSA or anybody snatched something from the air it would be gibberish, beyond their power to translate—unlike the foreign calls that Stony Man had monitored on his behalf. "Nazari's on his way to Hong Kong, airborne as we speak. He should be somewhere over India right now."

"To meet with Chan?"

"Chan called to set it up," Brognola said. "Whether he really wants to talk, or put Nazari on the spot and take him out, I couldn't say."

"It makes no difference to me," Bolan said. "By the time I'm done, it all comes out the same."

"You're going, then?"

"Best chance we'll have to wrap this up, right?"

"Absolutely," Brognola agreed. "You're traveling on U.S. papers, so you've got a ninety-day visa-free window for visiting Hong Kong, as long as you have enough money to cover your stay without working and don't try to pick up a job while you're there."

"That shouldn't be a problem," Bolan said. "What's the word on visitors from other countries?"

Brognola suppressed a sigh. "Someone thinking he should tag along?" he asked.

"It's possible."

"You mind me asking what the point would be in that?"

"To finish what we started," Bolan answered.

"What *you* started in New York, without him."

"Things change."

"And seldom for the better."

"Hal. The paper situation?"

"Right. Hang on." Brognola tapped keys on his laptop, bringing up the web page for Hong Kong's Department of Immigration. "Iran needs a visa," he said, "along with Iraq, most of the Middle Eastern countries, the old Eastern Bloc and a good chunk of Africa. You want me to go down the list?"

"Try Saudi Arabia," Bolan suggested.

Brognola checked it and scowled. "Thirty days, visa-free. Same requirement for funds and restrictions on working in Hong Kong."

"That ought to cover it," Bolan said.

"Okay. I'll say again—"

"No need. I'm handling it."

Brognola knew that there was no point trying to pull rank. Back in the bad old days when he'd been tracking Bolan for the FBI—first time he'd ever felt respect for someone he was hunting, working up to *helping* Bolan when it could have cost his life or his career—he'd recognized that the Executioner was a force of nature. Not entirely irresistible, in the way of a tsunami or a hurricane, although he had a similar effect on those he was determined to eradicate. Of course, he could be stopped like any other mortal man, but no one he had faced so far had been equal to the task.

You didn't *order* Bolan to do anything. That was the bedrock basis for him joining Stony Man originally. He was free to pick and choose assignments, to reject one if it didn't suit him and once he was on a job, unless he needed some kind of material assistance in a dire emergency, you simply wound him up and watched him go to work.

It was unorthodox as hell, but so far it was working.

So far.

Roping in a damned MISIRI agent from Iran was something else entirely. Brognola had been uneasy when they'd forged a short-term, one-time-only working deal in France. But now that they were going international…

The big Fed frowned and took a leap. "You know we're absolutely not recruiting for the team, right?"

"Never crossed my mind," Bolan replied. He didn't sound offended by the question.

"Right. Okay, then. If you need a hook-up when you land, for any gear…"

"Appreciate it."

"I'll look into that and get back to you ASAP. Starting out from where you are, you've got about six thousand miles to cover. One refueling stop and something like twelve hours in the air."

"We'd best get started then," Bolan replied.

"I'll leave you to it, and I'll be in touch," Brognola said. "Take care."

"I always do," Bolan replied. And that was almost funny, when you thought about it.

But Brognola didn't feel like laughing.

Not even a little bit.

Marseille, France

"How many dead?" Captain Aubert inquired.

"Twenty-seven, so far," Lieutenant Isabel Caron replied. "Another six are badly injured. Whether they'll survive or not, who knows?"

"And who cares?" Sergeant Pradon offered from the sidelines. "That is, if we're speaking only of the criminals?"

"It blots my record," Caron told him, not quite pouting.

"Worse than the exposure of the brothel?"

She glowered at Pradon but did not answer him. Instead she told Aubert, "We have at least two gunmen still at large. A witness saw them shoot one of the Chinese in the alley there, behind the temple."

"Temple!" Pradon snorted.

"Then—" she forged ahead, ignoring him "—they went inside and there was more shooting, as well as explosions. Finally they came back out and ran away."

"You have this witness still available?" Aubert inquired.

"She's under guard," Caron replied, and nodded to her left. "That cruiser, parked outside the pharmacy."

"I don't suppose she saw the vehicle that carried them away?"

"No, Captain. Quite sensibly, she did not follow them beyond that point."

"Ah, sensibility. Just when we need a spirit of adventure, eh?"

"We do have fair descriptions of both subjects. Not the best, I grant you, but—"

"By all means, broadcast them. And if you have a sketch artist available, try to obtain a decent likeness of them," Aubert answered.

He had a rotten, sneaking feeling that the men he'd

tracked from Paris to Marseille were gone already, or would soon be far beyond his reach. Descriptions, sketches, some of that might help with Europol or Interpol, but by the time he had the sketches in his hand—assuming that he *ever* got them—any subject capable of booking airline reservations could be anywhere on earth and burrowed deep, beyond the prying eyes of man hunters. Besides, the international police agencies were simply data-collecting intelligence bodies. Hollywood pap notwithstanding, they had no executive powers in any country. They had no agents in the field.

Aubert was stymied now, although he hated to admit it. If the men he sought were not apprehended somehow before leaving France, the odds against him ever seeing them in court were astronomical. He could apply for European Arrest Warrants, but only if he knew the subjects' names. Even then, it only helped if they were found in one of the European Union's member states, and Aubert knew that the chances of that happening were very small indeed.

The Arab-looking one, particularly, could be on his way to Pakistan, Afghanistan or God knew where by now, lost in the crowd, shedding whatever false identity he'd used for traveling, sprouting a beard and disappearing back into his daily life. The taller one, simply described as "white" by Chinese witnesses in Paris, may have been American, Canadian or British. Aubert had already begun the process of accepting that both killers might escape.

And he was vaguely troubled that the notion did not bother him so much.

What had they done, in fact? Killed criminals, of course, and damaged property belonging to those criminals. There was a rumor that they'd stolen an unspecified amount of cash in Paris—once again, from felons who would never have reported it or paid their proper taxes to the government. Conversely, they had rescued several youngsters and young women from a hellhole in Marseille, where most or all of them likely would have been slaughtered in due time, after a few more months of unimaginable misery.

Pradon was right about the murdered criminals, although it was not politic to say so. Aubert would not miss them, nor would any other member of a safe and sane society. If several dozen monsters were eradicated through the use of extralegal force, how ardently should he pursue the two exterminators?

"Come, Pradon," he said at last. "I need a drink."

"Yes, sir."

They had retreated several yards in the direction of their borrowed cruiser when Aubert stopped, turned and said, "Lieutenant? Will you join us?"

Caron glanced once more at the fire-gutted temple, shrugged and said, "Why not?"

Over the Hindu Kush, 42,000 feet elevation

KHALIL NAZARI HAD CHOSEN the Hawker 4000 jet for no special reason. It seated seven passengers besides himself, two pilots on the flight deck, traveling eastward at 540 miles per hour over the so-called "roof of the world." Below him, while Nazari lounged in luxury, the mountain range known to locals as Pariyatra Parvata reached toward the sky, but the jet soared well above it, still some seventeen thousand feet beyond the reach of its tallest peak, Tirich Mir.

It amused Nazari to imagine climbers roped together, plastered to the frigid, weather-blasted cliffs down there. Perhaps a yeti would be watching as his plane passed overhead and wondering what kind of giant bird it was. Or maybe not.

His guards were armed, of course, as per Nazari's deal

with Ma Lam Chan, but he had two more guards in the air before he'd left Kabul, one flying into Hong Kong from Bangkok, the other from Manila. They would land ahead of him, and unlike Nazari's party, neither one required visas to enter Hong Kong on their Thai or Filipino passports, respectively.

Not that visas were a problem for a man of Nazari's wealth and connections in Kabul. Authorities in Hong Kong were concerned with screening terrorists, not blocking megamillionaires from visiting their city to invest substantial sums of cash. A good friend of Nazari's in Afghanistan's Ministry of Foreign Affairs had visited the Chinese embassy in Kabul personally, to facilitate the paperwork without tiresome delays. Nazari had provided funds for the transaction and was not concerned with how those funds were finally apportioned.

He'd obtained exactly what he needed, which was all that ever mattered.

Killers were a dime a dozen in the world, as he had learned from living in Afghanistan and dealing with the scum of other nations as a drug lord. But assassins of the highest class were rare indeed, and those Nazari had dispatched to Hong Kong were the best in Asia. For the price he'd paid them, they had better be. The bonus waiting for whichever of them did the deed was a small fortune.

Of course, the thought had not escaped Nazari's mind that Ma Lam Chan might have a similar surprise in store for him. To stay alive in Hong Kong while his two advance men marked their target and proceeded to eliminate him, he had brought his finest soldiers as an honor guard of sorts. Four of them were Pashtuns who had fought the Soviet invaders, then moved on to private enterprise. The other three were former U.S. Navy SEALs, veterans of their country's two Iraqi wars, now mercenaries he had lured from employment with a private army run be a religious zealot in the States. All were hardened killers, perfectly remorseless, although lacking in the artistry of the two specialists Nazari had selected as his point men.

Those were *truly* special.

Yong Cao Tio was a Malaysian Chinese who resided in Bangkok. He'd been affiliated with the Sun Yee On Triad, until his masters found that they could not control him. Next, they'd tried to kill him, but the war that followed proved too costly for them, so they finally declared a truce. These days Yong took the jobs that pleased him, executing them with flair and surgical precision, living in a princely style on the proceeds from one or two assignments during any given year. Rumors suggested that he also killed for pleasure, or to keep himself in practice, which concerned Khalil Nazari not at all.

Mori Saburo was a Japanese no longer welcome in his homeland, since a teenage incident involving swords, a wealthy pedophile and four policemen who had tried to bring him in alive. In exile, Saburo had done piecework for the Yamaguchi-gumi faction of the Yakuza, expending over time to build a list of clients ranging from the Russian Federal Security Service to the American CIA. He specialized in deaths made to appear as accidents, but would accommodate a client to the full extent of his ability, assuming that the price was right.

Between the two of them, Khalil Nazari thought with perfect confidence, Ma Lam Chan was as good as dead.

Marseille Provence Airport

THE DASSAULT FALCON 50EX jet had a range of 4,025 miles, leaving them 2,027 miles short of Hong Kong on a flight from Marseille. Jack Grimaldi planned to refuel at New

Delhi, then fly on from there to land at Hong Kong International Airport. Call it eleven hours in the air, plus whatever time they had to spend on the ground at Indira Gandhi International.

His one regret was that he couldn't drop Heydar Bizhani off along the way.

Like, maybe, when they passed over the Persian Gulf. Let him swim home.

Why not?

It wasn't that Grimaldi minded Bolan working with another partner. Honestly. The big guy had teamed up with other helpers in the past, and the Stony Man pilot had never felt that he was being slighted. He was Bolan's transport and provided airborne backup as required, but didn't count on fighting in the trenches. That was seriously not a problem.

What he hated was allowing someone from the other side *inside*.

Okay. He realized that the MISIRI agent wasn't being briefed on Stony Man or anything related to it, but his homeland had been hostile to the U.S.A. for close to forty years now, and the situation looked as though it was getting worse, not thawing. Coincidence had put Bizhani on the track of Bolan's latest target, but that didn't make them friends—at least, not in Grimaldi's eyes. Bolan assured him that Bizhani had been carrying his weight so far, but what did that prove?

If a snake killed rats around your house, did that mean you should put it in your pocket?

Waiting for his clearance to take off, Grimaldi thought about the task ahead. Hong Kong was worlds away from France, and not just with regard to its geography. It might be deemed autonomous, but that did not prevent the Chinese Ministry of State Security from operating on the island, keeping track of foreigners and intervening as required in matters deemed essential to the national security. When a person thought about it, that could be anything Beijing decided might be adverse to their country's government or public image.

Such as a pair of foreigners attacking wealthy, well-connected triad leaders, for example. Or precipitating war between those home-grown gangsters and an Afghan drug cartel on Chinese soil. Grimaldi wasn't any kind of expert on the Far East, but he'd done his homework for this mission. There were forty thousand cops in Hong Kong, giving it the world's second highest ratio of officers to civilians, after London. Its Marine Region, with three thousand officers and 143 vessels, *was* the largest on earth. The department's Special Duty Unit, nicknamed "Flying Tigers," was a paramilitary outfit trained to deal with terrorists, hostage-takers and the like, including its own marine wing known as "Water Ghosts," whose members trained with U.S. Navy SEALs.

And if that wasn't bad enough, they would be up against the Wah Ching Triad on its home turf. The gang had only nineteen thousand members sprinkled through a city population that exceeded seven million, but each one of its members was dedicated to the Family, oath-bound to sacrifice himself in its defense. Add in the fact that each and every Wah Ching member was a hard-core felon—killers, rapists, narco-traffickers, gunrunners and professional extortionists—and what you had was an explosive recipe for mayhem in the streets.

Long odds? Hell, yeah.

And none of it worried Grimaldi half as much as Bolan's helper from Tehran.

Heydar Bizhani might not be a terrorist himself. Maybe he'd never pulled the trigger on a dissident who only wanted freedom in a country where religion merged with politics to craft a special brand of tyranny. Maybe he'd never personally sent a young man off with Semtex strapped around his torso, spiked with rusty nails that had been marinating overnight in feces, to annihilate a market filled with unarmed "infidels."

So what?

The people he worked for did all that, and worse, as matters of routine. Bizhani stuck with them, either because he shared their goals or simply didn't want to rock the boat. Grimaldi couldn't say which attitude disturbed him more, and thankfully, he didn't have to choose. The first move that Bizhani made to jeopardize their mission or to betray Mack Bolan, he was going down.

And he was never getting up again.

Victoria Peak, Hong Kong

"ALL IS IN READINESS?" Ma Lam Chan asked.

"As you instructed," Henry Kwok replied.

In fact, Chan had no doubt that his orders would be carried out to the letter. Kwok was the most efficient Vanguard of the Wah Ching Triad within living memory—and certainly the most ambitious. One to watch, on all accounts.

"Safe conduct for Nazari's party from the airport to their lodging. Nothing must befall them in the public eye."

"Of course, sir."

Chan had booked Khalil Nazari's party into suites at the Conrad Hong Kong, one of the world's top business hotels, for a taste of five-star luxury during their last days on earth. It was a small price to pay for long-term peace of mind—and for the profits he would earn by cutting back Nazari's operation, even for a little while.

Not that the world would drop into his hands with the elimination of a single Afghan warlord, but no other competition on the same scale presently confronted Chan. He had a flexible but satisfactory relationship with leaders of the Yakuza, a wary truce with the Sicilian Mafia and reckoned that he could negotiate a contract with the Unione Corse once Nazari was out of the picture for good. Afghanistan was still a problem, constantly producing opium and morphine with American protection, but the word from Washington suggested that the troubled country would soon be left to its own devices. If the Taliban regained control, as Chan devoutly hoped, production would be cut back to the rates from 1999, leaving the Golden Triangle once more the world's primary source of opiates. From there, Chan's leading rivals would be the Colombians and Mexicans, whose product—aptly labeled "mud"—was recognized as distinctly inferior.

"There was no difficulty with the Kudo-kai?" Chan asked.

"None, sir. They're pleased to help…in exchange for a thirty percent reduction in price on their next two shipments."

Chan smiled, watching the lights from Hong Kong Harbour. "You agreed, of course."

"As ordered, sir."

"And have they reached the city?"

"Landing as we speak," Kwok said.

The Kudo-kai ranked among Japan's smaller Yakuza clans, with fewer than seven hundred sworn members. But they maintained an elite private army, trained in both traditional ninja techniques and more modern methods of the Tokushu Sakusen Gun, an elite counter-terrorist wing of the Japan Ground Self-Defense Force. For the price Kwok had negotiated, they would deal with Nazari's entourage at a time and place of Chan's choosing, leaving clues enough to lead police away from the Wah Ching Triad without incriminating themselves. It was, in Chan's view, the ideal solution to a knotty problem.

It was all a matter of perception; smoke and mirrors for authorities in Hong Kong who could blame outsiders for whatever happened to the Afghan visitors. Chan knew the ruse would not play well in Kabul, with Nazari's underlings, but they would have a power vacuum to contend with before contemplating vengeance. If his luck held, the cartel he was decapitating might be swept away entirely by competitors—who would, in turn, care nothing for the means by which Khalil Nazari was removed. If anything, they might be grateful for Chan's help, or at the very least, inclined to let him live in peace.

And failing that…well, he could always teach another lesson to the desert dwellers. Once you pinned them down and ground their necks under your heel, they really weren't that special after all.

Indira Gandhi International Airport, New Delhi, India

THE DASSAULT FALCON 50EX jet touched down lightly and began its taxi toward the refueling station behind Terminal 1C. Bolan unfastened his seat belt and moved toward the cockpit, leaning in the doorway while Grimaldi steered the jet across a plain of asphalt.

"Have we got an estimate for turnaround time?" he inquired.

"About an hour, if we're lucky," the Stony Man pilot replied.

New Delhi's airport handled some thirty-four million passengers yearly, with perpetual construction expanding the layout to roughly triple that figure by 2030. One terminal was closed for renovation, and another had been marked for demolition once its shiny new replacement was completed. In the meantime, some fliers were routed through the Hajj Terminal, normally reserved for pilgrims on their way to Mecca for the holy pilgrimage their faith demanded of every Muslim who could manage it.

Since they were only passing through New Delhi, neither dropping any cargo off nor leaving any passengers behind when they departed, they were spared a trip through customs at the terminal for international arrivals and departures. Midway through refueling, a bored-looking immigration agent came around to check their passports and confirm their flight plan leaving India without another stop en route to Hong Kong. Satisfied, he wandered off to run some other errand, leaving them in peace.

"No sweat," Grimaldi said when they were clear.

Bolan glanced at his watch, ticked off the time zones in his head. "Nazari should be…what? A couple hours out from landing?"

"More or less. With the jet that Hal described, he wouldn't have to stop for fuel between Kabul and Hong Kong."

Bolan didn't like falling behind, but there was nothing he could do about the laws of physics. Jets, regardless of their speed, took time to fly between points A and B. Khalil Nazari had the jump on them by starting out some 3,200 miles closer to their common destination. Even with Grimaldi on the flight deck and three engines pushing the Falcon, they still couldn't compress the space-time continuum.

Real life was a drag that way, sometimes.

As if reading his mind Grimaldi said, "You know they'll need some time to settle in and feel each other out. That is, unless they jump right into killing each other."

"Save us the trouble," Bolan said, half smiling.

"Stranger things have happened. And speaking of strange, what becomes of our third wheel when this gets wrapped up?"

"He goes home, I suppose," Bolan said.

"Telling tales about the nice Americans he met while he was fighting evil."

"You think I've told him something that I shouldn't?"

"No, man. Definitely not."

"We're all right, then," Bolan replied. "Unless the two of you have gotten cozy when I wasn't looking."

"Right. As if."

"So he goes home, and say he tells them what he knows. What's that amount to? Our descriptions?"

"And the plane," Grimaldi said.

"A drug seizure. Hal's bound to change the registration number after this, regardless."

"It's not that simple. If he's got a cell phone," Grimaldi replied, "he's got a camera. For all you know, he sent your mug shot to Tehran five minutes after meeting you."

"We'll deal with it."

"That means dealing with *him*."

"And we've been over that. I'll handle it, if necessary."

"Fair enough. But don't let Sergeant Mercy talk you out of it."

That had been Bolan's *other* nickname, in the same war where he'd earned his label as the Executioner. He'd been that kind of soldier, willing when the opportunity arose to aid a wounded enemy or shepherd terrified civilians from a scorched-earth battleground to safety. Some regarded that side of his character as paradoxical. For Bolan, it was just a part of being human.

Grimaldi checked the fuel pump's gauge and said,

"Okay, we're good to go. Another twenty minutes, give or take, we should be in the air."

But still running behind.

Bolan called on his training to relax him, sticking to the limits of the possible. They'd be in Hong Kong when they got there, not a second sooner, and he wouldn't gain a thing from worrying about it in the meantime.

If his enemies killed off one another while he was in the air, so be it. He would turn around as soon as it was verified, and head for home. But if they were negotiating terms, a means of carving up the world between their two cartels, then Bolan had some time.

And they were in for a surprise.

CHAPTER SIXTEEN

Hong Kong International Airport

A stretch limousine awaited Khalil Nazari's arrival at the airport. An associate of Ma Lam Chan's was standing by, together with a customs officer, to ease Nazari's passage through the busy, large passenger terminal. With passports stamped and luggage cleared, Nazari's party moved from air-conditioned comfort in the terminal, across a narrow stretch of humid sidewalk, to the limo's purring luxury for transport to the city and their waiting hotel suites.

Nazari's guide was Henry Kwok, apparently the Wah Ching Triad's second in command. It would have been unusual for Chan himself to greet arrivals at the airport, and Nazari took no umbrage at being met by a subordinate. He would have done the same thing in Chan's place, establishing his status with a gesture indicating that he had other, and equally important, things to do.

As they proceeded into Hong Kong, Henry Kwok droned on about their posh accommodations, dinner plans with Ma Lam Chan and the following day's meeting where they would begin substantive talks. He dropped no hints concerning Chan's agenda: how the triad leader thought they should divide prospective territories or prevent conflicts in any future partnership.

It hardly mattered anyway, since Chan would soon be dead.

Nazari had received no calls from Yong Cao Tio or Mori Saburo since they'd accepted their assignment, nor did he expect to hear from them again, except in case of an emergency. They were professionals and independents in the truest sense—had nearly balked at a collaborative effort as it was, until they'd heard his price—and Nazari knew he would be contacted when the job was done. He had already transferred half of each assassin's payment in advance to their selected banks, and would be pleased to pay the rest when they delivered on the contract.

It was only money, after all, and the demand for heroin worldwide ensured that Khalil Nazari would never be short of cash.

In due time they arrived outside the Conrad Hong Kong, which towered sixty-one floors above the street. It amused Nazari that he would be sleeping that night within sight of Hong Kong's High Court and the Queensway Government Offices building, barely two hundred yards southwest of the Wan Chai police headquarters. The confluence of politics and crime reminded him that things were not so different in the Far East, after all.

But by the following day, or the one after, there would be a change. When Ma Lam Chan had been eliminated, seemingly by members of the Yakuza, the balance of power would shift, both in Hong Kong and throughout the world of narco-trafficking. Next stop, eradication of the threat from South America.

The Conrad Hong Kong was part of Pacific Place, a complex including two other five-star hotels, three Grade-A office towers, 270 five-star serviced apartments and a four-story shopping arcade. As with everything in Hong Kong, it made Kabul seem, to Nazari, both far away and rather primitive, but skyscrapers and neon were not everything.

Power was more than money, more than real estate. It was a quality that some men cultivated, while inferiors sat back and let it slip between their fingers. Ma Lam Chan might be a big man on his little island, but he was about to find himself outclassed and earmarked for extinction.

He was an endangered species in his own domain.

Justice Place, Hong Kong

MORI SABURO STOOD across the street from Pacific Place and watched the stretch limousine disgorge its passengers outside the Conrad Hong Kong hotel. A concierge greeted the new arrivals, directing uniformed porters as they collected the party's luggage and wheeled it into the lobby. Saburo recognized Khalil Nazari, counted seven members of his entourage and raised his cell phone, speed-dialing a programmed number.

"Yes." The voice that greeted him was flat, unquestioning.

"He's here."

"Affirmative," the bland voice said, then it was gone.

Nazari was their sponsor, not their target, but Saburo wanted to confirm his presence in the city. Meanwhile, Yong Cao Tio had eyes on Chan and was considering the best way to attack him. They had worked together once before and understood each other well enough, although there was a certain rivalry between them under normal circumstances.

This was not a normal job, much less a normal payday if they pulled it off.

In fact, Saburo never took a casual approach to homicide. His first killings, at age fifteen, had been a matter of necessity, protection of his younger brother from the lecherous attention of a so-called holy man. Saburo still recalled with pride the pedophile's expression after he was skewered with Saburo's great-grandfather's *kai gunto* sword, a relic from the war against America. The officers who'd turned up to arrest him had been equally amazed: two of them died, and one, Saburo understood, now wore a steel claw in place of his right hand.

How many more had died over the years since that adventure? If he'd felt like keeping score, Saburo could have worked it out. He had been blessed with an eidetic memory, forgot nothing and could recall specific moments from his past in perfect detail when it pleased him to. He had become an artist at his chosen trade, not only with the sword and *tanto,* but with firearms and explosives, poisons—any tool at all, in fact, that came to hand. Saburo also held black belts in Shotokan karate, kendo and ninjutsu, if he ever happened to be caught unarmed.

A rare occurrence, granted, but there were occasions when it simply was not feasible to carry weapons.

In Hong Kong, of course, that was no problem.

Firearms and ammunition were strictly controlled in Hong Kong, by statute, with lawful ownership restricted to holders of a license furnished by the Department of Justice. That license, in turn, was issued only to persons who displayed an understanding of firearms safety, tested in a theoretical and practical training course. At least, so said the island's Firearms and Ammunition Ordinance, enacted in 1999. In practice, though, legal restrictions only caused black-market trade to flourish, whether it applied to chemicals, commercial sex or guns.

At present Saburo was armed with a Norinco QSZ-92 semiautomatic pistol, chambered for Chinese 5.8 mm DAP92 armor-piercing rounds. He also carried a Fairbairn-Sykes fighting knife, its double-edged blade honed to razor sharpness, and a steel telescoping baton that could gouge eyes or fracture bones with equal ease. As for more specialized equipment, he would wait to see what the particular occasion might demand.

It was true that their styles conflicted to some extent, with Yong more likely to make a ritualized display of his handiwork, while Saburo placed a premium on minimizing risk and effort. Why dissect a target when an IED or long-range bullet to the head would do the job as well, without needlessly complicating his escape? There'd been no time, so far, to talk in depth about their plans for Ma Lam Chan, but taking out the Dragon Head of the Wah Ching Triad meant going up against his soldiers in the city they called home.

Still not impossible, but much more difficult. And costly for Khalil Nazari.

He was paying the equivalent of one million U.S. dollars per man. It was a record payday for Saburo, and perhaps the most dangerous job he had accepted—although he had risked his life on each and every one of them.

And dead, of course, was dead.

High risk required more preparation, more finesse. With or without Yong's help, Saburo had full confidence in his ability and ultimate success.

One Dragon Head served on a silver platter, coming up.

South China Sea, 42,000 feet altitude

"WE'RE JUST ABOUT an hour out," Grimaldi announced over the jet's intercom.

Bolan glanced down at the expanse of blue-green ocean, unable to tell if tiny flecks of white were fishing boats or cresting waves. There were islands, as well, sprinkled randomly between the Philippines and the coast of Vietnam, but none approaching the size of Hong Kong.

"It's almost finished, eh?" Heydar Bizhani asked him from across the aisle. "You must be pleased."

"I'm not ready to celebrate just yet," Bolan replied. "The hard work's still ahead."

"But you have plans."

"Same plan, but on a larger scale."

It had to be, when they were playing out the final act at Wah Ching Central, where the syndicate's forces were concentrated and collaborated with at least some of the forty thousand law-enforcement officers assigned to keep the peace in Hong Kong. How the cops would play it when the shooting started still remained unknown. They obviously had to make a show of cracking down on violence, but whether they would do it by the book or take their marching orders straight from Ma Lam Chan was anybody's guess.

At least Bolan was confident that he would be well armed. Hal Brognola had furnished the name and address of a dealer on Sing Woo Road in Happy Valley who stocked ample supplies of arms and munitions at flexible prices. No menu was available for his perusal in advance, but he could work with any reasonably modern hardware, and there should be no shortage in Hong Kong.

China had been manufacturing knock-offs of various American, Russian and Eastern European small arms since Mao Zedong's revolutionaries captured control of the country in 1949. Prime examples included their Type 59 service pistol, a Russian Makarov with minor cosmetic changes, the Norinco HP9-1 shotgun, an unlicensed copy of the Remington Model 870, the Type 56 assault rifle, China's copy of the world-famous AK-47, and the Type 80 machine gun, mimicking Russia's PK model. Truly indigenous small arms included the QBZ-95 assault rifle and

QCW-05 submachine gun, both modern bullpup designs issued to Chinese soldiers and police.

Bizhani's voice cut into Bolan's planning for the fight ahead. "I think your comrade still suspects me of some foul intentions, eh?"

"Our countries have a history," Bolan said, "but he's handling it. He's a professional."

"As all of us must be. Professionals."

"Your people can't be loving it," Bolan suggested.

"They have reservations," Bizhani admitted, "but I have not been recalled. As to the welcome I receive at home when we are finished…well, who knows?"

"It's all about results, right?"

"In America, perhaps. We, on the other hand, must get results while following the will of Allah as revealed by Ali Khamenei."

"He's your ayatollah?"

"The *Grand* Ayatollah," Bizhani corrected him.

"The one and only?"

"No. In fact, there are approximately seventy grand ayatollahs living in the world today. Six in Najaf, Iraq, alone."

"Must get confusing," Bolan said.

"It might," Bizhani granted. "But Ali Khamenei has also served as our Supreme Leader since 1989, when he resigned the presidency."

"Moving up."

"Indeed. If he or one of his subordinates decides that I have breached Sharia in some way by joining forces with an infidel, regardless of the cause…"

Bizhani left it hanging there, his frown the final punctuation.

Under other circumstances, that might be the point where Bolan offered an alternate solution to Bizhani's problem, but that door was closed. There'd be no welcome for him from the team at Stony Man. Maybe an outside chance the CIA would take him as a walk-in, if he gave them everything he knew about the inside workings of MISIRI, but that seemed about as likely as Bizhani suddenly deciding to renounce his faith in Islam.

So no bargain, then. They'd land in Hong Kong, do their best and see what happened next. No quarter asked or offered in the end.

Another day in Bolan's world.

Victoria Peak, Hong Kong

"AND ARE THEY pleased with the accommodations?" Ma Lam Chan inquired.

"I believe so," Henry Kwok replied. "Nazari has the presidential suite, as we arranged."

"And women?"

"They brought none and made no inquiries," Kwok said. "I tried to hint, but it is difficult with Muslims."

"Truly," Chan conceded. "Possibly I'll find some way to broach the subject over dinner."

He cared nothing for Khalil Nazari's sex life per se, but Chan knew that he had to appear to be the perfect host at every turn throughout the Afghan's visit. Up until the moment when it ended for his adversary with the last surprise he'd ever face.

"Speaking of dinner," Kwok said, "the arrangements are in place, sir."

"Fook Lam Moon?"

"As you requested."

The restaurant's name translated to English as "fortune and blessings come to your home." Chan hoped that supplication would be granted when Khalil Nazari had his last great meal there, and relaxed in preparation for their conference the next day. It would help him if his enemies were lulled into a sense of calm and confidence, anticipating a negotiation that would benefit their interests. Let them relax before the ax fell and it would be easier for all concerned.

Chan, for his part, would not relax his guard. He knew Nazari's reputation and expected treachery. To that end, he had placed two dozen of his own men at the Conrad Hong Kong—some installed as paying guests, others disguised as porters—to maintain surveillance on the Afghan party and be ready at a moment's notice if it seemed they were about to strike at him.

As for the other aspect of betrayal...

"What about the airports?" he asked Kwok.

"We're monitoring all incoming flights, sir, with assistance from the Security Bureau. Kalitla Air and Air Atlanta Icelandic handle all commercial flights from Kabul. Pakistan International Airlines also rates close surveillance."

"And if friend Nazari uses more imagination? What then, Henry?"

"All incoming passengers are screened routinely, sir. Airport security checks documents and uses facial recognition software."

"You presume they are infallible?"

Kwok blinked at that and answered, "No, sir."

"Then it is possible Nazari might employ technicians from another country, traveling on other airlines. Yes?"

"Yes, sir."

"Who might, if called from some location closer to our shores, arrive ahead of him?"

Kwok's eyes had narrowed. "It's possible. Yes, sir."

"And would it not be advantageous to inquire among our friends who use the services of such technicians, to discover whether any they may know are visiting our city at the present time?"

"I will begin at once, sir. If I may say—"

Chan raised a manicured hand to silence him. "Waste no time on apologies," he said. "Start with our contact in the 14K clan. If he knows nothing of this matter, try Chen Siu-Kei with the Ang Soon Tong. Failing there, reach out to our associates within the Yakuza."

"Yes, sir. If there is nothing else...?"

"Only success," Chan said.

"And if there's nothing to be learned?"

"Then I am confident you will learn nothing. Put my mind at ease, Henry."

"Yes, sir."

Chan knew there was an outside chance, however tiny, that Khalil Nazari meant to meet with him in good faith, to resolve their conflict peacefully. There was a possibility, as well, that Chan might be struck by a meteor en route to meet Nazari at the restaurant that night, but only a demented idiot would bet on it.

A wise man dealt with all potential dangers, emphasizing those that seemed most likely to occur, ignoring those that dwelled within the realm of fantasy. And if Nazari had neglected to prepare a secret plan for killing Chan... so what?

It only made the Afghan that much simpler to eliminate.

Chan was determined. Hong Kong would be Khalil Nazari's final resting place—or, possibly, the depths of the South China Sea. He'd leave the details to his well-paid experts, satisfied they would give him the desired result.

He had a world to win, and much to lose if they should fail him.

Ma Lam Chan had always loved the high-stakes games.

Hong Kong International Airport

HEYDAR BIZHANI WAS concerned about his Saudi passport, even knowing that it was the best Tehran could furnish with official blanks from Riyadh. As it happened, though, the Chinese Immigration agent only spent a moment thumbing through the passport's pages, stamping one, and nodding when Bizhani told him he was visiting on holiday. The same was true for Michael Stack and his pilot friend, who cleared the check without a hitch.

They left the pilot with his aircraft, Stack explaining to him that he had booked a room at the Regal Airport Hotel to stay "near the action." After clearing Immigration, Bizhani followed Stack to the auto rental agency, where they retrieved a slate-gray Audi A4 four-door sedan with a five-speed manual shift. Its trunk was roomy, and their next task was to fill it with the equipment needed for their stay on Chinese soil.

Bizhani did not ask how Stack had acquired the firearm dealer's name—one of his cryptic sat-phone calls, presumably—but he could not help laughing when he heard the address.

"Happy Valley? I believe that you are pulling me."

"You mean pulling your *leg,*" Bolan replied. "And no, I'm not."

"Why Happy Valley?" Bizhani asked.

"I can only tell you what the guidebooks say. It's sports related, somehow, part of Hong Kong where you find the cricket grounds, two stadiums, a lot of recreation clubs. I'd guess it harks back to the British days."

"And Sing Woo Road?" Bizhani pressed his point. "Is *woo* not love, in English?"

"Usually. But we pitch it, not sing it."

"Singing, as you may know, is a controversial subject in my country."

"You mean protest songs?"

"Singing of any sort. After the revolution, all concerts and public broadcasts of music were banned. Foreign, traditional—it made no difference. Grand Ayatollah Khomeini warned of its seduction and corruption. Of course, that ban only succeeded in creating a black market in recordings and musical instruments. After Khomeini's death there was some minor liberalization of the rules, but the president Ahmadinejad banned Western music once again, late in 2005. Today, only specific versions of traditional and regional music are approved for broadcast over the IRIB."

"And what's that?" Bolan asked.

"Islamic Republic of Iran Broadcasting," Bizhani replied. "The only state-sanctioned outlet for radio and television."

Bolan frowned. "This is the system that you risk your life for? Where you're told what you can watch or listen to?"

Bizhani shrugged. "Sharia leads us on a quest for purity," he said. "It includes physical hygiene, dietary laws, dress codes, inheritance and marital relations. It is all a matter of faith."

"What happened to free will?" Bolan inquired.

"I hear the Christians speak of this," Bizhani said, "most often when they wish to sin. Of course, each person has the freedom to behave as he or she may choose, but there are consequences. Laws dictate what is acceptable and what is punished as a threat to orderly society and our relationship to Allah. Is it not the same in your America?"

"We haven't settled that," Bolan replied. "Some want their personal beliefs imposed on everyone, while others claim a right to privacy in matters they deem strictly personal. We have our share of preachers telling people how to live, some of them in it for the money, but I wouldn't say they have a death grip on the government."

"Two very different systems, it would seem," Bizhani said. "Yet, here we are together, hunting the same enemy."

"In Happy Valley," Bolan said, and smiled.

"But not, I think, happy for very long."

Victoria Peak, Hong Kong

YONG CAO TIO had been to Hong Kong many times, but he was still bemused by the lingering British influence. Nearly two decades after the handover to Beijing, it was impossible to move around the island city without facing incessant reminders of colonial rule by the West.

Queen's Road. Connaught Road and Upper Albert Road, both named for British princes. Wellington Street, christened for the victor at Waterloo. Even Hollywood Road, invoking the decadence of America, although it was named a decade before settlers occupied the now famous California capital of motion pictures. Passing through the city, working there, Yong felt as if he was immersed in something filthy, but the pay was excellent.

Besides, he'd been corrupted long ago. There was no turning back, even if he wanted to.

Which he did not.

Yong loved his work, from planning an assassination to the final moment when his hands snuffed out another life. He would have killed for free—had done so frequently, in fact—but getting paid extravagant amounts for doing what had always pleased him most in life was extra icing on the cake.

His task, this day, was to shadow the target, Ma Lam

Chan. It should have been more difficult, considering Chan's power and influence in Hong Kong, but for that very reason, Yong supposed, the man he'd come to kill was not as cautious as he might have been. The Dragon Head of the Wah Ching Triad trusted his men to keep him safe, without investing much of his own effort toward that goal.

A critical mistake.

Yong had decided that they should not try to kill Chan at his home, where money bought the best security. It would not be impossible—a long-range rifle shot, perhaps, or possibly an RPG—but Yong preferred a more direct approach. Whenever possible, he liked to see the target's eyes as life faded behind them and was finally extinguished. It was a treat he granted to himself when it was feasible.

Or, failing that, he would at least be close enough to hear his quarry beg for mercy.

At the moment he was watching Chan's palatial home through 10 x 50 power binoculars, tracking the movement of bodyguards circling the grounds. From his vantage point at Blake Garden—predictably named for one of Hong Kong's British governors—he had a good view of the walled estate, including the house and two-thirds of the property surrounding it. He had already glimpsed Chan once, his round face unmistakable, and Yong was looking forward to their next encounter, when the big man's life would end.

But not this night.

He and Saburo had been told to let Chan keep his dinner plans with their employer, lulling him into a sense of confidence. A premature attack might spoil whatever plan Khalil Nazari had in mind. Yong neither knew nor cared what that scheme might involve, as long as he was paid in full for his part of the job.

So the banquet would proceed as planned. But in the

morning, when the two sides gathered to discuss their business, then all bets were off. The only rule Yong recognized from that point forward was to spare his principal from any harm during his execution of the task assigned. Beyond that, he was not a bodyguard or an insurance agent, but the key to a successful job was getting paid.

And it was difficult to bill a corpse.

Granted, Yong had managed to collect from the estates of two dead men who'd owed him money, after applying some moderate pressure, but he didn't fancy taking on an Afghan drug cartel if it could be avoided. Should Nazari die on Yong's watch, there was every chance that his successor would be grateful for the opportunity to rise—but not grateful enough to pay Yong for what would be widely seen as a mistake or worse.

So, no explosives at the meeting and no hosing down the crowd with automatic fire. A subtler touch would be required, and Yong was just the man to do it.

As for Mori Saburo, they could work around the traditional hatred between their peoples, but it did not make them friends. Saburo was a major-league competitor of Yong's, and if something tragedy befell him in Hong Kong, although Nazari was unlikely to pay Yong a double salary, losing a rival would be good for business down the road.

Something to think about while Yong was working out his final moves against the Wah Ching Triad's Dragon Head.

Maybe two dragons for the price of one.

CHAPTER SEVENTEEN

Aberdeen Promenade, Hong Kong

Gambling was banned by law in Hong Kong, except through the Hong Kong Jockey Club, which took bets on horse races, soccer matches and a lottery. Private bookmaking was illegal, as were all casino games—none of which prevented their operation in the city, for players who knew where to look. The Lucky Spot on Aberdeen Promenade was one such place, a tourist nightclub with a small but well-equipped backroom casino on the premises. Hong Kong police, normally zealous in performance of their duty, managed to ignore the club for reasons best known to themselves.

The Executioner supposed it might have been because the place was owned by Ma Lam Chan, which made it perfect for a Bolan hit.

The Happy Valley arms dealer had furnished everything Bolan thought he might need in Hong Kong. With Bizhani, he'd picked out a pair of QBZ-95 assault rifles and two sound-suppressor-equipped QSZ-92 pistols for backup. For work at longer range, Bolan had chosen a QBU-88 sniper rifle chambered for 5.8 mm ammunition, fed from a 10-round box magazine and topped with a telescopic sight. Accurate out to a 1000 meters, the QBU-88 delivered a five-grain projectile traveling 2,900 feet per second, striking with 1.395 foot-pounds of energy.

For heavy hitting, Bolan had picked out a Type 69 RPG, the Chinese version of Russia's RPG-7, a shoulder-launched weapon that loaded a 40 mm rocket-propelled grenade with an 85 mm warhead, handling a variety of high explosive and incendiary projectiles. Closer work was covered by a crate of Type 59 fragmentation grenades, again copied from a Russian design, in this case the RGD-5. Each lethal egg weighed roughly two-thirds of a pound, was packed with TNT, and had a four-second pyrotechnic delay fuse. Its kill radius was three meters, with serious penetrating wounds reported out to fifteen meters—more than ample when it came to clearing rooms.

Aberdeen Promenade was an urban waterfront park. Bolan found a parking space where they could jog back from the Lucky Spot in seconds, if it came to that, and nosed the Audi A4 into it. Night was already falling over Hong Kong, and the city was a blazing neon light show. Viewed from space, Bolan surmised, it had to look like the maw of a volcano spewing lava toward the sea.

He took a moment, double-checking gear before he left the car. A fully loaded 30-round box magazine was seated in the bullpup rifle's stock, and Bolan carried four more in the pockets of his raincoat. On a whim, he had attached the sound suppressor to his pistol holstered under his left arm. Clipped on to his belt, he wore a couple of the frag grenades he'd bought in Happy Valley, just in case.

The players at the Lucky Spot were not his targets, but a triad club was bound to be protected, and he never tackled any target knowing he would be outgunned. Bizhani, similarly armed, seemed calm enough as they set off toward the casino, walking with Aberdeen Harbour to their right, a party boat ablaze with lights just passing by. Two women at its railing raised their glasses, laughing, and Bizhani waved back to them from the shore.

"A hard life, eh?" he said.

"It will be, in a minute," Bolan answered.

There was a gorilla in a tux outside the Lucky Spot. If he had worn a derby, he'd have been a doppelgänger for the mute karate champ in *Goldfinger,* only inflated to a six-foot stature, with a head as round and solid-looking as a bowling ball. He frowned at Bolan and Bizhani, holding up a square, blunt-fingered hand.

"You need ID, please," he informed them.

"What kind of ID?" Bolan asked.

"Passport, driver's license. Something to show you are not HKPF."

"Sounds interesting," Bolan said, and reached under his raincoat, pulling out the QSZ. "Will this do?"

When the bouncer simply glared at him, Bolan got tired of it and told him, "Get inside." He gave the guy some room, and was prepared for it when the gorilla snarled and spun, lifting his right leg for a kick that made him look like someone's dog about to douse a fire hydrant.

The QSZ coughed once and dropped him in the club's foyer, a lifeless slab of meat in evening wear. Somewhere inside, a woman saw him fall and squeaked a shrill cry of alarm. Bolan holstered his pistol, hauling out his rifle as Bizhani did the same.

"Okay," he said. "Let's shut this party down."

THE RESTAURANT STOOD less than a mile east of Ma Lam Chan's home on Victoria Peak, in the Wan Chai District of northern Hong Kong Island. Anticipating his Islamic guests' dietary restrictions, Chan had called ahead to guarantee that pork would not appear in any form upon their special menu for the evening.

The chef had offered him no argument.

"Where are they?" Chan inquired, checking his watch.

"Late leaving the hotel," Henry Kwok replied. "Mr. Nazari sends apologies."

"Does he?"

Chan wondered if the Afghan's tardiness was meant to be a calculated insult or a gesture of asserted dominance. Under other circumstances, Chan might have been gravely irritated, but since he already planned to see Nazari dead before the next day's sun went down, it hardly mattered. He could wait a few more minutes for his meal, lulling his enemies into a fatal sense of overconfidence.

Kwok's cell phone hummed from somewhere underneath his jacket, and he fished it out, giving the LED display a glance. "They're coming, finally," he said. "Five minutes out, according to the driver."

"Let's be seated, then," Chan ordered. "I will not stand waiting for them like a maître d'hôtel."

Chan had two separate tables reserved, in different rooms at the restaurant. One was for himself and Henry Kwok, with Nazari and whomever the Afghan chose as his chief lieutenant. The other was for Nazari's armed escorts and an equal number of Chan's men, not counting those he had salted among the usual staff and standing by outside, ready to move in the event of an emergency. Chan had considered finishing Nazari at their dinner, but decided it would be rude to the restaurant's proprietor and bring unnecessary heat down on his clan. Better to handle matters during the negotiations, scheduled for a site more private than one of the city's most popular night spots.

It had been some time since Chan had ordered the deaths of so many targets at once. The last occasion had involved a conflict with Malaysia's Sio Sam Ong Triad, better known as the "Three Little Emperors" after its triumvirate of bosses. Chan had settled that dispute by sending a crack team of killers to Panang, where they'd massacred the leaders and six of their top-ranking sub-ordinates, leaving the clan in disarray. There had been threats of vengeance at the time, but they were soon for-gotten in the power struggle that erupted with selection of new Dragon Heads.

And what had worked once, Chan believed, should work a second time.

He was seated at the table's head when Khalil Nazari entered with a younger, bearded man trailing a step be-hind him. Henry Kwok stood to greet them, but Chan re-mained sitting, wearing a vague, neutral smile. Despite what Kwok had said before, Nazari offered no apology for being late, nor did he make an effort to shake hands. The latter lapse was no surprise, Chan being well aware that many Muslims balked at touching other persons who were not related to them in some way.

"I'm pleased that you could join us," Chan allowed.

"Of course," Nazari said.

"You've met my Vanguard. And your aide is...?"

"Latif Tarzi," Nazari said. "He has my total confi-dence."

"I trust your other men are well provided for?"

"They are most pleased with the accommodations, yes."

"And was your flight pleasant?"

"An unexpected journey," Nazari said. "But I trust that it will be worthwhile."

"A hope we all share," Chan replied, lifting the menu from his placemat. "Now, to order. Who likes shark fin soup?"

As Bolan soon discovered, the gorilla in the tux was not the only triad guard watching the Lucky Spot. The first wail from a female player at the roulette table, followed by a short burst from Bizhani's autorifle toward the ceiling, started a stampede toward the casino exits and brought half a dozen gunners on the run.

Bolan was ready for them, rifle at his shoulder, with the fire selector set on "1" for semiautomatic, squeezing off his first round at a short guy carrying a shotgun as he ran along a second-story balcony encircling the casino. Bolan's 5.8 mm slug ripped into the gunner's chest, seventy grains of copper-jacketed steel tumbling with catastrophic effect through flesh and bone. The dying man was down and out as Bolan shifted to a second target coming up behind him, this one carrying a submachine gun.

Before he had a chance to use it, Bolan shot the second man through his lower jaw, nearly detaching it in an explosive burst of crimson, spinning him through a one-eighty as he fell, his head wobbling loosely on his shoulders. If he wasn't dead already he was close, between the spinal damage and the hydrostatic shock his brain had suffered on impact.

To Bolan's left, Heydar Bizhani had engaged a pair of shooters who'd emerged from a door on the ground floor marked Private. Both were armed with pistols, ducking in and out around the club's panicked customers, angling for a clear shot at the two intruders. Bolan saw one of them go down, blood spraying from his neck and upper chest, then he got busy with the other guards circling around the balcony above them.

They were firing now, in desperation, without any visible regard for hapless patrons of the club. A woman ran in front of Bolan, wild-eyed, and a bullet drilled her neck, the kind of shot most gunmen couldn't make deliberately if their lives depended on it.

Which, in this case, one life did.

Bolan nailed the hasty shooter with his third round from the rifle, missed dead center, but the tumbling slug still did its work, smashing the gunman's clavicle and severing his brachial artery, ripping his right shoulder out of its socket and slamming him onto his back. If the shock didn't kill him, he'd bleed out in minutes, his pistol spinning out of reach to make him harmless while his life ran out in a scarlet river.

Number four was close enough behind his third kill to get spattered with the gore, recoiling automatically instead of cutting down his enemy on instinct. Bolan took advantage of the lapse to hit the shooter with a solid double tap that sat him down, a stunned expression on his face before he toppled over backward, dead before his shoulders hit the carpet.

The last guy standing didn't look much like a fighter. He was older, hair and mustache gone to gray, most of his onetime muscle gone to flab; maybe the manager, but he was still determined not to let the Lucky Spot go undefended. Moving past the now deserted gaming tables, his patent leather shoes sloshing in pools of blood, he came at Bolan and Bizhani with a grim look on his face, raising a shiny pistol when he'd closed the gap enough to make a clean shot possible.

Both automatic rifles opened up on him at once, stopping the gray-haired shooter in his tracks. He crumpled underneath that fire, the bullets ripping through him while his knees collapsed and pitched him forward, landing with a wet slap on his face. A final tremor raced along his spine and he was done.

"Looks like we broke the bank," Bolan said. "Want to bag some of that cash before we go?"

Bizhani grinned and grabbed a cash bag from its shelf below the nearest roulette table, cleaning out the till in nothing flat. As they were leaving, Bolan took one of the frag grenades he carried on his belt and pulled its pin, gave the bomb a long toss from the foyer toward the rear of the now-empty gaming room, then closed the door behind them as they hit the street.

"Remodeling," he told Bizhani as they walked back to their Audi.

And a little something for the Wah Ching Dragon Head to think about.

MORI SABURO HAD FOLLOWED Chan's party from home to Fook Lam Moon, the restaurant standing alone on its block, rising boxlike from the pavement. He had watched the limousine deliver half a dozen passengers, then leave, while Ma Lam Chan and his companions went inside. Saburo was not joining them for dinner, being under orders not to strike Chan on the first night that Khalil Nazari was in Hong Kong, but he saw already that it would be possible to kill the Wah Ching Dragon Head.

Power inevitably spawned a kind of arrogance that was extremely difficult to manage. Even someone like Chan, with ample cause for paranoia in a world of enemies and jealous allies, was inevitably tainted by a sense of confidence that left him vulnerable. Chan had bodyguards, of course, but he felt relatively safe in Hong Kong, left himself exposed in situations like the present outing, where a skilled assassin could relieve him of his life.

He would not protract the job longer than another day. Saburo's time was money, and he never wasted it.

He wondered briefly where Yong Cao Tio had concealed himself. Saburo had not seen his partner since their first brief meeting, and was not inclined to phone him now. Saburo trusted him to be available when needed. They would meet once more this night, after the banquet, drawing up their final plans for Chan and any soldiers brave enough to die with him.

Before arriving at the restaurant, Saburo had added a QCW-05 submachine gun to his mobile arsenal. When the time came, if it was agreed to work in close, Saburo reckoned he could shred Chan and his bodyguards in seconds flat, before most of them realized what was happening.

And he would certainly enjoy it, though Saburo thought that Yong Cao Tio might have other plans.

No matter. This was a cooperative effort, and his pay was not reduced if Yong killed Chan before Saburo had the chance. Khalil Nazari had agreed to pay them both in full for satisfactory results, and he was wise enough to know the consequences of reneging on a contract. Powerful he might be, and well guarded, but no man could hide forever from a skilled, determined killer—and much less so from two.

Time passed, and finally another limousine arrived outside the restaurant, this one bearing Nazari and his soldiers to their meeting with the Wah Ching overlord. Saburo faded back into a shadowed doorway on the far side of the street, while his employer entered the restaurant to feast and make believe that all was well between him and the triad. It occurred to him that Chan might have a trap in place, prepared to slip the noose around Nazari's neck this night. And what would he do then?

Nothing.

The payment he had already received, half in advance, would compensate Saburo for a wasted trip to Hong Kong. Without being paid the balance, he had no incentive to kill Chan or any other person who had done nothing to offend him personally. If his principal was taken out of play, their contract would be null and void.

Simple.

But in his heart, Saburo hoped that no such thing would

happen. He was geared up for the kill and knew he would feel cheated if he lost the opportunity to follow through.

Murder, after all, was a labor of love.

PREPARING SHARK FIN SOUP was an exercise in skill and patience. Raw shark fins were processed by removing the tough skin and denticles, trimming them to size and shape, bleaching them to a desirable color, then softening the flesh to make it palatable. Though virtually tasteless, the fins were commonly regarded in Chinese culture as an aid to increasing energy and sexual potency, improving the diner's complexion, lowering cholesterol, preventing heart disease and cancer. Those qualities, coupled with the time and care required for proper preparation, made shark fin soup a favorite of emperors from the Ming Dynasty onward, served in modern times at weddings and banquets where wealthy hosts sought to impress esteemed guests.

Ma Lam Chan ordered the soup because he could afford to, even though it gave him gas.

This night he was midway through his appetizer, chewing a piece of gelatinous meat, when Henry Kwok frowned and thrust a hand inside his jacket, pulling out his cell phone. He had set the phone to vibrate. Checking the LED display, he muttered an apology to Chan before taking the call.

Chan watched his aide as Kwok listened, his aspect darkening, silent until the caller finished speaking and he said, "I understand. You'll have to deal with it for now."

Breaking the link, he leaned toward Chan, whispering even though he spoke in Cantonese. "Sir, there has been a shooting and explosion at the Lucky Spot."

Chan kept his face blank, conscious of Nazari peering at him from the far end of the table. "Oh?" he said, keeping his tone deliberately casual.

"Police are on the scene," Kwok told him. "Six or seven of our men are dead."

Chan forced a smile, asking, "And it is being handled?"

"For the moment. Alex Ho is dealing with the HKPD."

"All right. He knows them well enough to cope with this. We'll meet with him later tonight, after we finish here."

"Yes, sir."

"Is there some problem?" Nazari asked in what sounded almost like a hopeful tone.

"Nothing that need concern us," Chan replied. "A minor incident at one of our establishments. It has no impact on our business."

But even as he spoke, Chan wondered whether that was true. Could it be mere coincidence, a deadly raid occurring within hours of Nazari landing in Hong Kong? Or had Nazari brought the war along with him, to punish Chan for what he saw as raw Wah Ching aggression in New York and France? Would he lash out this way before they even had a chance to talk—or, more importantly, before Chan had an opportunity to cut him down?

Chan had arranged a signal with his soldiers, as a hedge against the possibility of treachery tonight. He merely had to touch the cell phone in his pocket, press one button, and the men he had stationed in or near the restaurant would strike, killing Nazari and his men on sight. It would be costly—at the very least, Chan would be forced to renovate the restaurant, cover whatever damages his soldiers caused and bring forensic cleaners in to certify the place as safe for future customers. These days, with AIDS and other diseases running rampant, spilling blood was tantamount to an environmental crime.

Chan saw the glance Nazari shared with his lieutenant, caught them frowning back and forth at each other, but made no move to summon help. Not yet. Some conversation passed between them before Nazari shrugged and bent back to his shark fin soup. Dipping his spoon, he said, "I trust this minor problem won't delay our meeting in the morning?"

"I see no reason why that should be the case," Chan said.

Nazari nodded, seeming satisfied, but it was difficult for Chan to read his face. Westerners spoke of Asians as inscrutable, perhaps because white men were fond of wearing raw emotion on their faces, but to Chan, the true inscrutables were Arabs, their faces baked and weathered by the blazing desert sun, hardened by centuries of warfare in an unforgiving climate, dying for the dunes and rocky hills of home.

No matter. He was finished with his soup, and it was time for abalone with braised goose feet and mushrooms on the side.

Why let a massacre upset his appetite, when there was nothing he could do about it now?

THE MING LEE BUILDING was unique: a twelve-story apartment block whose flats were all reserved for triad members. Ma Lam Chan held the deed through a firm he had bankrolled while keeping his name off the paperwork, but residence was not restricted to members of his own Wah Ching Family. Bolan's information, gleaned from Stony Man via Hong Kong police files, indicated that members of the 14K, Ghee Hin Kongsi, and Sun Yee On triads also occupied quarters within the building.

Sitting ducks.

"You do not plan to go inside?" Heydar Bizhani asked him.

"Nope. I'm rattling cages here. There's nothing to be gained by going at them head-to-head."

They stood atop a fourteen-story office building, situated kitty-corner from their target, on Woo Hop Street. Bolan held the Type 69 RPG grenade launcher, loaded with a high-explosive round, while Bizhani clutched two more of the rocket-propelled grenades, each weighing roughly six pounds. At Bolan's feet, the QBU-88 sniper rifle lay within easy reach, ready for action in a heartbeat.

The range was sixty meters, give or take. The odds of Bolan hitting his target at that distance: 100 percent. He had no concerns about innocent flesh in the line of fire, since the Ming Lee Building was a singles-only dormitory. Triad soldiers who got married were expected to make other living arrangements before they tied the knot, deliberately separating loved ones from the underworld milieu.

"Okay," Bolan said. "Party time."

He was loading TBG-7V single-stage thermobaric rounds, so-called "fuel-air" warheads designed for antipersonnel applications in urban warfare. The rockets traveled at 115 meters per second, with an expected penetration of fifty-nine inches through reinforced concrete or brick. With the Ming Lee Building neither armored nor fortified, Bolan expected dramatic results.

And he got them.

The first RPG hurtled downrange, trailing fire, and punched through a window on the target building's topmost floor, detonating in a darkened room, its shock wave blowing out a dozen other windows on that floor. Bolan saw flames roiling inside the damaged apartment, devouring its walls and furnishings as he reloaded, sighted on the eighth floor, and fired again.

The second warhead detonated with a flash that sent flames leaping from windows at the building's southeast corner, scorching paint and plaster on the beige façade. Each thermobaric charge produced a blast wave of a significantly longer duration than those unleashed by normal condensed explosives, designed to increase the number of casualties and the damage inflicted on manmade structures. They relied on oxygen from the surrounding air, rather than a built-in fuel-oxidizer premix, therefore consuming oxygen from the environment even as their targets were incinerated.

Fry or suffocate: a miserable choice.

By the time Bolan fired his third RPG, aiming at a fourth-floor central apartment, he could hear fire alarms bleating from the Ming Lee Building, warning its occupants to evacuate. As the last rocket exploded, spreading flames and panic, he was setting down the launcher, reaching for the sniper rifle at his feet.

And there came the first frightened tenants, hitting the pavement and milling around in confusion; some with guns in hand, others still grappling with clothes they'd shed before hell broke loose in their midst. Bolan framed one of them in the crosshairs of his telescopic sight and stroked the weapon's trigger, sending five grams of steel-cored death downrange at 2,900 feet per second.

The triad soldier's skull exploded on impact, like a melon with a cherry bomb inside it, and his nearly headless corpse collapsed onto the sidewalk, startling his comrades into flight before they heard the echo of the rifle shot. Bolan admired their quick reaction time, but it was not about to save them. Nine rounds remained in the rifle's magazine, and the Executioner planned to use them all.

His second target took one in the back, between the shoulder blades, and he hit the pavement like a baseball player sliding into home, leaving a blood trail in his wake. The third man stood with a pistol in his hand, looking for someone handy to receive a bullet, but instead he took one to the face, his lower jaw ripped free as if by a deadly, invisible ax. He fell beside the first gunner to die outside, firing a wild shot into darkness as he dropped.

And it became a turkey shoot from there. Some of the hardmen scuttled back inside the burning structure they'd just fled, taking their chances with the smoke and spreading fire. Others ran off in all directions, maybe hoping that their comrades would distract the sniper and allow them to escape. A few dived under cars parked at the curb, and Bolan left them there to watch the carnage spread.

He used the rifle's final seven rounds within eight seconds, clipping runners on the fly, neither knowing nor caring if they were Chan's men. All were triad thugs, all criminal parasites, dying as they'd lived, by violence. When Bolan and Bizhani left the roof, the street below them was a slaughterhouse, illuminated by a rising wall of fire.

CHAPTER EIGHTEEN

The bad news had overtaken Ma Lam Chan on his way home from the restaurant, and it refused to stop. First came news of the rocket attack and shootings at the Ming Lee Building, where police were still busy counting the dead and wounded. Next, the angry calls began from leaders of the other triad clans whose members had shared lodgings at the building. Chan had heard already from the 14K and Sun Yee On, knowing the Ghee Hin Kongsi would be calling soon.

All were furious at losing men. All blamed Chan because, based on the first raid at the Lucky Spot, his Wah Ching Family was the primary terrorist target. And as yet, he had no viable response to their complaints.

In New York and in France, the violence against his men had sprung from Afghan origins—or so Chan had believed. But would Khalil Nazari be so rash as to initiate an all-out war while he was sitting down with Chan to speak of peace between them? Assassination of a rival leader during treaty talks was one thing, demonstrated by his own plan to eliminate Nazari, but such bold attacks on Chan's home ground, infuriating other triads in the process, seemed both counterproductive and foolish.

And whatever he thought of Nazari, the Afghan was nobody's fool.

Not for the first time, Chan allowed himself to wonder if there might be other hands at work, some element that neither side thus far was able to identify. He had considered bringing up the subject in tomorrow's conversation with Nazari, then decided it would be a waste of time. In fact, the recent spate of violence might be useful to him as a cloak for his elimination of the Afghan drug lord.

Who could blame him if Nazari walked into the middle of a fight and died as a result?

Henry Kwok rapped lightly on the office door, distracting Chan from homicidal fantasies. Chan swiveled in his chair and beckoned Kwok inside. "What news?" he asked.

"The Ming Lee Building is a total loss, sir," Kwok replied. "Our friend at the Fire Services Department says incendiary rockets were employed. Something that requires a chemical extinguisher. Part of the structure still remains, but it will surely be condemned."

Chan thought about insurance, certain that it would pay nothing on a clear-cut act of terrorism. His attorneys had approved that waiver after telling him that such events were so unlikely he need not consider them as realistic threats.

How many millions lost because of that assurance, to save pennies on the premiums?

He wondered how long lawyers could be kept alive and screaming on an operating table.

"And the dead?" he asked, after a moment of reflection.

"Ten shot down outside," Kwok said. "Thirteen from the building so far, but the search is still ongoing."

"Ours?"

"Five on the street, with three 14K, two Ghee Hin Kongsi and one Sun Yee On. With those inside, the fire… our man says dental records will be needed to identify them. Otherwise, who knows?"

"And no one saw the men responsible?" Chan pressed.

"The rockets and the rifle shots came from a nearby rooftop," Kwok explained. "Police have found the shooter's nest and cartridges. The shells were 5.8 mm, standard PLA issue. The rockets, probably, came from a Type 69 RPG. Again, standard issue. Some passersby witnessed the incident, but they were on the street, the shooter fourteen floors above them and in darkness."

"Shooter? You think one man did all this?"

Kwok shrugged. "The witnesses saw only muzzle-flashes and the rockets flying then exploding. One man could have done it. Maybe two, or even more."

"And nothing else was left behind to help identify this man or men?" Chan asked.

"No, sir."

"It's unacceptable! To suffer this, then say the man responsible has simply vanished? No! *Someone* knows *something.* I want every soldier on the street within the hour. None eat, sleep, or earn a cent until this crime is solved and punished. Do you understand?"

"Yes, sir!"

"Then go. You have your orders."

Still, Kwok hesitated. "Sir, about tomorrow's meeting…"

"It proceeds," Chan said. "What other choice is there? I will win something from this situation, even if I have to kill the bastard myself."

THE *KOWLOON QUEEN,* 115 feet of pristine luxury, sat moored with half a dozen smaller yachts, inside the typhoon shelter fronting Victoria Park. Faint lights were visible from somewhere belowdecks, but Bolan saw no crewmen stirring on the boat—or would it be called a ship at that size, since it was capable of sailing on the open sea?

No matter. Either way, the *Kowloon Queen* was going down.

"It seems a shame," Bizhani said. "She's beautiful."

"You're sentimental about boats?" Bolan asked.

"It's all that desert. I was seventeen before I saw the Persian Gulf for the first time," Bizhani said.

"But now, you've been all over."

"It's ridiculous, I know. But still, there's something, isn't there? About the carefree sailing life?"

"I wouldn't know. Maybe, if you've got all the time and money in the world."

"And that's the point. Chan and Nazari *do* have all the time and money in the world."

"Not anymore," Bolan replied. "Stand clear."

He shouldered the RPG, took aim and slammed a high-explosive round into the yacht's hull amidships, just below the waterline. It raised a geyser first, then penetrated and exploded in the engine room, sending its blast wave up through two decks, lighting fires along the way. The vessel shuddered like a wounded animal, then started taking water through the gaping hole in its port side, listing in that direction as it foundered.

"Such a shame," Bizhani said.

"Get over it," Bolan advised him, lowering the rocket launcher as he palmed a hand grenade.

It was an easy toss from where they stood at dockside. Bolan lobbed the lethal egg into the yacht's stern well, nearest to the fuel tanks, waiting for the detonation to pierce decking and ignite another fire below. Some of the shrapnel flew skyward, but Bolan and Bizhani were beyond its killing reach. They stood and watched the dying ship wallow for another moment, sinking now, and still no crewmen visible, before they turned away and walked back to their waiting car.

Losing the yacht would be more of an irritant than any kind of crippling blow for Ma Lam Chan, but the craft would have cost him two or three million dollars, depending upon its accoutrements. Then factor in the damage to his personal prestige while he was trying to impress Khalil Nazari, and it had to sting.

But not enough to bring Chan down. Not yet.

Bolan could have attacked the triad leader's home, or gone after Nazari at his posh hotel, but he was saving that strike for the following day's main event. By then, with any luck, Chan's paranoia would be operating in high gear, preparing him to lash out at the Afghan visitors while Bolan did the mopping up.

But first he had a message for the Wah Ching Dragon Head. They had not spoken yet, and he'd decided it was time to introduce himself, after a fashion. Not by name, of course, or even nationality. A little chat to push his adversary that much closer to the panic button, while his tidy world went up in smoke around him.

Fair play? Forget about it. Stalking human predators meant hunting for them in the jungles—or the moral sewers—that they occupied. It meant adopting tactics they could understand and tightening the screws beyond what they could bear. Burning their houses down with everyone inside.

It was familiar territory for the Executioner.

KHALIL NAZARI SAT on a plush sofa in the Conrad Hong Kong's presidential suite, watching Hong Kong burn on a fifty-inch LED flat-screen TV. He was not sure precisely what to make of it, but there was something pleasant in the graphic images, broadcast in crystal-clear high definition. They encouraged him and very nearly made him smile.

Of course, it was not *all* of Hong Kong burning. That would have been too extravagant—and dangerous, as well. So far, the English-language channel he was watching had reported the destruction of a gambling club and an apartment building, both cautiously described as properties "allegedly" belonging to an unnamed triad syndicate. Nazari's personal research left him in little doubt that Ma Lam Chan had suffered grievous losses while they'd dined, and from the commentator's breathless observations, it appeared there might be worse in store.

Nazari hoped so, willing Chan to suffer bitterly before he died.

Beyond that streak of malice, he was privately delighted that the raids—in which he had no part—would serve as cover for his plan to liquidate the Wah Ching Triad's leader. Nothing could connect him to the night's attacks, since he was absolutely innocent of any role in them. The following day, when his hired assassins did their work, police and Chan's loyal followers would scurry hopelessly around the city, seeking leads, inevitably linking Chan's death to the acts of violence that preceded it. Khalil Nazari, meanwhile, would be safely on his way back home.

Perfect.

"The town's falling apart," Latif Tarzi observed.

"Let it. It serves our purpose."

"Will Chan proceed with the meeting tomorrow?"

"What choice does he have, when we've come all this way? He would lose face by canceling now."

"And if he decides to retaliate?" Tarzi inquired.

"Against whom? We have nothing to do with these incidents."

"No. But he may not believe in coincidence. If he sends soldiers against us in force…"

"At a five-star hotel? I think not," Nazari said. "He'd have to be mad."

"The Chinese do not think as we do. If he blames us for losses he's suffered in France and New York, he may draw a connection."

"The wrong one, Latif."

Tarzi shrugged. "Does it matter, once fighting begins? And besides, we *are* planning to kill him."

"But *he* doesn't know that. You worry too much."

Tarzi muttered something that Nazari didn't catch. "Speak up!" the drug lord snapped at his subordinate.

"I said we should have stayed at home with all this going on."

"Ah, but it *wasn't* going on when we left Kabul. Are you frightened now?"

Tarzi glowered at that. "I would prefer to be on more familiar ground, Khalil. Hong Kong is like Calcutta. Everything's too rushed and crowded. And I don't trust these Chinese."

"You won't be forced to deal with them much longer," Nazari pointed out.

"Just remember that we're not the only people capable of treachery. These Chinese were killing emperors before Afghanistan existed."

"I am not an emperor."

"You may do until they have another one to kill," Tarzi replied.

"And you are giving me a headache. Stop it, for your own sake."

Tarzi knew when he had pushed a thing too far. Nazari might have kept chastising him, regardless, but Nazari's cell phone started buzzing and vibrating on the coffee table, near his knees. He checked the number on the LED display and recognized it, answering cautiously.

"Hello?"

"You've seen the news?" Mori Saburo asked without preamble.

"Yes."

"Have any plans changed for tomorrow?"

"None," Nazari said.

Saburo cut the link and left a dial tone humming in Nazari's ear. The Afghan closed the cell phone and replaced it on the table. He felt Tarzi observing him but holding back his questions.

"One of the mechanics checking in," Nazari said. "They go ahead as planned."

"We'll need to be prepared, in the event of retaliation," Tarzi said.

"Of course. Although, if all goes well, it should not be a problem."

As he spoke, Nazari pictured the confusion that would reign after Saburo and Yong dealt with Chan at the meeting. The number of guards on the scene had been limited by prior agreement to seven for each cartel leader. Even allowing for duplicity on Chan's part, once the Dragon Head was taken out of action it should make no difference. Nazari's men could deal with odds of two or three to one with no great difficulty, and unlike the triad bodyguards, they'd be prepared for what was coming.

By the time police came looking for Nazari at the Conrad Hong Kong, if they even tried to find him, he should be long gone, winging his way back to Afghanistan. Kabul had no extradition treaty with Beijing, so he'd be safe once he had cleared Chinese airspace.

Not only safe, Nazari thought, but sitting on top of the world.

YONG CAO TIO sat in darkness, watching the gate of Ma Lam Chan's estate for any sign of movement. Two guards stood smoking just inside the gate, occasionally answering a walkie-talkie that the taller of them carried; probably a supervisor from the big house making sure that they were

still awake. Beyond that, and a few lights in the house itself, there were no signs of life on the estate.

Yong had been following the steady flow of news from
downtown Hong Kong on his smartphone, keeping abreast
of the action, half wishing he could be part of it. For a moment, at the first reported outbreak, he'd wondered if Mori
Saburo had gone off without him, to hunt on his own, but
a quick text message had refuted that idea.

That meant more players in the game, and that was...
interesting.

Yong supposed that the attacks on Chan could be Nazari's doing, though it made no sense to him. If he and Saburo were meant to kill Chan in the morning, why would
Nazari do anything now to put the triad leader on alert? It
only made their work more difficult, and might even result in cancelation of the gathering where they were meant
to strike.

If that turned out to be the case, if Yong discovered that
Nazari had prevented them from completing their mission,
Yong would demand full payment for his services regardless of the outcome. He was not responsible for foolish acts
by one of his employers, but he *would* be paid.

Or else.

Before that prospect could distract him, Yong considered the alternatives. Suppose Khalil Nazari had no part
in the attacks on Chan's holdings around the city. Who,
then, was responsible? Although Chan had to have countless enemies, his wealth and power limited the number
who could cause him any major injury.

Yong ruled out law enforcement automatically. They
might use heavy weapons in a siege—against a band of
barricaded terrorists, for instance—but they would not
ordinarily attack without making arrests, serving their
warrants in accordance with the law. In Hong Kong, more

specifically, Chan would have been forewarned by officers he had bribed to be his eyes and ears inside the force.

So, criminals. And once he had ruled out Nazari, that left whom?

A rival triad was his next thought, but the latest news from Queen's Road West told him that members of at least three different clans had lost their lives in the Ming Lee Building attack. Unless one of the other twenty-odd crews had declared war on three cartels simultaneously—including the massive 14K group, with some twenty thousand soldiers—that option also made no sense. That kind of suicidal war had not been seen in decades, and the timing of it struck Yong as preposterous.

He thought next of the Yakuza, with more than one hundred thousand men divided into twenty-odd organizations. Some had battled with the triads, but in recent years their leaders had preferred accommodation that ensured profits for all, rather than wasteful bloodletting for little or no gain. Yong's knowledge of the Japanese convinced him they were not responsible.

And so, a mystery.

That made his job more challenging, to say the least. Yong was committed to eliminating Ma Lam Chan, even as someone else—perhaps even a team of killers—had begun dismantling his cartel in the Wah Ching Dragon Head's backyard.

Yong thought about the ancient Chinese curse: may you live in interesting times. The trick, he told himself, would lie in living *through* them.

BOLAN PARKED THE Audi A4 outside the International Finance Centre Mall and sat, watching the Dao Lin Bank directly opposite. The bank was closed, of course, lights burning in the spacious lobby, but it would not welcome customers again for six more hours. Even then, no normal residents of Hong Kong would be taking money in or out of that particular establishment, which served primarily to launder money for the Wah Ching Triad under Ma Lam Chan.

Palming his smartphone, Bolan keyed a private number for the Dao Lin Bank's unlisted owner and its key depositor. He waited through three rings until a gruff voice answered.

"Shi?"

"I need to speak with Mr. Chan," Bolan said in English. "It's important."

"Who is calling?" asked the flunky on the other end.

"Tell him," Bolan replied, "that it's about his bank."

"You wait."

He waited. Bolan didn't mind if Chan had gear in place to trace the call. He planned to tell the triad leader where he was, regardless, not that it would be of any help to Chan. The best part of a minute passed before another, smoother, voice came on the line.

"Who's calling, please?"

"My name's irrelevant," Bolan stated. "I just called to tell you you're about to lose a few more million dollars."

"Am I?"

"You can take it to the bank. The Dao Lin Bank, that is. You'd better hurry, though."

Instead of rising to the bait, Chan asked, "Are you the man behind my recent difficulties?"

"Just the messenger," Bolan informed him. "And the message is, you're going out of business."

"You think so?"

"I'd bet my life on it."

"You have already done so. May I ask who sends this message?"

"Let's just say the postmark's from Kabul."

"And you expect me to accept your word for that?"

"Your call," Bolan replied. "Listen to this."

He set the smartphone on the Audi's roof and hauled the loaded RPG out of the backseat, shouldered it and sighted on the bank's front doors. From thirty yards or less, he barely had to aim the rocket launcher. Seconds after hoisting it, he'd sent a thermobaric warhead hurtling through the lobby of the Dao Lin Bank to detonate against its row of cashier cages with a roar that echoed through the street.

Lifting the phone once more he said, "You'd better send the fire department. Maybe wake up your accountants and your IT guys. Find out what they can salvage from the wreckage."

Bolan didn't understand what Chan said next. He guessed it wasn't complimentary and cut the link before Chan could revert to English, leaving him cursing dead air at the other end while Bolan packed his rocket launcher and slid in behind the Audi's steering wheel.

When they were on the move, Bizhani asked him, "Do you think he believed you? Will he blame Nazari?"

"Maybe, maybe not. He'll think about it, anyway. For now, that's all we need."

Sirens were racing toward them now, a fire truck barreling down Finance Street with all lights flashing, and another in the distance, following behind it. Bolan knew they would need more than water to contain the blaze he'd lit inside the Dao Lin Bank. He trusted that the firefighters were smart enough to check it out before they rushed inside, particularly since they should have known by now about the warheads used against the Ming Lee Building.

How much had he cost Chan with the bank explosion? Some of the triad's funds were doubtless floating through the maze of cyber limbo, safe from anything as mundane as a fire, but Chan would certainly lose some cash, along with anything from documents and jewelry to gold bars that he'd stashed inside the Dao Lin vault. Tack on the building's damage, and it was another solid hit against the Wah Ching cash machine.

And yet another wedge driven between the triad and Khalil Nazari.

In several hours Bolan would be taking on the cartel leaders when they met to talk of peace, assuming they were still speaking to each other, right.

In any case, Hong Kong was on its way to get another taste of Hell.

Pacific Place, Hong Kong

KHALIL NAZARI FOUND that he could wait no longer. Staring at the television in his suite, the commentators switching from one scene of carnage to another, he could not resist the urge to speak with Ma Lam Chan. His plan for dealing with the triad chief depended on their sitting down to meet as scheduled, and Nazari feared that Chan might skip the meeting—even flee the city—in the face of all he'd suffered since they'd left the restaurant.

Chan's phone rang half a dozen times before one of his house men picked it up and took Nazari's message, running off somewhere to fetch the boss. Another silent interval ensued, and when Chan's voice came on the line at last, Nazari sensed a certain hesitancy that had not been present in their other conversations.

"Yes? Hello?"

"I've been watching the news," Nazari said.

"Reporters make it sound worse than it is," Chan said.

Nazari wondered whether that was true. In Kabul, he would have exerted influence to minimize reports of any damage to his holdings. Was it different in Hong Kong, or was Chan simply pretending for Nazari's benefit?

"I'm glad to hear it," the Afghan said, lying through his teeth. "I trust our business may proceed, then?"

"Certainly. Without a doubt," Chan replied.

"And the security…?"

"Will be substantial, I assure you."

That would pose a greater challenge to Nazari's hired assassins, but he'd picked the best for just that reason. Both were known for their ability to circumvent the best precautions their appointed targets could devise. Saburo, it was claimed, once killed a deputy minister of trade and industry in Singapore, at the target's closely guarded office, during lunch hour. Yong was renowned for severing the head of a Yakuza first lieutenant and leaving it on his *oyabun*'s desk—at the gang leader's home in Osaka.

"I am pleased to hear it," Nazari said as he watched another building burn on television. A bank this time, from what he could make out of the announcer's comments.

"You need have no worries about safety in Hong Kong," Chan said.

"In which case, I rest easier tonight."

"Until the morning, then."

"Until the morning," he repeated, then switched off his phone.

"Latif!" Nazari called out to his second in command.

Tazir emerged from the suite's dining area, holding a bottle of San Miguel beer. "Yes, Khalil?"

"Chan tells me we are perfectly secure."

"Does he?"

Nazari nodded. "Call the men and get them up here. They can sleep in shifts, watching the elevator and the door."

"A wise precaution."

"And tomorrow, on our way to meet with Chan, I want them all on full alert. At the first hint of danger, they must act accordingly."

If things went badly and Nazari could not reach his jet immediately, he would need a place to hide. Afghanistan had no diplomats in Hong Kong, but Pakistan was represented with a consulate at 338 King's Road, in the island's North Point district. In the worst-case scenario, Nazari guessed that he could travel that far from his meeting site with Chan, call in the favors owed to him by Pakistan's Directorate for Inter-Services Intelligence and gain asylum there until the heat died down. It was not an ideal solution, but survival was the key.

And if his luck held, if his two assassins earned their pay, Nazari should have nothing more to fear from Chan by midmorning. The Dragon Head's hours were numbered, his time running out.

Nazari hoped that he could watch Chan die, but that was optional. The fact of Chan's extermination was reward enough.

And he would celebrate it properly once he was safely back at home.

CHAPTER NINETEEN

Stony Man had worked its magic to discover that the sit-down between Ma Lam Chan and the Nazari team would be occurring at a moderate-to-smallish conference center overlooking Tamar Park, a five-minute ride north of Nazari's hotel in the Admiralty district. A pretext call for reservations had revealed the place as being booked that day by one of many firms Chan owned in fact, if not on paper. Lunch was being catered in by On Lot 10, one of the city's top ten restaurants.

"It's them," Bolan confirmed after an early drive-by at the site revealed a team of shifty-looking, although well-dressed, triad guards hanging around outside the building.

"And the time?" Heydar Bizhani asked.

"It doesn't matter," Bolan answered. "We'll be ready for them. Let them get inside and settle down, then pop in and surprise them."

"Hoping to ignite hostilities," Bizhani said.

They were examining their weapons as they talked, with Bolan in the Audi A4's front seat and Bizhani in the back. The Executioner had left the RPG and extra rockets in the rental trunk, after deciding there was no way to conceal it on their entry to the conference building. Otherwise, though, they were going in loaded for bear—or, in this case, for jackals. They had topped off all their magazines, attached the sound suppressors to their pistols, cocked each weapon and secured its safety as required until the action started. On his belt, each man had clipped as many frag grenades as he could comfortably carry with the other hardware—six, in Bolan's case, with the assistance of suspenders he had purchased at an all-night store, to keep the weight from dragging down his slacks too much.

It wasn't standard GI gear, but it would do.

Bolan had traced Nazari's party—once again, through Stony Man's connections—and discovered that the crew consisted of eight men. Say seven soldiers, with the boss calling the shots. Chan, as the home-team manager, could field as many gunmen as he felt the need for, given the suspected Wah Ching population of Hong Kong. Bolan surmised there would be rules in place to keep Nazari's side from feeling overwhelmed, but in light of the recent hits he'd taken, Chan might be inclined to fudge the numbers.

And, of course, there was the likelihood that one side or the other—maybe both—had death cards hidden up their sleeves.

All things considered, it should be an interesting day.

Watching the street outside the conference center through a pair of compact field glasses, Bolan observed the long white limousine arrive at half-past eight. The Afghans disembarking from it stood out among locals passing on the street, further identified by one of Chan's facto-tums coming out to bow and gesture them inside. Bolan picked out Khalil Nazari from the pack and noted that the others' added bulk under their jackets from the weapons they were carrying.

Eight minutes later Bolan watched a second limousine arrive. This one was black and slightly longer than the white one, as befit a prince of Hong Kong's underworld. Not quite the king—at least not yet—but Chan was clearly hoping for advancement if he either made a bargain with

Nazari or devised someway to take the Afghan drug lord out of play.

Bolan could help him with the latter part. As far as being crowned, however, Chan would have to make it through the morning in one piece, all on his own.

DURING THE TEN-MINUTE drive from his home to the conference center, Ma Lam Chan mapped out the final phase of his campaign in silence, staring through the tinted window of his black stretch limousine but seeing only carnage in his mind's eye. He pictured Khalil Nazari falling in a hail of bullets, while his men went down around him, helpless to defend their master. There would be nothing they could do to save Nazari—or themselves—when Chan's trap sprung and claimed them all.

The men he'd stationed in and near the conference center carried silenced weapons, minimizing any risk that the police would be involved. Aside from renting out the center for the day, Chan had brought in his own men, and a few trusted young women, to replace the usual staff. One well-paid manager aside, himself an ally of the Wah Ching Family, there would be no civilian witnesses to anything that happened once the faux peace talks began.

Chan also had a clean-up crew on standby, one of those that specialized in crime scenes and eradication of biohazardous waste. Often employed by the police, the firm had also worked for Chan on multiple occasions, eliminating evidence that could have sent him to prison for life. When they were finished, later on that afternoon, it would be as if nothing had happened at all.

Except that his market share of the heroin trade would expand overnight.

"Remember," he instructed Henry Kwok, "to smile and

seem amenable to anything the bearded barbarian says. We must appear to be good hosts until the need has passed."

"I wish we could dispose of them immediately," Kwok replied, "instead of going through with this charade."

"Patience," Chan said. "Nazari in particular must see no hint of treachery in your expression, and hear nothing in your voice. The others—" Chan made a dismissive gesture with one finely manicured hand "—all take their cue from him."

"I understand, sir."

"You will make a leader yet, Henry," Chan said.

The limousine slid to a halt outside the conference center, its engine idling while the shotgun rider exited and came around to open Chan's rear door. Two of Chan's soldiers joined the first one on the sidewalk, checking all directions for potential threats, and then beckoned him to follow them. Chan found the center's manager waiting to greet him, managing to hide his nerves quite well under the circumstances.

Cash would do that almost every time.

Chan nodded in response to his effusive greetings, then asked, "Have our guests arrived?"

"Indeed, sir. They await you in the main hall, on the mezzanine."

"The caterers?"

"Are in the kitchen, sir. Preparing the food."

Chan had selected the menu himself, choosing some of his personal favorites: tea-smoked duck, Kung Pao chicken and cold beef tripe. He could have added the twice-cooked pork, for all it mattered to his Muslim guests, since none of them would live to taste the food, but fine attention to detail was one of Chan's keys to success.

Before that lunch was served, Khalil Nazari and his soldiers would be dead. Chan wondered if he should enjoy the meal himself, while they were hauled away for rendering and ultimate disposal in the sea.

Too much of a good thing, perhaps?

Passing through glass revolving doors, he thought it would be best to wait to see how well his plan was carried out. If he still felt the urge to celebrate when it was done, why not enjoy himself?

MORI SABURO ROLLED his shoulders underneath his knee-length leather coat, adjusting the harness he wore underneath. It supported two QCW-05 submachine guns with suppressors attached, one slung beneath each of Saburo's arms. His Norinco QSZ-92 pistol nestled upside-down in a horizontal holster at the small of his back, while the Sykes-Fairbairn dagger was sheathed to his left forearm. As a last resort, on his right ankle, the killer wore a nylon holster supporting a Glock 28 subcompact pistol loaded with ten rounds of .380 ACP. The pockets of his coat, specially reinforced to bear the weight, held extra magazines for all four weapons.

It was dagger work at first, as he approached the rear service entrance of the conference center. He walked up to its loading dock as if he owned the place—which, in his mind, was already the case. It might belong officially to Ma Lam Chan, but he would soon be dead, along with anyone who tried to shield him from his bloody destiny.

Chan had two guards covering the center's back door and they scowled at Saburo as if he were something they would scrape off their shiny wing-tip shoes. He smiled—or tried to, being decades out of practice—then attacked with stunning speed. The dagger in his hand, before they saw it coming, opened the taller gunman's throat, then lanced through the other man's green silk shirt into his heart. Saburo danced away before he could be spattered with their blood, then wiped his dagger on the short one's slacks and left them lying where they fell, no longer relevant.

He tried the door, found it unlocked and slipped inside, knife ready if he met another challenger. The conference center, while not large by Hong Kong standards, was a minimaze of corridors and meeting rooms that might have dazzled one less perfectly prepared. Thanks to the internet, however, its floor plans were readily available to all potential customers—or anyone who might desire to interrupt a sit-down with a rude surprise. Saburo had the layout memorized, knew where to find the kitchen on his own before its sweet aromas beckoned him, and moved in that direction first.

Khalil Nazari wanted every precaution taken in eliminating Chan, and not so incidentally ensuring that Nazari walked away from the engagement safe and sound. That meant eliminating any Wah Ching soldiers on the premises—or those with any will to fight, at least—to clear a path for the Afghan's escape.

Beginning now.

Saburo reached the kitchen's entrance, ducked inside and found two Wah Ching gunmen supervising preparations for the feast. He shot them both before they had a chance to challenge him, one round apiece from each of his two silenced submachine guns, dropping them with dazed expressions on their faces.

And the next surprise was his, as half a dozen kitchen workers reached for weapons hidden underneath their aprons or white chef's coats, clearly bent on blowing him away. It was a brave attempt, but fruitless as Saburo swept the room from left to right with one weapon, the other swinging right to left, hacking and mincing flesh with their converging streams of fire. Bloodied corpses tumbled to the white-tiled floor amid a rain of punctured pots and pans, brown sauce, white rice and half-cooked meat. Saburo scanned the bodies, making sure that none would rise again to threaten him, then switched out magazines for both his SMGs and backed out of the charnel house, in search of other prey.

Ten down, and he was starting to enjoy himself.

Recalling that the best was yet to come.

TWO DEAD MEN were lying on the conference center's loading dock when Bolan and Bizhani arrived, both clearly victims of a blade wielded by someone who knew his business. They had to walk through blood to reach the back door, where it stood ajar.

"Looks like somebody started without us," Bolan observed.

"An unexpected complication," Bizhani said. "Shall we leave them to it?"

"That's not reliable enough," Bolan replied. "We might as well go on in and join the party."

Two steps in, Bolan smelled the gunpowder scent of battle, mixed with something else burning. He followed his nose to a kitchen where bodies were scattered with guns around them, and spilled sauce was crackling on top of a stove. That meant another complication if the smoke set off a fire alarm, so Bolan grabbed a nearby fire extinguisher and stepped around more corpses, sprayed the range with foam until the flames were out, then set the canister aside.

"Two gunmen here," Bizhani said, pointing toward the first bodies they had passed on entering the kitchen. "But the rest of these also were more than cooks, I think."

"I'd say you pegged it," Bolan agreed. "And if they were all Wah Ching, it means somebody's cleaning out the Family."

"Again, I ask if we should leave them to it."

"You were sent to stop Nazari," Bolan said. "Odds are that he's the one behind all this."

"In which case, we must thank him personally. Let's proceed."

They left the kitchen, now secure from an alarm, and moved along a corridor that led them past more doors, pantries and offices, all standing open to suggest the kitchen killers had been active clearing rooms as they'd passed by. The hunt had not produced any more victims by the time they reached a set of escalators leading upward to the center's second floor, facing an empty lobby leading to the street.

Bolan would have preferred a normal staircase, safely tucked away from public view, but he would work with what they had. The other choice was riding in an elevator, which seemed doubly dangerous under the present circumstances, with at least one killer working on the premises ahead of them. Holding his silenced pistol, Bolan stepped up onto the escalator, with Bizhani just behind him, and began to rise from the ground floor up to the mezzanine.

From what he'd seen so far, Bolan suspected that Khalil Nazari had anticipated treachery from Chan, or else had planned to kill his rival from the get-go, under pretext of a meeting to resolve their feud. Whoever he had sent to do the job was clearly bent on leaving no one to describe the incident; a plan Bolan approved of as long as those who fell were all Wah Ching thugs, not innocents caught in the line of fire. But now he'd have to deal with the assassins, too, as well as their employer and the triad's Dragon Head.

A complication, right. And one that could prove lethal if he didn't watch his step.

KHALIL NAZARI GLANCED discreetly at his watch before speaking. "Our problem," he said at last, "appears to be largely territorial. We both need markets for our merchandise, and those we find most desirable have a limited threshold for new customers."

"You are doing quite well in Iran, I believe," Chan replied.

"For the moment, it's true. The police have become more efficient, however, and the regime more extreme. You're aware of the strict ban on smoking in public, including while driving or riding in cars?"

"You still have India and Pakistan, both markets virtually closed to me," Chan pointed out.

"India," Nazari said almost dismissively. "There are buyers, agreed, but I lost five hundred kilograms to police last month. Heroin aside, their Narcotics Control Bureau lists two hundred and thirty-six controlled drugs, imposing a sentence of six months for first-offense minor possession. In Pakistan, unruly peasants now produce their own poppy crops. They are competitors more than customers."

"You must be suffering," Chan said, nearly concealing his sarcasm, but not quite.

Nazari longed to wipe the smug look from his adversary's face. Knowing that it would soon be done, he inhaled a slow breath, sipped from the cup of coffee in front of him and answered, "I still turn a profit, naturally, but the field is narrowing in what you might call my part of the world. The same is true in part, I think, for you in parts of Southeast Asia."

"Yes, you are correct," Chan said. "Although our mainstay is produced there, it is not the best of markets. All the younger people want so-called designer drugs or methamphetamine."

"And now we have more competition to contend with," Nazari said, "from the Latin side, Colombia and Mexico. Their product is inferior, I'm sure you would agree, but also cheaper, and it satisfies the craving of consumers in the U.S.A. who don't know any better. Already, the Western Hemisphere's cartels are making inroads into Canada and Europe."

Chan could hardly contradict him on that point, as if it mattered. And, in fact, he replied, "That is precisely why I asked you for this meeting. If we're able to cooperate, perhaps delineate specific territories for our sales forces, it should be mutually beneficial to us both."

"I cannot argue with the mathematics," Nazari said, stalling for time. "But how do you propose that these divisions should be drawn up on a map?"

"I think we must begin with ruling out incursion on our obvious home territories," Chan replied. "You dominate the traffic in Afghanistan, and thus throughout the Golden Crescent, just as we, my triad brothers and I, rule the Golden Triangle. As I imagine the division, you would service Central Asia and the Middle East, including North Africa, Russia east of the Ural Mountains. My clan would cover Southeast Asia, with Australia and New Zealand, plus existing Chinese settlements in Canada and the United States."

Nazari frowned. "That still leaves nearly half the world, including Europe, western Russia and Sub-Saharan Africa."

"China, as you're no doubt aware, enjoys economic relations with many African nations. Immigrants from China also inhabit eighteen Sub-Saharan countries, roughly five hundred thousand in all. Where they have settled in substantial numbers, we already trade and would continue doing so. Other markets—Chad, for example—we cede to whoever may claim them."

"Without interference?" Nazari asked, dragging it out.

"If we reach an agreement."

YONG CAO TIO had come in through the building's roof access, an agile spider rapidly descending in his search for prey. He carried an AK-9 assault rifle fitted with a quick-release sound suppressor and loaded with 9 mm subsonic ammunition to approximate true silence when firing.

Entry was simple for an expert with a set of lockpicks, through the door used by maintenance workers to service the conference center's roof-mounted air-conditioning system. Stairs led downward from there to an unoccupied floor, its meeting rooms empty that morning, where Yong passed on to reach a service elevator. There was no guard at the elevator's door, apparently because no one had thought of any danger coming from above them.

Yong freed the AK-9 from its concealment underneath his jacket, standing easy in the elevator car as it descended to the next floor, one above the mezzanine. He could have gone directly to the floor where Chan was meeting with Khalil Nazari, but he had agreed to first eliminate whatever reinforcements Chan might have in place outside the target chamber, and this seemed a likely place to start. Dozens of shooters could be waiting for Nazari there, and if Yong wanted to get paid, he had to guarantee that nothing happened to the Afghan cartel boss.

As usual, the elevator *ding*ed to signal its arrival on the chosen floor. Yong stood to one side of the door as it hissed open, made a smaller target of himself and watched for any lookouts in attendance. Two Chinese men stood in front of him, hands on holstered guns, looking surprised, but neither had a chance to draw before Yong punched a silenced round through each one's chest.

A third, off to the left, had seen them fall, and he was coming on the run, clutching a compact submachine gun, as Yong cleared the elevator. This man was a better soldier, but he hesitated at the sight of death emerging into view, and that cost him his life. A double tap from Yong's Kalashnikov came close to disemboweling him, and the Wah Ching thug dropped like a sack of refuse tumbling down a garbage chute.

How many more?

The last man down had squealed as he fell, and the sound brought two more shooters from an office to the right of where Yong stood. They blundered into harm's way without understanding what had happened to their comrades, and they died with blank expressions on their faces, leaking blood onto the polished granite floor.

Yong cleared the other rooms in seconds, finding no more targets on the hoof. The first phase of his job completed, he moved off to find the escalator that would take him to the mezzanine and Ma Lam Chan.

It wasn't every day he got to kill a triad Dragon Head, and Yong was anxious not to let Mori Saburo beat him to the prize.

THE ESCALATOR WASN'T SLOW, but seemed to take forever. Bolan knew he could have climbed stairs faster, but he didn't push it, standing still and going with the flow, pistol in hand and pressed against his thigh. He'd nearly reached the top when a Chinese man in a stylish suit, clearly expensive, scurried into view as if to intercept him. That was going to be problematic, since the new arrival's hands were empty and his nicely tailored jacket showed no bulges that suggested hidden weapons.

He began with indignation, asking, "May I ask what you are do—" then saw their guns and took a quick step backward, muttering what sounded like a curse in Cantonese.

"Wah Ching?" Bolan asked as he topped the escalator, leveling his pistol at the frightened man's chest.

"No, no! I am the center's manager."

"So, manage. Where's the sit-down?"

"Sit-down?"

"Meeting. Confab. Where is Chan holding his powwow with Khalil Nazari. Quick, now!"

"This floor. Take the hallway to your right." He pointed. "They are in the Kowloon Room."

"Lead on," Bolan commanded.

"But I—"

"It's a simple choice," Bolan advised him, holding steady with the silenced pistol.

"Yes, of course."

The manager moved past them, walking stiffly, scared eyes darting every which way. As they reached the corridor he'd pointed to, the guy suddenly bolted, shouting what could only be a warning to a group of four tough-looking men downrange. Bizhani shot him on the run, a short burst from his autorifle, and the triad troops ahead of them scrambled for weapons as the manager went down, rolling in blood.

And it was on.

The Wah Ching gunners were surprised, but they were also pros at urban warfare, gangland style. They drew their weapons quickly, covered one another, but they weren't in Bolan's league and never would be. He got off a 3-round burst before the manager's fresh corpse had come to rest between him and his targets, gutting one triad thug with 5.8 mm rounds and flinging him aside with all the grace of a scarecrow caught in a twister.

Next in line was a squat-bodied soldier clutching what looked like a MAC-10 machine pistol, or maybe a Japanese Minebea PM-9. The fine distinction didn't matter as he raised it, tracking Bolan and Bizhani with the weapon's stubby barrel, his index finger on the trigger.

Bolan dropped into a crouch and fired another short

burst down the hallway, bullets ripping through the Wah Ching hardman's sturdy legs. The target fell hard, lost his weapon as it skittered from his hands and curled into a fetal ball, reaching for shattered knees. The sound he made was like a lamb at slaughter, bleating without letup until Bolan drilled a mercy round into his skull.

Bizhani had engaged the other two, meanwhile, catching one as he ducked toward a doorway nearby, ending his retreat in a wallowing death slide. The last man standing took advantage of his comrade's death to cut loose with a pistol, rapid-firing down the corridor, but he was scared and hasty, wasting bullets on the walls to either side of Bolan and Bizhani.

Bolan had him slotted, was about to drop him, when Bizhani fired another burst and put the man on his back, his legs kicking through their death throes as the life poured out of him through jagged holes.

It was time to hustle now, no further need for stealth with the hellacious racket they'd already made. Time to locate Chan and Nazari in the Kowloon Room, before they had a chance to field defenders and escape to fight another day.

CHAPTER TWENTY

Khalil Nazari was about to check his watch again when gunfire echoed from the corridor outside the Kowloon Room. It pleased him, seeing Ma Lam Chan bolt upright from his chair and lose a shade of color from his face before he started barking orders at his men in Cantonese. Latif Tarzi was on his feet a second later, beckoning Nazari's soldiers to surround their leader and protect him, come what may.

Nazari, for his part, was only worried about Chan. The racket in the hallway, he assumed, meant that his mercenary specialists were closing in, dealing with Chan's outlying troops before they closed in for the final kill. The drawback lay in his uncertainty concerning just how many soldiers Chan had placed throughout the conference center as a hedge against intruders—or, perhaps, as part of a design to trap Nazari and be done with him for good.

But now it was too late for any Wah Ching treachery. Nazari had, as usual, beaten his adversary to the punch.

It would have pleased him greatly to reveal his stratagem, but at the moment he was more concerned with getting out of there alive. He could enjoy the thrill of victory when he was airborne, leaving Hong Kong far behind him. At the moment it was useful—make that necessary—to maintain a posture of suspicion, verging on outrage.

"Chan, what's the meaning of this?" he demanded. It pleased him to see the confusion on Chan's pallid face.

"No cause for worry," Chan replied, an obviously foolish statement in itself, with gunfire echoing outside. "I have security in place."

"You won't mind if I trust my own men," Nazari said haughtily. "We're leaving now."

"You can't!" Chan blurted. "We have not finished our discussion yet!"

"Discussion? In a battle zone?" Nazari was already moving toward the nearest exit from the Kowloon Room, surrounded by his bodyguards. "Next time, you fly to Kabul, where security is guaranteed."

He left Chan staring after him, unable to suppress a smile now that his back was turned. The doorway he'd selected led into another conference room, which in its turn provided dual exits, one to the hall where he could hear a battle under way, the other to a service corridor that should, with any luck, grant access to the street. When Chan called to him one more time, Nazari stonily ignored him, waiting for the door to slam behind his party, cutting off the Wah Ching leader's voice.

Nazari had not known precisely what he should expect from Yong and Saburo, something more subtle perhaps, but a full-on frontal assault was satisfactory as long as it succeeded in its goal. There would be no payment to either assassin if Chan slipped through their hands. Beyond that, any damage they inflicted on the Wah Ching hardmen was irrelevant, but not unwelcome to Nazari.

Never leave an enemy in fighting form if you could kill or cripple him instead.

And now, before Chan had an opportunity to work out what was happening, the time had come to flee.

BOLAN SWEPT PAST the corpses of Chan's outer guards, making his way swiftly toward the Kowloon Room. He followed a babble of voices, aided by multilingual signs on the corridor's wall, with Bizhani following close on his heels.

Killing the unarmed manager had been a judgment call, maybe a hasty impulse, but it couldn't be undone. Bolan would probably have spared him in the circumstances, but it did no good to agonize over the moment now. There were enough targets ahead of them, presumably all armed and dangerous, to hold his full attention.

Halfway to the door labeled Kowloon, Bolan slowed a little, catching the tone of raised voices behind it. He couldn't understand a word they said, but the agitation was plain enough, with one voice shouting down the others, clearly giving orders.

Ma Lam Chan? Bolan would keep his fingers crossed.

With ten yards to go, suddenly the door burst open, spilling men into the corridor. They all had guns in hand, and there was no time for a head count as they spotted Bolan and Bizhani closing in on them. Someone in the front rank snapped an order, and they fanned out in a skirmish line, firing with no attempt at pinpoint marksmanship.

Bolan dropped to the cold, hard floor as bullets swarmed over his head, hoping Bizhani had been quick enough to do the same. His bullpup autorifle stuttered 3-round bursts, starting with twenty-four rounds in the magazine after his confrontation with the guards laid out behind him. If Bizhani lived and held up his end, they could manage it. If not...

A bullet struck the floor to Bolan's left, stinging his cheek with granite shards. He rolled away, still firing, and took down the gunner who had fired that round, three 5.8 mm tumblers ripping into his groin and pelvis, wrenching a scream from the gunner's throat as he fell over backward, shattering fluorescent ceiling fixtures with a last burst from his SMG.

In front of Bolan gunmen scurried back and forth like targets in some madcap shooting gallery, except that these returned fire on the run, filling the air with slugs. One dropped, and then another, making others stumble as they ducked and dodged for cover. Bolan tracked them, glad to hear Bizhani's rifle chiming in, dropping its share of targets on the firing line. It only took one shot from any of the Wah Ching guards to put Bolan away, but if his luck held—

Seconds into the engagement, ringing silence settled on the hallway killing ground. In front of Bolan's smoking gun, a couple of the fallen gunmen still convulsed and trembled, but the fight had all gone out of them, bled off through bullet holes. The Kowloon Room stood open, still producing sounds of scuttling movement from inside, as more hardmen made ready to defend their leader.

Or was Ma Lam Chan already gone?

The only way to answer that required another gamble for the highest stakes.

Rising, he glanced around to find Heydar Bizhani also on his feet and closing in on the gaping doorway.

CHAN WATCHED THE DOOR slam shut behind Nazari and his entourage, then turned on Henry Kwok. His aide was standing with cell phone in hand, frozen as if he could not think of what to do.

"Have you called in the reinforcements?" Chan demanded.

"No, sir. But—"

"Do it now!"

"Yes, sir." Kwok paled before his master's wrath and pressed a single button on the phone, speed-dialing for the backup they'd arranged in the event of an emergency.

The question preying on Chan's mind: would help arrive in time?

And yet another: who was dueling with his soldiers in the corridor outside the meeting room? Was this a trap laid by Khalil Nazari, or was someone else involved? Was his suspicion of outside involvement being borne out here and now? And if so, how would he escape?

Chan gave no serious consideration to Nazari's safety. If the Afghan died while trying to evacuate the conference center, then so be it. That had been his plan originally, and he still might benefit from the arrangement if his soldiers kept their wits about them. Otherwise, if both of them survived, he might be able to arrange another meeting—and another ambush—for his primary competitor. Next time, perhaps, using Colombians or Mexicans to shift the blame.

But first Chan had to find a haven from whoever was attacking him; someplace to hide in absolute security.

Should he go home? It was not far, but since his enemies had found him here, he was not sure it would be safe. Chan had prepared for such emergencies, never believing that they would be necessary, but he'd seen enough competitors die from a dose of carelessness to know that preparation was the all-important key.

"Henry!" he snapped at Kwok. "The men?"

Kwok blinked at him and answered, "Some of them are coming, sir."

"*Some* of them?"

"Others do not answer," Kwok explained. "The kitchen team, the guards at the back door…"

Chan felt a chill of fear. So many men not answering could only mean one of two things. They had either deserted him—which was unthinkable and tantamount to suicide—or they were dead, cut down before the shooting started in the corridor outside the Kowloon Room.

That thought put Chan in motion, bolting toward the nearest exit.

Kwok moved to follow him, but Chan stopped him. "I'm leaving," he stated. "You stay and deal with this."

Kwok blinked at Chan, then swallowed hard and answered, "As you wish, sir."

"Call me when it's finished," Chan instructed.

Four of his soldiers, preselected, followed Chan, leaving the rest with Kwok to face their enemies and rally any reinforcements who arrived in time to help. Survival was the top priority. As always, Ma Lam Chan was looking out for Number One.

"WE PASSED ANOTHER hall back there," Bizhani cautioned Bolan as they neared the entrance to the Kowloon Room. "There'll be another exit from this chamber, yes?"

"You want to cover it?" Bolan asked.

"If it's not too late. Don't wait for me."

"Okay. Go on."

Bizhani turned and ran back toward the corner where two hallways met, then turned off to his left and disappeared from sight. Bolan was on his own now—for the moment, anyway—not knowing whether the Iranian had some trick up his sleeve or truly wished to help by cutting off the enemy's retreat. It made no difference to Bolan either way, since he was focused on the racket coming from the Kowloon Room, where triad soldiers spoke in high, excited voices, plotting hasty strategy.

He fed his weapon a fresh magazine and jacked a round into its chamber, edging toward the partly opened door. When he was almost there, a rush of movement farther down the corridor made Bolan pause, refocusing on a group of men who passed along another hallway, moving from his right to left and out of view.

It was Khalil Nazari and his men, bent on escape.

Making his choice, Bolan unclipped a frag grenade and primed it, launched himself into a sprint directly past the doorway to the Kowloon Room and tossed the high-explosive egg inside, left-handed, as he passed. Before it detonated, he had nearly reached the junction where he'd seen Nazari pass, slowing to check for traps before he followed in their wake.

No one was waiting for him when he peered around the corner, the grenade's shock wave still ringing in his ears. He saw the last man in Nazari's party turn another corner, seemingly oblivious, and Bolan set out after him, moving with cautious strides. He thought about Bizhani, maybe taking on the triad gunners by himself, and knew he'd made the only choice available under the circumstances.

Wrap this up, then double back to finish it.

Sudden silence in the corridor ahead of him made Bolan pause. The air had turned electric with a kind of trembling anticipation that he'd felt before in ambush situations. Maybe it was his imagination, but he didn't think so. Angling to put himself inside Nazari's mind, he pictured his adversaries waiting just around the corner, braced to intercept pursuers, and he made his move.

A sprint, a leap and a long slide took Bolan out into the hallway intersection, ready with his autorifle as the gunmen clustered there fired hastily, too high and wide to damage him. He hosed them down with 5.8 mm slugs, watching them jerk and fall together, some of their incoming rounds striking closer than others, but all off the mark just enough to leave Bolan still breathing.

Still firing.

He'd been wrong about one thing. Khalil Nazari had not left a team behind to cover him while he moved on. The drug lord stood in front of Bolan now, with seven corpses sprawled around his feet, watching a total stranger rise to face him.

With an empty rifle.

When he realized that, Nazari dropped to one knee, reaching for a weapon that his nearest bodyguard had dropped as he was dying. Bosses didn't carry weapons of their own, apparently, where he came from.

It was a grave mistake.

Bolan's Norinco autoloader cleared leather and spit a single, silent round, closing the gap between them at a speed of nearly sixteen hundred feet per second, drilling through Nazari's forehead and his frontal lobe, canceling any final thoughts he might have had. Stone-dead before he knew it, the Afghani cartel boss slumped over backward, sprawling with the men who'd failed to save him.

Bolan heard more shooting now and doubled back the way he'd come, racing time to reach the Kowloon Room.

HEYDAR BIZHANI REACHED the hallway's corner, peered around it and spied a solitary figure moving toward the nearest entrance to the Kowloon Room. The man wore a long leather coat, had a shiny shaved head and carried what appeared to be a mini version of Bizhani's own assault rifle in each hand, muzzles lengthened by the tubes of sound suppressors.

One of Chan's men?

Standing thirty feet away, Bizhani watched the gunman turn to face what he regarded as the conference room's rear entrance. In profile, he saw that the man was Japanese, so not a member of the Wah Ching Triad, with its strict adherence to bloodlines. A mercenary, then—but acting for which side?

The man lowered one of his weapons, freeing his left hand, and reached out cautiously to grasp the doorknob.

Believing there would never be a better time, Bizhani stepped into the corridor, his rifle shouldered, finger on the trigger for a shot to bring the prowler down without a fight.

The movement, when it came, was so fast that he scarcely saw it happening. His target spun, dropped to a crouch and raised his weapon in a single fluid motion, triggering a short burst from the hip. Bizhani answered with a longer burst, feeling the slugs rip into him along his belt line, then his knees gave way and he was lying on his side, watching the Japanese man wobble in his squat, then sit awkwardly, one leg bent underneath him.

Bleeding.

Hastily, before his enemy could fire again, Bizhani triggered half a magazine, raking the man's head and face with hideous results. The bald head lost its shape and a substantial portion of its contents as the seated figure rolled away and slapped wetly against the floor.

Bizhani tried to stand, but slipped in something wet and warm, losing his balance. Cursing through clenched teeth, gripping his rifle in one dripping hand, he set off crawling toward the back door of the Kowloon Room.

YONG CAO TIO surprised a clutch of Wah Ching soldiers double-timing to obey a summons from their master, unaware of danger lurking on their flank, inside a recessed doorway. He stepped out behind them with his AK-9, stitching the last two men in line with a short burst that dropped them in midstride, their arms flailing as they fell. The others spun to face him then, but they were already too late.

Yong strode to meet them as he chopped them down with automatic fire, his teeth bared with raw ferocity that cowed his targets, even as they died. He was like nothing they had seen before, the last grim sight their eyes would ever register, behind the muzzle-flashes of his nearly silent rifle. Spent brass jangled on the granite flooring, leaving a shiny trail behind him, dancing to the muffled death tune that his weapon played.

Yong dropped the empty magazine and snapped a fresh one into the Kalashnikov's receiver, stepping over and around the corpses of his latest kills. A portion of his mind kept score, adding the bodies to his tally, idly wondering whether the *Standard* or the *Ming Pao* daily would publish a list of names in due time, for addition to the scrapbooks that he kept, commemorating his achievements. Ma Lam Chan might be the target he was paid to liquidate, but Yong did not like to ignore the little men who fell along the way.

Standing outside the Kowloon Room, Yong smelled the tangy chemical scent of a TNT blast. He edged into the room through the drifting haze and saw scattered bodies, these torn by shrapnel, some of them still clinging feebly to life. Moving among them, he examined faces, rolling over this or that one in his search for Chan, but finding no one whom he recognized. Those still alive, he left that way, to either die or find a way out on their own.

Clearly, a hand grenade or similar device had detonated in the conference room, but Ma Lam Chan was not among its victims. So where was the Wah Ching Dragon Head?

Fleeing the center—but how?

His quickest route would be out to the street, but that was also the most dangerous. Police would be arriving soon, if they were not already on the scene. Instead, Yong thought about the center's underground garage, pictured a car waiting for Chan below street level, ready to evacuate him through a tunnel accessing Tim Wa Avenue. From there, Chan could flee south, then east or west, as he desired.

But was there time to stop him?

Yong could only do his best. And if experience was any guide, his best was very good indeed.

The other exit from the Kowloon Room was closer to his destination. Yong went out that way, startled to see Mori Saburo sprawled outside the doorway, lifeless in a spreading pool of blood. Away to Yong's right side, an Arab-looking figure struggled to approach the doorway, laboring along on hands and knees. Yong shot him once and saw him crumple, wheezing air through ruptured lungs, and left the two of them behind.

More cash for him, perhaps, if he could catch Chan in the underground garage.

And one less prime competitor for any future jobs.

RETURNING TO THE Kowloon Room through smoky silence, Bolan took the back way, hoping he would meet Bizhani. On arrival at his destination, what he found instead was two bodies, the nearer of them Japanese. He moved past that one, glanced into the conference room and saw that his grenade had done its work, but failed to locate Ma Lam Chan among the fallen.

Now what?

Exiting, he saw the second of the bodies in the hallway moving just enough to indicate a spark of life remaining in its tattered flesh. He took a closer look and recognized Bizhani through a veil of blood that masked his face. Crouching beside the stricken man, Bolan did not require a medical degree to know that he was on the verge of death.

And still, he tried to speak.

Bolan leaned closer, asking, "What was that?"

Bizhani raised one hand as if it weighed a hundred pounds, pointing along the hallway with a dripping index finger. "That way," he said, wheezing, blood gleaming on his lips. "Gunman...after Chan."

Before Bolan could ask another question, the MISIRI agent slumped and hissed a rattling sound, the last breath leaking from his lungs. Bizhani's eyes already had that unmistakable glazed look as Bolan rose and turned away from him.

A sign at the next hallway intersection offered choices, one of them directing passersby to the parking garage. Bolan called up the center's floor plan in his mind and saw the garage's subterranean exit, pictured Chan escaping into Hong Kong, lost in teeming crowds, winging away to parts unknown.

Unless Bolan was quick enough to stop him.

He left Bizhani, knowing there was nothing more that could be done for him. His government would almost certainly deny him, just as Bolan's would if he fell in the line of duty, far from home. It was a fate accepted at the get-go, ultimately meaningless when lives were weighed and measured by the universe.

Bolan passed the elevators, found the service stairs where he could set his own pace and descended toward the building's basement level, fairly flying down the steps, his rifle at the lead. When he was halfway down four zigzag flights, more gunfire sounded from below him, the ringing echoing inside a larger hollow space.

Chan and his men? But who could they be fighting, with Nazari and his backup team dead? He flashed back to the solitary corpse outside the Kowloon Room, a bloodied face that hadn't looked Chinese. And what did *that* mean?

Curious, he picked up speed, chasing the sounds of battle underground.

Ma Lam Chan was cornered. He had no idea how it had happened, but his route to safety had become a trap, and he had no idea if he'd be able to escape.

It had seemed simple, at the outset. He had reached the limousine, flanked by his soldiers, and was just climbing inside the car when someone started shooting at them from behind one of the giant concrete pillars that supported the garage's roof. The sniper's first shots flattened both tires on the limousine's right side, before he targeted the engine, leaving it a mess of dripping oil and gasoline.

As he had scrambled from the vehicle, Chan cursed himself for not investing in a model that was bulletproof. He had grown soft, there was no doubt of it, residing in the lap of luxury. And would that error cost his life?

A lull in firing motivated Chan to try communicating with his would-be killer. Shouting from his place behind the crippled limousine, he asked, "Who are you?"

Momentary hesitation, while the shooter thought about it, then the answer came back.

"Yong Cao Tio. You know my name?"

Feeling the short hairs bristle on his nape, Chan said, "I do. You are a businessman."

"It's true," the legendary killer granted.

"We could make a deal," Chan offered. "Double what your sponsor's offered you, to let me go in peace."

"It's tempting," Yong replied. "But I still have a reputation to protect."

"*Triple* the contract price," Chan shouted back, "to let me go and kill him instead."

While he spoke, Chan gestured to his soldiers, sending them around to flank the gunman, who appeared to be alone. If he could keep the man talking long enough—

"I do love money," Yong Cao Tio replied. "But in the circumstances, there are ethics to consider. Now, before we're interrupted—"

Chan expected gunfire, hopefully from his men taking out the opposition, but instead a loud explosion echoed through the underground garage. Instead of ducking, Chan popped up to catch a glimpse of what was happening and saw a body tumbling, airborne in a cloud of smoke, dropping into the open no-man's-land between the killer's last position and Chan's bullet-riddled limousine. The form struck concrete with a sodden, final sound and moved no more.

"One down. Yong, wasn't that the name?" another voice, distinctly Western, called to Chan. "And on the cash, no deal."

Now who was this? Chan felt himself about to snap. He called out to his men in Cantonese, commanding them to kill this man, whoever he might be, and finally be done with it. As frightened as they had to have been, they followed orders, charging from their various positions, firing as they ran to do their master's bidding. Automatic weapons chattered, numbing what was left of Ma Lam Chan's hearing. He barely realized it when the shooting stopped, could scarcely understand the sound that reached him in the ringing, smoky silence afterward.

Footsteps, drawing closer by the second.

Chan wished that he had a weapon and then remembered for the first time in his panic that he kept guns hidden in the limousine for just such an emergency. He pulled open the nearest door and had begun to lean inside when that grim voice reached out to stop him.

"Don't bother," it said.

He turned to face a white man, over six feet tall, athletic-looking, with an automatic rifle leveled at his face.

"May I at least know who you are?" he asked the stranger.

"I'm your judgment," Bolan said. "This is where it ends."

"You think so? You're insane if you believe that you

can stop the triads. We've survived for centuries. We are immortal."

"Guess again," the stranger said, and shot Chan in the face.

No one remained to hear the Executioner's retreating footsteps or to see him as he left that slaughterhouse with sirens drawing near.

EPILOGUE

South China Sea, 40,000 feet altitude

"So I was wrong," Grimaldi said an hour out of Hong Kong, headed for Manila. "He played his string out to the end."

"Nobody faults you for suspecting him," Bolan replied. "It was the only way to go."

"You took him on, though. He was helpful."

"Yeah, he was."

Grimaldi had their homeward journey plotted out by stages: Hong Kong to Manila, Manila to Brisbane, Brisbane to Wake Island, Wake to Honolulu, then on to Los Angeles. The Dassault Falcon jet would be fueled several times before it touched down on U.S. soil again, but it would get them there.

"What happens to him now?" Grimaldi asked.

"You know the drill," Bolan replied. "Deniability. Tehran can't have a man in Hong Kong, much less France."

"That sounds familiar," the pilot conceded. "Same for us, I guess, one of these days."

"It's what we all agreed to."

"Yeah, I know. It just seems kind of rude somehow, you know?"

"Rules of the game," Bolan replied. "One thing that never changes."

Maybe, he thought, MISIRI had some secret archive for

its heroes, as viewed through Iranian eyes, where Heydar Bizhani would be honored for his sacrifice. The CIA gave secret medals to some of its agents, which they couldn't talk about while still in active service—or, in some cases, for the remainder of their lives. So had the KGB, back in the day, and other secret intelligence agencies. Deniability had always been a hard and binding rule.

But not the only one.

Another rule, at least in Bolan's world, was that no victory could ever be considered permanent. Bad men and women could be taken off the game board, but they were replaced as soon as they went down. Cartels could be annihilated, but the vacuum they created with their passing would be filled by other predators, feeding on greed and weakness. That truth was as immutable as any law of physics or biology.

Evil endured. It could not be destroyed, only postponed, diverted from one target to another. Human nature made it so. Until that hurdle could be overcome, the world would always need an Executioner.

And Bolan, while he lasted, was prepared to fill that role. Because he could.

* * * * *

The Don Pendleton's®
Executioner®
DESERT IMPACT

Smuggled U.S. military weapons turn a cartel kingpin into a Mexican warlord

The murder of several border patrol agents seems like an average Mexican cartel ambush...until the killers' weapons turn out to be U.S. military-grade. There's a leak in the local army base, and it needs to be plugged.

When an ally is killed, Bolan realizes he has underestimated the threat. Whoever is behind the attack is not only smuggling weapons, but building an army to spread their reign of terror into America. With an unofficial war about to break out, he must plan a strike to take down the empire.

GOLD EAGLE®

Available July wherever books and ebooks are sold.

The Don Pendleton's Executioner®
ARCTIC KILL

White supremacists threaten to unleash a deadly virus…

Formed in the wake of World War I, the Thule Society has never lost sight of its goal to eradicate the "lesser races" and restore a mythical paradise. This nightmare scenario becomes a terrifying possibility when the society discovers an ancient virus hidden in a Cold War–era military installation. Called in to avert the looming apocalypse, Mack Bolan must stop the white supremacists by any means necessary. Bolan tracks the group to Alaska, but the clock is ticking. All that stands between millions of people and sure death is one man: The Executioner.

GOLD EAGLE®

Available August wherever books and ebooks are sold.

GEX429

7998

Don Pendleton
COLD SNAP

Posing as ecoterrorists, a renegade military group ignites economic crisis between Japan and the United States

Ecoterrorism becomes the perfect cover for a renegade Chinese and North Korean military group. Striking Japanese whaling and oil vessels on the high seas, the terrorists plan to trigger an economic war between Japan and the United States. But when a Japanese delegation is attacked on U.S. soil, Able Team gets the call to hunt down those behind the lethal ambush while Phoenix Force goes in to stop the mass targeting of sailors and fishermen on the Pacific. With the mastermind behind the scheme still unknown, Stony Man Farm can only hope the trail of bodies will lead them to their target.

STONY MAN®

Available August wherever books and ebooks are sold.

GOLD EAGLE®

GSM132